# AGAINST THE CLOCK

## WILMINGTON FOOTBALL
### BOOK 1

## BRITTANY KELLEY

# BRITTANY KELLEY

*For Cecil- don't worry, soccer is next*

## AGAINST THE CLOCK

Published by Brittany Kelley

www.brittanykelleywrites.com

Copyright © 2023 Brittany Kelley

Illustrated by @lucielart

Design by Sarah Kil Creative

Edited by Happy Ever Author

For sub-rights inquiries, please contact Jessica Watterson at Sandra Djikstra Literary Agency.

❦ Created with Vellum

# AUTHOR'S NOTE

Hello readers!

I do my best to write sports romance with heart, heat, and a lot of laughs, but this book does contain themes that may upset certain readers. Thus, I've included a list of potential triggers so that those who wish may peruse and decide whether or not to continue to read.

\*\*\*\*\*\*\*\*\*\*\*\*\*\*\*\*\*\*\*\*\*\*\*\*\*\*\*\*\*\*\*\*\*\*\*\*\*\*\*\*\*\*\*\*\*\*\*\*\*\*\*\*
\*\*\*\*\*\*\*\*\*\*\*\*\*\*\*\*\*\*\*\*\*\*\*\*\*\*\*\*\*\*\*\*\*\*\*\*\*\*\*\*\*\*\*\*\*\*\*\*\*\*\*\*\*\*
\*\*\*\*\*\*\*\*\*\*\*\*\*\*\*\*\*\*\*\*\*\*\*\*\*\*\*\*\*\*\*\*\*\*\*\*\*\*\*\*\*\*\*\*\*\*\*\*\*\*\*\*\*\*

## SPOILER
## ALERT

\*\*\*\*\*\*\*\*\*\*\*\*\*\*\*\*\*\*\*\*\*\*\*\*\*\*\*\*\*\*\*\*\*\*\*\*\*\*\*\*\*\*\*\*\*\*\*\*\*\*\*\*\*\*
\*\*\*\*\*\*\*\*\*\*\*\*\*\*\*\*\*\*\*\*\*\*\*\*\*\*\*\*\*\*\*\*\*\*\*\*\*\*\*\*\*\*\*\*\*\*\*\*\*\*\*\*\*\*
\*\*\*\*\*\*\*\*\*\*\*\*\*\*\*\*\*\*\*\*\*\*\*\*\*\*\*\*\*\*\*\*\*\*\*\*\*\*\*\*\*\*\*\*\*\*\*\*\*\*\*\*\*\*

Content Warnings:
-explicit sex
-parental illness
-divorce (past relationship, hero)

-injury
-sexual harassment
-mild violence
-cyberbullying
-needles (medical)
-emetophobia
-alcohol consumption
-light kink

# CHAPTER 1

## DANIEL

This is gonna fucking hurt.

The moment I'm more worried about taking a hit than fucking up a pass is the moment I wonder if the pundits and TV personalities and long-retired gridiron gladiators are right.

This could be my last season.

The noise of the crowd, the sound of my own breathing in the helmet, the rush of blood in my ears all goes quiet. Deadly silent. A massive linebacker bears down on me, a snarl turning his lip up, his sheer size the only thing I can focus on.

They seem to get bigger every year. And every year, I just get older.

My teeth grind against my mouthguard. I lift my gaze from his red face, past the tidal wave of lime green and blue headed toward me, looking for a receiver.

The taste of potential glory is metallic in my tongue, tinged with menthol-scented pain reliever creams. A half-second ticks by.

*There.*

Number nineteen's open, the rookie wide receiver, Tyler

Matthews. My brain reacts faster than my sluggish arm, my team's defense reacting quicker still.

The ball cannons from my hand, and no sooner have I launched it than the hope for glory fades into fear. I jerk sideways, throwing myself out of the path of the linebacker who looks like he would like nothing more than to grind my ancient ass to dust on the fucking turf.

Well, ancient by pro football standards. At thirty-nine, I'm hardly old, but I might as well have one foot in the grave, if I listen to the shit reporters can't seem to stop spewing at me during every post-game press conference.

The linebacker moves faster than a man his size should be able to.

*Shit.*

I pick up the speed, unwilling to take the hit. Unwilling and unable. I cannot afford another injury. If the body keeps the score, then a football player's body keeps it with a vengeance.

A blur of blue-gold pom-poms signals I've crossed into the sidelines, and I chomp the mouthguard, trying to stop my momentum without tearing the ACL I've already fucked over so many times that my goddamned medical release file is thicker than that beast of a linebacker's skull. Not to mention my damn shoulder.

Metallic pom-poms fly past my face, and a girlish scream rings out.

Shit. *Shiiiit.*

I need to smash into a cheerleader even less than I need to reinjure any of my joints.

I veer left, hopping slightly, my eyes fixed on the scantily clad women in my team's colors.

And plow straight into someone else.

In my periphery, a shiny black object goes flying. In front of me, there's a tangle of limbs clothed in more than the cheerleaders, and I'm still falling.

All I can see is the terror in her wide brown eyes, the way her lush pink lips are parted in an 'o' of surprise.

All I can think is that I'm about to tackle one of the prettiest girls I've ever laid eyes on.

Just fucking great.

# CHAPTER 2

KELSEY

*his is not good.*

The huge football player slams into me and all the breath leaves my lungs in a guttural noise that's nothing compared to the crunching sound of the iPad I've been taking notes on when it smashes next to me.

I can't move.

"Ah, shit," a low male voice says and I blink, trying to figure out what the hell just happened. "Shit, I'm so sorry. Are you okay?"

There's a football player on top of me.

And not just any football player, either.

The goddamned quarterback of the Wilmington Beavers, the one that I'd have to be dead not to know about. The oldest quarterback in Beavers history, who's apparently fragile enough that they're worried about his feet falling off or something else equally stupid.

He's on top of me, nearly resting his entire weight on me, and I can't breathe.

"Answer me, gorgeous," he says. "Are you okay?" He blinks,

and even through the lines of the face mask, I can tell his eyes are an icy blue unlike anything I've ever seen.

He doesn't *look* old.

I gasp, then cough, my lungs finally deciding to work again. Thank fuck.

"Dammit," he says, frowning. "I knocked the wind out of you, huh?"

I nod and he finally backs up slightly, his face no longer mere inches from mine. I try to sit up, and to my surprise, he wraps one muscled arm around my back, kneeling next to me like there's nothing more important than my well-being.

"I'm okay," I say, somehow embarrassed despite the fact this is most definitely not my fault.

"I'm Daniel Harrison," he says easily, like this is totally a normal way to meet someone.

"I know." I cough again. Damn. I forgot how much it sucks to have the wind knocked out of you.

"What's your name, gorgeous?" he asks, grinning at me, a plastic mouthguard dangling from his helmet.

"Er," I say, staring at him. He's just so giant. On TV, the players look big, sure, but when one is wrapped around you, looking at you with sparkling blue eyes, it definitely takes a slight readjustment in thinking.

"Er?" he repeats, laughing like I've just made the funniest joke ever.

His hand dips to the lanyard around my neck. Gloved knuckles graze my collarbone, and my breath catches again. This time, it has nothing to do with my lungs and everything to do with the sheer proximity of this man. A very manly man. A very, *very* manly man.

Maybe he knocked the sense out of me, too.

"Kelsey Cole," he says, eyes finding mine again. "Kelsey Cole, from USBC-Philly. You're a sideline reporter?"

"Uh-huh. But not sideline. Investigative. I just happen to be...

here." It's hard to look away after being tackled by a giant of a man with biceps as big as my thighs.

Who could have guessed?

"Investigating on the sidelines," I add, then try not to roll my eyes at myself.

"You're not hurt?" he asks again, clearly bemused by my answer. "Didn't hit your head?"

"I don't know," I say honestly. "Shouldn't you be more worried about yourself?" The question comes out reflexively, and we both stare at each other for a split second before he bursts into laughter.

"Kelsey Cole." My name is soft on his lips, barely audible over the roaring of the crowd, which seems to have flipped a switch and turned back on, or at least, my brain's awareness of anything beyond the man kneeling next to me has. "I like your name... and your sense of humor."

"I'm a regular clown," I tell him, then try not to cringe at the idiocy of that statement.

Daniel laughs though, grinning at me like I'm the best thing he's ever seen.

Maybe he did hit me harder than I thought. Or maybe he just has a really great smile.

A medic in Beavers team colors of navy and gold shows up, squatting next to me.

"Finally," Daniel tells him, "she got hit pretty hard." None of the softness is in his voice now.

"Are you hurt?" the medic asks him instead.

I blink.

"She's the one who took the hit," Daniel snarls at him. He turns back to me, his lips turned down in a frown. "Kelsey Cole, there is nothing I'd rather do than sit here and make sure you're okay, but I have to go back to work."

The medic looks between us, clearly confused about why the quarterback is still here. Frankly, that makes two of us.

"Don't worry, gorgeous, I'll take you out to dinner to make it up to you."

"Uh?" I manage, confused about how dinner equates to getting the wind knocked out of you.

"Exactly," Daniel says, grinning broadly. He reaches a hand out, and for a moment, I think he's going to touch my face.

He drops his hand, though, and stands up, every inch the athlete. He winks at me, then takes off at a run.

I watch him go, transfixed by pants that, despite all the reasons I hate football, I can't deny are a blessing to anyone interested in men. My gaze floats to the display overhead.

The Beavers scored a touchdown while I was down for the count.

Or while I was too busy staring up into the too-handsome face of Daniel Harrison.

"Oh my god, Kelsey, are you hurt?" Savannah, one of the cheerleaders that's agreed to speak with me for my story, pushes through the small crowd surrounding me.

The medic, who's finally decided to do his job now that Daniel Harrison told him to, is shining a flashlight into my eyes and I swat his hand away, annoyed.

"Just surprised," I tell her.

"You okay?" the medic asks, clearly put off by my efforts to stop him.

"I'm fine," I tell him and he finally backs off, stowing his tiny flashlight away.

"That looked like it hurt," Savannah says, grabbing me under the armpit and pulling me up with surprising strength. It shouldn't be surprising. The cheerleaders are pure muscle and glitter. I have a whole hell of a lot of respect for them... which is why I'm here.

To do a job.

Just like Daniel Harrison.

Not sit on my butt on the poky grass.

"You sure?" Savannah asks again, giving me an eagle-eyed once-over.

"I'm good," I tell her, then frown when I see my damned iPad shattered on the ground next to me.

"I'm so glad," she says, giving my shoulders a quick, gentle squeeze before darting back to the line of ten cheerleaders and immediately picks up the dance where she left off.

Grimacing, I roll my shoulders, trying to pop my neck. My favorite grey pencil skirt is covered in bits of turf, and I have a sneaking suspicion it now sports an ass-shaped green imprint. I brush my butt off as best I can, putting a safer distance between me and the men insistent on beating each other to a pulp for the crowd's entertainment.

I *hate* it here.

I chance a look back at the rabid crowd behind me, and even though the Wilmington Beavers are the losingest pro football team in recent history, the stands are packed with gold-and-blue-clad fans, screaming their lungs out at each fresh impact on the field.

It brings back the worst memories.

There's a newly sore spot behind my shoulder. Maybe I'm not so fine.

I'm definitely going to feel it tomorrow.

I blow out a breath, trying to get my adrenaline and rampaging heart under control. Somewhere on the field, a whistle blows and the vicious play grinds to a halt.

Music blares so loud I wince, and the cheerleaders in front of me shimmy with military precision. I bend over to pick up the cracked iPad, way more gingerly than the sparkly uniformed women dancing their hearts out. A piece of turf hangs from the case. I pluck it off, letting it fall to the ground.

With a little shake, not nearly as sexy as the cheerleaders, I try to clear my head.

I am here to do my job. My job, right now, is to expose the American Football League for the way they treat their cheerleaders. My job, right now, is to get glossy pictures and footage of the cheerleaders, as well as document first-hand the way the women are treated by fans and team management. Sure, the perpetually down-on-their-luck Beavers were the only team that would issue me a press pass and access to their cheerleaders, probably because they have a lot fewer problems than most... but it's a start.

And if my exposé takes the AFL down a notch? Or at least gets these women dancing their tushies off better working conditions?

Then it'll be worth it all. Even worth the eventual soreness from being tackled.

My job is not to be breathless, thinking about a certain quarterback. My job is to expose one more facet of how the AFL is a totally messed up meat grinder of a circus.

My phone vibrates in my pocket, and a quick glance at my watch tells me it's my father. As if I summoned him with the mere thought.

He would hate that I'm doing this because of him. Well, not completely because of him.

But he's definitely part of it.

A flick of my finger silences the call and I stare at the dancers, resolute. Resolute despite the fact that my gaze keeps dragging over to a certain handsome, tall, blue-eyed quarterback.

I bet he forgets me before the end of the third quarter.

# CHAPTER 3

## POST-GAME PRESS CONFERENCE WITH QB DANIEL HARRISON: BEAVERS V. CONDORS

Interviewer 1: Daniel, how do you feel about your performance in this game?

Daniel Harrison: You know, we went out there and we did what we get paid to do. We worked hard, we ran the plays, the receivers made sure their routes were open. Defense worked hard, the coaches worked hard—

Interviewer 2: Do you think you worked hard enough?

<laughter>

Daniel: I think I did. I think I did. You know I've been doing this for a long time, right?

<laughter>

Daniel: I thought you might. But I'm proud every time I put on my helmet. I'm proud to be a part of this team, and I'm proud of what the guys and I did out there today.

Interviewer 1: You didn't win. You haven't won the last three games, none since you were traded. Do you think you have what it takes to lead this team to any wins this season?

Daniel: Of course I do. Otherwise I wouldn't still be out there working my ass... sorry. Working my butt off every day with these guys that are fresh out of school. Jacob Matthews is out here at twenty-three, trying to kick my—well, you know—every day. His brother Ty is pushing thirty and he's out here trying to kick it every day too. Every day, we put in the work, I put in the work, and if I thought I was done, I would retire. I'm not going to punish a team of men I respect by doing a half-ass... sorry... by not going out there and doing my best. That wouldn't be right. That's not me. It's early in the season. I think we're just getting started.

Interviewer 2: But you're not just getting started.

<laughter>

Daniel: Yeah, yeah, I know, get out the coffin already.

Interviewer 2: Seriously though, Daniel, it looked like you didn't want to get hit. You ran off the field... and you ran into a reporter. Do you think you can still take the hits, or are you running scared into the Beavers cheer team?

Daniel: <heavy sigh> If I didn't want to get hit, I wouldn't be playing, Tom. That's what this game is. That's why we do this. We suit up, we get on the field, and we go to war. This is what we do. This is what I love.

Interviewer 3: And the reporter you hit? Did she suit up to go to war?

Daniel: <scratches his five o'clock shadow> Of course not. But don't worry about her. I'm going to do everything in my power to make it up to her. That's all guys, thanks.

# CHAPTER 4

## KELSEY

I n the cube farm life, time feels more like a construct than ever. I'm at my desk in the station office, working on what feels like a million different things. Time's passing, yes, but with the glow of the computer screens and the fluorescents overhead, it sure as heck doesn't feel like it. My stomach grumbles in protest of the early lunch I took—the only sure indicator that I haven't slipped into some weird vortex where time doesn't exist.

Yawning, I lean back in my chair, stretching my arms way out behind me.

And brush up against something solid. Someone solid.

"Yeaaack!" I yelp, jumping to my feet. I fling my AirPods out and whip around. They skitter across the desk. My hands go to my chest, my heart racing a mile a minute.

Only to see Daniel Harrison.

He grins at me.

My heart skips a beat.

"We have to stop meeting like this," he says, tucking his hands in his pants pockets.

A regular suit. A nice one, navy-blue, with the barest hint of pinstripe. It shows off his broad shoulders, his trim waist. A light blue button-down, unbuttoned just enough to show a hint of thickly muscled chest.

"What?" I finally manage. "Meeting like what?"

"I hit you at my place of work, now you hit me at yours. People are going to talk."

I glance around, because despite the fairly late hour—after six on a Friday—there are plenty of people around. He's right, too. The people are, in fact, already talking. Leslie whispers behind her hand to Bruce from marketing, who stares at Daniel Harrison like he's seeing a god in our midst.

"How did you get in here?" I ask, narrowing my eyes at the visitor pass affixed to his jacket.

He points at the pass. "I asked to?"

"Right," I say. "And because you're the quarterback for the Beavers you can just get in wherever you want?"

He blinks, as surprised by my acidic tone as I am.

"Sorry," I sigh, pushing my likely frizzed-out hair out of my face. "It's been a long day."

"Well," he says slowly, that mega-watt smile starting to grow on his face again, the one that sends his fans into overdrive, "to be completely honest with you, Kelsey Cole, I told them I had an invitation."

"From whom?" I ask, then my jaw drops as I put it together. "From *me*."

We have become *quite* the internet sensation—the feral Beavers fans putting together fan cam recuts of the moment he ran into me over and over again. I've been tagged so many times in random TikToks over the past week that I've nearly deleted the app four different times.

He tilts his head, a searching expression on his face, like he's just now realizing this might not be the wonderful gesture he thought it was.

"Listen, if I read this wrong—" His eyes go round. "You're married," he says. His gaze dips to my left hand.

"What? No." I hold up my bare hand, as if expecting to see a ring there.

"Boyfriend," he says, rapid-fire, his intense blue gaze pinning me in place where I've backed up almost into my computer screen on the desk. "You have a boyfriend, and it's serious."

"No?" I say, growing more confused by the second.

"Girlfriend?"

"Nope, just me."

He runs a taped-up index finger around the inside of the collar of his shirt. "Man, you were making me sweat that. So you *are* good with me taking you to dinner?"

I cross my arms and raise an eyebrow.

His gaze dips to my boobs, which I've accidentally pushed up. I clear my throat and put my hands on my hips instead.

One eyebrow rises on his face, and he's so overwhelmingly outsized, too handsome, too tall, too *much,* I can't help but take a step back.

"Why are you asking me to dinner?" I counter, raising my own eyebrow like we're in some quick-draw eyebrow duel. "Is it because you feel bad for nearly murdering me last weekend?"

"Go to dinner with him," Leslie whisper-shouts.

"I will if you don't," Bruce says too loudly.

Fucking Bruce from marketing. I keep myself from rolling my eyes, but it's an Olympic effort.

"We can bring them too, if you want," Daniel says, leaning slightly against the cube, a cocky half-smile on his lips.

He doesn't seem real. His brown hair, so dark it's nearly black, is sprinkled throughout with silver, as is the start of a beard on his jawline. It doesn't make him look old though, not like everyone in Philly and Delaware has been saying on the news and Twitter and TikTok…

Nope.

Daniel Harrison looks like he's in his prime.

"Let's go," I finally say. If I don't, Leslie and Bruce are going to make things even more awkward. Better to get out while we can. "Just dinner." I shake my finger at him. "No funny business."

"I would never try to be funny," he says gravely. "You know where I work, after all."

"Are we invited?" Bruce asks.

"No," Daniel and I say at the same time, not bothering to break off our staring contest.

"See? We're already thinking alike." He flashes that brilliant celebrity QB smile, and I would be lying if I said it didn't make me a little weak in the knees.

"Oh? You were thinking about going on the record for the piece I'm working on, then? Great." I bat my eyelashes at him, and for a moment, I think I've pushed a little too far.

His face turns serious, his gaze searing.

But that's not the look of a man who's pissed off.

That's the look of a man who's seen something he wants.

"Is that what it's going to take? A few quotes from me? A bargain?"

I toss my hair over my shoulder, acting a whole hell of a lot more confident than I feel. What I'm actually feeling is completely out of my depth.

"Yep," I say. "I want a few quotes."

"But the whole night won't be on the record?" He squints at me.

"Nope."

Yeah, that's me, the queen of witty repartee.

"Deal," he says, holding out a hand. I take it, prepared to shake.

What I'm not prepared for? The way he takes my hand like it's spun glass, then raises it to his lips, pressing a kiss against my knuckles.

"You sure I can't come?" Leslie asks. "Is anyone else hot? Is it hot in here?"

"Shut up, Leslie," Bruce tells her.

"Let me just get my purse," I croak, trying to regain control over the situation. Yeah, the situation. That, and my suddenly blazing desire.

I mean, a soggy leaf on the ground would take one look at Daniel Harrison and think naughty thoughts. If Daniel Harrison bent his big ole body down and kissed the leaf, the leaf would be shook.

Great. Now my thoughts are completely scrambled.

"What, exactly, are you working on that you need my quotes for? You're not a sports reporter. I did some research on you."

"No, I'm not," I say. "I would be terrible at that." I finally manage to finagle the screwy bottom desk drawer open and tug my bag out. I scoop up my poor AirPods, dumping them into my purse. My not fancy, not expensive, not even particularly nice purse.

I look at Daniel Harrison.

I look at my beat-up bag.

I'm not dressed up.

"Are we going somewhere fancy?" I gesture to my jeans. Sure, they're my nice work jeans, just uncomfortable enough to be nice for casual Friday… but Daniel Harrison is in a suit.

"Not particularly, no," he says. "You didn't answer my question."

I stand up, tossing my purse strap over my shoulder and tugging my oversized blazer down. "Me answering questions wasn't part of the deal."

His mouth twists to the side, a faint smile still there. "That's true."

"But," I say, stalking past where Leslie and Bruce still gape at me, "in the interest of being a good conversationalist and an honest member of the press, I will tell you." I wheel around, putting on my best intimidating face as I shake a finger at him. "But you have to promise to answer my questions, even if you don't like what I'm writing about."

It's hard to be intimidating when faced with six and a half feet of man.

His cheeks suck in like he's biting them to keep from laughing. I slowly lower my finger.

"I'm a man of my word," Daniel says, taking a step towards me, forcing me to look up at him. And up. "I'll answer whatever questions you have for me. On… or off the record." His eyebrow quirks up at that, and I swallow past the heavy tension between us. I think he just fired a shot with that eyebrow. I think he won our unspoken eyebrow duel.

*This can't be real.* There's no way the charm he's turning on is for *me*.

I couldn't avoid the gossip after the game, after the press conference he gave, where he all but said he would take care of me. Hell, my coworkers were dying to know what he meant. TikTok was dying to know what he meant.

I wanted to know too.

But this is probably some stupid stunt to get good publicity before the next game. To turn the tide of public attention in his favor and use me as a prop to do it.

I square my shoulders.

"I'm writing an investigative piece on the way pro cheerleaders and dance teams are treated by the franchises. From criminally low pay to outdated double-standards and even quid pro quo arrangements, professional cheerleaders are treated like anything but pros." It comes out in a waterfall of words, faster and louder than I meant it to.

He blinks. "Good for you," he says. "Those are some of the hardest-working people on the sidelines."

I open my mouth to argue the point, then realize he's made it for me.

"Exactly," I say, tilting my chin and reevaluating everything I know about him. "Was that on the record?"

"Sure," he says. He closes the distance between us and his hand finds the space between my shoulders, gently propelling me toward the elevator. "You really thought I wouldn't want to go on a date with you once you told me that?"

"Uh—" A date? I try to wrap my head around that. A *date*?

"You'd have to try a lot harder than writing about something people should know," he continues, like he hasn't just run a dump truck over all my notions of what the hell is happening. Daniel steers me towards the elevator and I plod along next to him, his touch light on my back.

His hand doesn't feel disrespectful or rude or *anything* but good. Heat blossoms under my shirt where his fingertips graze over the fabric until I turn around, leaning against the cool wall where it's safe.

The elevator doors have closed in front of my face before I regain enough cognitive function to speak again.

"A date?" I echo.

To my surprise, a glimmer of embarrassment flits across his face and he shrugs his powerful shoulders. "Well, I should have done a better job asking you, if you are still confused about why I'm here. In fact, I should just start over."

"I thought you were just being nice? After tackling me?" A date? My mind's stuck on that word, a skipping song with two words.

Heat explodes through his gaze and he focuses all that intensity on me.

We're alone in the elevator and he deliberately, slowly presses the red emergency stop button. The elevator grinds to a halt and I start to wonder if I need to go to the doctor, because I am once again breathless around this man.

My eyes get wide as he places one hand on the wall behind me, his body leaning so close to mine that I catch the spicy scent of expensive cologne: coriander and sandalwood, and something else beneath it, masculine and fresh.

I inhale deeply, wanting more.

He pushes a strand of my hair from my forehead, his thumb brushing against my temple as I watch him, unable to look away.

"Hi Kelsey," he says in a low rumble, and he's so close I can feel the vibration from his chest. "I'm Daniel Harrison. I'd like to take you on a date."

"Uh-huh," I say.

His lips quirk up at one side. "Do you want to go on a date with me?"

"Yep," I reply breathlessly, and he lets out a low chuckle that makes my toes literally curl in my heels.

"Good," he says. His face turns serious, his eyes still twinkling with humor. "But no funny business."

"No funny business," I agree, and I've never made a more idiotic ground rule in my life.

I would like the funny business. I would like all the funny business with this man, right now, in this elevator, at work.

I reach out from behind his huge body and press the emergency stop button, bringing the elevator back to life.

I do not need to start making bad choices in my work elevator.

Agreeing to this date might be a bad enough choice. I told myself I'd never, ever get involved with a pro sports player, much less a football player.

And Daniel Harrison?

I study his face, still inches away from mine, smiling like he finds my off-kilter self amusing. He is easily the most handsome man I've ever seen in my life, and I didn't realize just how disarming all that was until now, stuffed in an elevator with him, wearing a suit and asking me on a date.

"I like you out of the football uniform."

His eyebrows rocket up. "You trying to get me out of my clothes? You're sending me mixed signals, Kelsey."

I snort a laugh, some of the tightly wound sexual tension dissipating with his easy humor. He backs up and I take a deep breath as my ability to think clearly returns.

"So, do you want me to meet you at this place? I need to fill my car up—"

"Are you kidding? And deprive me of the opportunity to show off my hard-earned car to a beautiful woman?"

A blush heats my cheeks at the compliment. Out of all the women Daniel Harrison could date, I'm nowhere near the top of the pile. I mean, I think I'm pretty enough, but hell, he dated a Victoria's Secret model a few years ago. They were splashed all over every magazine in the grocery store check-out for months.

"You can drive if you want to, though," he says, clearly misinterpreting my silence.

The elevator dings and the doors slide open with a mechanical grind that lowers my confidence in the functionality of the elevator every time I use it. The fading fall light filters through the lobby of the USBC-Philly offices, hitting the marble floor at just the right angle to momentarily blind me.

When I look through the window, there's something else nearly blinding me. A big white truck, the chrome trim sparkling.

"I don't know why I expected a Maserati."

"Is the truck a problem?"

"No," I say honestly, and shake my head. "A Maserati would have freaked me out."

"So you're saying you'll let me drive you? On our date?" He nudges me with his elbow, and I glance up at him to see a huge smile on his face.

I can't help but smile back.

"I am a very safe driver," he says. "Gotta protect this money-maker." He gestures to himself, a very serious expression on his face.

I bark a laugh, and he chuckles too.

"Yeah, you can drive," I say.

"Did the moneymaker comment convince you? Making notes for later," he taps his temple, nudging me with his elbow again as we walk toward the truck that's inexplicably parked right in front of the building.

"More like my feet hurt from these heels and your car is right there." I crane my neck as we continue towards it. "And I'm pretty sure it's in a no-parking zone."

Not that our security officer seems to care. In fact, he gives Daniel a two-finger salute as we walk by his desk.

"Noted." His laugh's infectious and unself-conscious, and he exudes such an air of quiet confidence that it makes me stand up straighter.

All I can think is that Daniel Harrison would be easy to fall for... and that it would hurt like hell once he inevitably decided to find a new flavor of the week.

# CHAPTER 5

## DANIEL

**K**elsey settles into the car like she's sitting on a bed of acupuncture needles.

"You know, the med team with the Beavers, they like these mats," I say conversationally, putting the truck into drive, "that have all these little plastic pins all over them. They're supposed to help circulation or lymph or whatever. Fluid build-up. They like to have us lie on them after rehab sessions. I think the real reason is so that we want to say we're feeling better more quickly so we don't have to lie on them."

Her pretty pink lips twist to the side in disgust. "That sounds awful."

"You look like you're sitting on one right now."

A laugh peals out of her, and I grin at catching her off guard. I like that she puts up with my gentle ribbing. My ex-wife would have just gotten mad. Familiar shame floats through me. I would have deserved it with her, though.

"Do they work?" she asks, her face angled away from me, watching the buildings pass by as we sluggishly make our way through Philly traffic.

"The mats? Yeah. I think they do. It's a shock for the first few seconds when you lie down on one, though. One of the guys on the team, Ty, he bought one and swears by it. Calls it his girlfriend."

She laughs again, and the sound is bright. Her head turns back to me, and her gaze is curious as it skates over my face. There are dark circles under her eyes, ones that say she hasn't been sleeping well.

"How are you feeling?" I ask her, guilt surging through me. "Did you get checked out after I hurt you?"

Her answering smile is soft, like she's surprised by the questions. Like she's surprised I care about how she's feeling.

It surprises me how much I do care about it.

"I did," she says. "The Beavers sports medicine trainers," she flicks her hand, "whatever they're called, they made me submit to a quick exam. Nothing more than a few bruises. I'm good."

"Shit." My gaze darts from the road to her. "I'm so sorry, Kelsey." I hate the idea of her being bruised from me, her skin blue and green from taking a hit like that at my hands.

I like the idea of finding every single bruise and working my lips across her skin, kissing her better. I cough.

"I should have been paying more attention to the game," she says. "It's all good."

The sardonic way she says game tells me she is not, in fact, all good.

My hands flex on the wheel and I resist the urge to grab her hand and make her tell me what's bothering her.

*What the fuck is wrong with me?*

Am I feeling so possessive and protective of her out of some guilt about what happened? It's fucking weird. It's out of character.

"Football is dangerous," she continues, crossing her arms over her chest. "It was stupid to forget that, even temporarily."

"You don't like football," I say randomly. Better that than

insisting on rubbing some of the Icy Hot I keep in the center console all over her body.

Her reaction is immediate. The gentle smile on her face disappears, her gaze shuttering. "What makes you say that?"

I bite my tongue, trying not to tell her that I was searching for anything to say besides, "I wanna fuck you right now, in my truck," and landed instead on intuition I wasn't sure I still possessed.

"A guess," I say instead, turning onto the Benjamin Franklin Bridge.

She's silent for a moment, staring out at the boats leaving a frothy wake in the Delaware River.

"Where are we going? There are so many good restaurants in the city," she says, her expression confused.

She doesn't want to tell me why she doesn't like football. That's fine. Not everyone likes football. A little weird, considering she's on a date with me, a professional football player, but I'll get her to tell me eventually.

Maybe it'll be fun.

Hell, maybe it's better she's not one of the jersey-chasing groupies.

"There are," I agree. "But this place is my favorite. The Matthews brothers—do you know them? Probably not, considering…" She shoots me a look, and I clear my throat before continuing. "They both play on the team. Unusual that they signed brothers, but they're a lot of fun. Anyway, they took me to this place during training camp, and they make some of the best cheesesteaks and pork rolls I've ever had."

"Now that's heresy." Kelsey laughs, and I swear to god, I could get addicted to that sound. "Driving to South Jersey for cheesesteaks? I didn't think you were a deviant."

"I wouldn't steer you wrong, Kelsey Cole," I say, and it comes out much more sincere than I meant.

The press would probably say I'm getting soft in my old age, but this woman… I like the idea of her. I like all my ideas about her.

I want to steer her exactly right.

Or maybe I'm just fucking hard-up and willing to cling to the first curvy body I've slammed up against in over a year.

I sneak another quick glance at her, her dark blonde waves partially obscuring her face. My hand twitches on the wheel, the desire to push it back behind her ear, to lose myself in the softness of her body so intense I have to grit my teeth.

"My ex wouldn't have wanted to eat at this place," I say, then mentally kick myself.

"The supermodel?" she asks.

"This is off the record," I say, trying to gloss over the fact that only a fucking idiot brings up their ex on a goddamned first date.

"Sure," she says, her eyebrows raised. God, I like her eyes. I like how they're the warm brown of hot cocoa, maybe with a kick of spice you didn't expect. Mexican hot chocolate.

"Not the supermodel. My ex-wife."

"Not a fan of cheesesteak?" she asks.

"Not a fan of local dives," I say. "Although, I have to say it: Cheez Whiz isn't for everyone."

"Cheez Whiz is the way," she says solemnly, then grins up at me.

"This is the way," I agree, fucking loving the way she beams even brighter, like I flipped a switch on her.

"I didn't peg you for a fan of Star Wars," she says.

"What's not to love? Everybody loves Star Wars. Besides, that green guy is cute as hell." I almost tell her it's enough to make me want to settle down and make babies but manage to reign myself in before it slips. That would be a first date disaster I probably wouldn't make it back from.

I do not want to fuck this up.

I don't know everything I want to know about Kelsey Cole, but I sure as shit know that.

"What else do you like?" she asks. "That seems like a good

place to start on our… date." She says the word quietly, like she's still testing out the idea.

"You," I answer without hesitation, and the grin she gives me in response is the brightest I've seen yet.

It's warmer than the sun.

# CHAPTER 6

KELSEY

"Gardening?" I ask again, totally caught by surprise. "Really?" I'm having a hard time imagining this suit-wearing athlete hanging out around flowers. Like Ferdinand the Bull. One of my favorites from when I was little. I can still remember sitting in my dad's lap while he read it to me.

"Yeah," he says, a little gruffly, though he's still grinning at me. "In the spirit of honesty, and still off the record, Kelsey Cole, I got into gardening after my divorce. I went into therapy and realized…" He clears his throat, the sound of his turn signal filling the sudden silence.

"This is awkward, isn't it? Me talking about therapy and my divorce." He frowns.

I shake my head, pursing my lips. "No, actually. It's refreshing."

It is, too. I like that he is being upfront. I like that he's not hiding who he is, or his past, even if it's less than sparkling.

"Well, my therapist said that maybe I was too all-or-nothing with football. Made me realize my ex-wife… she knew football always came first for me. It had to. It was my first love, my career, my everything. So I took up gardening because watching things grow… it made me feel like I could do something besides throw a ball. It's rewarding, you know? Planting a seed, watching it bloom."

I settle against the side of the door, curious about this man. Who would've thought a gardening hobby would be such a turn-on?

"What?" he asks, his gaze flicking from me to the road. "You have a look on your face. Is that weird?"

"Not at all. Makes me wish I had more hobbies. I have room for maybe a plant in my apartment. *A* plant. Definitely not a garden." I snort. "How do you even have time for that?" I almost add that I know how much time football truly eats up, eroding relationships and everything else, relentless and all-consuming.

I stop myself before I say it.

His expression turns rueful, and he's quiet again for a moment. "That's part of the challenge, at the moment, at least. Finding time for things I love besides football."

He casts me a sidelong glance, and butterflies take flight in my stomach at the heat in his gaze. Like maybe he wants something… *more* from me than one date.

I shouldn't think like that. He hardly has time for his plants.

Relationships take a lot more than water and sunlight.

Gravel crunches under the truck's tires and I turn my attention away from Daniel, realizing with a slight twinge of embarrassment that I've been straight-up staring at him for the last five minutes.

He's pretty easy to look at.

The restaurant appears to take up the main floor of an old house. Chipped white paint peels from the siding, but a jaunty red striped awning juts into the night air, an open sign blinking in the window.

"Want to go in?" he asks.

"Sure," I say. "Why not?"

Before I have time to even grab my purse, Daniel's out of the truck and jogging around to open my door. I squint at him, unsure if this is some weird sign that he's super old-fashioned and out of touch.

"The ground here isn't great for heels," he says apologetically, offering me a hand.

"Oh, thanks," I manage. His hand is warm and strong, and his touch is electric. I try not to gape at him, wondering if this... *attraction* is one-sided.

*Does he feel it too?*

I gingerly step out of the truck, wobbling slightly on the gravel parking lot.

A bell on the door jingles as he holds it open for me, revealing a very small, very normal looking deli. There's no line, no tables, nothing but the counter full of meats and cheeses. The guy at the counter looks like he stepped straight off of a *Sopranos* set, and when he greets us, he sounds like it, too.

"What'll it be?" he booms, his Jersey accent so thick that it takes me a second to recover.

"Cheesesteak with hot peppers and Whiz for me," Daniel says confidently.

I stare at the chalkboard menu behind the guy, his gold chain glittering in the overhead lights.

"Listen, lady, we're good at hoagies. We're good at steaks, like what your..." His face scrunches up in surprise, his black and silver eyebrows hitting his receding hairline. "You're not just her boyfriend. Holy shit, Frank, come 'ere! Look who it is."

A younger man, a smaller replica of the one at the counter, appears, his eyes round as saucers. "Daniel fucking Harrison! No shit! You getting a cheesesteak with Whiz? Holy shit!"

"The pork rolls with long hots are real good too, Daniel's girl-friend," the man behind the counter tells me confidently.

"Oh, I'm not his—" I start, but the younger guy interrupts me.

"Listen, a friend of Daniel fucking Harrison is a friend of ours. Girlfriend or not, you should get the pork and long hots." His nose scrunches. "Do you like spice?"

Daniel looks like he's holding in a laugh, and I'm too bewildered with the enthusiastic response over our sandwich orders to do more than watch the duo behind the counter.

"Yeah, I like spice."

"Oh shit, Daniel fucking Harrison!" he says again, shaking his head. "Your girl can handle the heat! Love to see it, love to see it." He takes a phone from his pocket, and before either of us can react, he snaps a picture of the two of us. "My wife's not gonna believe it unless I show her photo evidence, you know."

"Don't be a jackass, Dom," the older guy chides. "Can't you see my guy is out on a date? Jesus, Mary, and Joseph. Sorry about him. You want the pork and long hots?"

"Sure," I say.

Next to me, Daniel's shoulders are shaking slightly, and when I glance up at him, he's biting his cheeks. Something about it sets me off and I slap a hand over my mouth to stifle my own laugh.

"I'm gonna throw in some Utz chips for you two, too. Weren't you here a month or two ago with the Matthews brothers?"

Daniel nods. "Yeah, and I had to bring her down here for the best cheesesteak I've ever had. Couldn't think of a better way to impress my future girlfriend."

I blink, trying to process that statement. His future girlfriend? No. He's just schmoozing with this guy. No dude I've ever dated has bothered to try and lock it down on a first night out. That's just weird.

The man slams his hand on the counter, beaming at Daniel. "Now that's how you give a man a compliment! Wait till I tell my kids that. They're always going on about Pat's downtown, and I say, no, the secret to a good steak is in the—" He raises his eyebrows again, then mimes zipping his lips and locking them tight. "You know what? You can't get trade secrets out of me, no sir. The Beavers gonna win this next game?"

"Sure hope so." He grins at the guy, but there's a slight edge to it now, an edge that says he doesn't want to talk about football.

Weird. Even now, my dad wants to talk about football every waking moment, despite it taking nearly everything from him.

The man behind the counter rattles off the price for our meal, thankfully distracting me from that line of thinking.

"I can pay," I say, and am glad he didn't try to take me somewhere where prices weren't even on the menu. My bank card can definitely handle a nine-dollar pork sandwich.

"My treat." Daniel pulls out his wallet. "You can get the next date, if you want."

Next date? I don't know what to say to that. I don't know what to think about any of this, other than I'm attracted to Daniel like crazy, and that I know the only way all this charm he's expending on me plays out is with me waiting for a text that will never come.

My phone vibrates in my purse and I pull it out, a text from my best friend Cameron lighting up the screen.

> Leslie said a certain QB just kidnapped you from work

Daniel edges in closer, clearly feigning disinterest in the message on my screen.

"Kidnapped seems like a strong word," he says. "You went with me willingly." His eyes dance with laughter. "If that's what you're into, though…"

"Then maybe you should let me tell her that," I say tartly. "Instead of peeking at my screen like a creeper."

He holds up both hands, a sheepish look on his face. "Sorry, sorry, you're right."

I mock-glare at him, purposefully turning my phone screen away to type back a response. Cameron and I moved out here at the same time, me from a small town in West Texas, her from Northern Virginia, and we bonded immediately at work. Now she's one of my best friends.

> I'm freaking out a little

> If he really kidnapped you, you better tell me. I'll get the SWAT team out there to find you

> He didn't kidnap me. We're on a date... he called me his future girlfriend

> Damn, that's hot

> You know how I feel about football

> Yeah, but isn't he like geriatric? How much longer can he play? Does he want grandkids?

> Also who cares? Ride that pony. Have some fun. You don't have to commit to anything

> Just that d

A GIF of a girl on a mechanical bull appears on my screen, and I roll my eyes.

> you better tell me all about it. All about it. No detail left unsaid

I snort, pinching the bridge of my nose, ignoring the notifications blowing up my TikTok app, though the sight makes me brighten a bit. Most of the Beavers fans' interest seems to have died over the past few days, so maybe one of my short videos on the cheerleader situation finally went viral. Or one of the other investigative pieces from last week, maybe the one on the corruption at the Philly Farmer's Market. I want to check it, but... god, it would be so embarrassing if it were just another fan cut of Daniel tackling me.

"Everything good?"

"Yeah," I say. "SWAT team call averted."

"That would have been awkward," he says easily.

"Here ya go," the guy at the counter says, holding up a large brown paper bag. It smells amazing, and my stomach twists with hunger.

"Thanks, man," Daniel says, taking the bag and holding out his hand for me. I take it, biting my lip. Heat blossoms low in my stomach.

I might not like the idea of dating a football player... but the chemistry between the two of us is undeniable.

The mere touch of his hand sends my pulse speeding. The brush of his bicep against my shoulder leaves my chest tight with anticipation. I blow out a breath as he helps me back into his truck, trying to keep my head on straight.

If I can't get myself together, I'm going to end up doing something I regret.

But damn, it might be fun.

# CHAPTER 7

## DANIEL

**M**y heart's in my throat as I turn the truck onto the sketchy-seeming road, marked only by a plain mailbox out front and a row of orange-leafed sugar maples.

I'm starting to get nervous, and it's because I want her to like me.

She's proven me right about everything I thought about her so far: Kelsey is smart, and kind, and quick to laugh—on top of being gorgeous and down-to-earth.

She's like a breath of fresh air. Plus, she smells good. Really good.

"Is this a park or something?" she asks.

"Well, so, I probably should have told you this before I brought you here, but I, uh, I didn't think it all the way through, maybe."

"That's not exactly inspiring confidence," she says, her eyes narrowed. "Don't forget, my friend Cameron is standing by with the SWAT team." She holds up her phone.

"This is my home," I tell her instead. "A lot of the guys like to live close to the training center, but I… wanted some peace and quiet. So I moved out here."

The asphalt road turns to pavestones, and I grin at her wide eyes as she takes in the house before her. Thank fuck I called my yard guys this morning and asked about getting twinkle lights put up in the front garden. It looks magical.

"Do you always have Christmas lights up in the… garden?"

"Nope. I thought I would go the extra mile to try and impress a woman." Nervousness fills me, and a low chuckle erupts from my throat. "Is it working?"

"Mmm," she says, her brown eyes reflecting the warm yellow glow of the garden.

"It's not as nice now as it was this summer," I tell her, unable to stop talking. It's like I've forgotten how to turn on the charm, like I've been transported back to the first time I ever took a girl out for dinner, and all I wanna do is impress her.

*Like me*, I want to say. *I like you. Like me back.*

"Usually it's full of flowers and herbs, but now there's just the sort of ruddy autumn colors as everything's going dormant."

"Are you kidding me?" she asks, swinging her head towards me as the truck rolls to a stop. "This is beautiful."

I laugh, relieved, beaming down at her expression, full of wonder.

I like impressing her. I like that look on her face.

I want to see more of it.

"I should have worn different shoes," she says ruefully. "I didn't plan on hanging out in a garden."

"That's okay," I tell her. "I'll carry you to the table."

I get out of the truck before she has time to refuse, hoping she'll let me. Wanting to hold her, wanting to feel her pressed up against me.

Giddy with the chance to make it happen, I brush a hand through my hair before I open her door, trying to center myself, trying to play it cool.

There's nothing cool about me right now. I want this woman.

The door opens and Kelsey's staring at me, looking slightly bewildered. "You want to carry me to the table," she repeats.

"If you don't want to ruin your shoes." I shrug, pretending like it's no big deal, pretending like my heart isn't hammering against my chest with anticipation and *want*.

"I could go barefoot."

"No," I shake my head. "What if you step on something? I can't have you calling an audible on our date before you have a chance to try the life-changing sandwich in that bag." I nod my head at the brown paper bag in her lap.

"Call an audible?" she repeats, the corners of her mouth lifting as she grins.

"Yeah." My mouth twists to the side. "It's a football term, sorry. You can take the quarterback out of the game but you can't teach an old dog new tricks."

"That's a mixed metaphor," she says, laughing. "And you're not old. Not at all. And I know it is... I know plenty about football."

I raise my arm, pretending to flex for her. "So you trust me to carry you into the end zone?"

She arches an eyebrow, her brown gaze turning fiery. "Are you trying to say you think you're going to score tonight?"

All the humor in me dies at the thought of it. Fucking her. Tasting her. Seeing if those brown eyes get as wide and full of wonder when I'm making her come.

We're both staring at each other, and I don't know what to say. All I know is that I want her so fucking bad it hurts.

"That's not what I meant," I finally manage. "I just don't want you to hurt yourself because I didn't do a good job of taking you out on our first date."

She sighs, then holds out the bag with our food. I take it, unsure of what she's planning.

"I'm not sure if this qualifies as funny business or not," she says, a mock-serious expression on her face. At least, I sure as shit hope it is mock-serious.

I hold both hands up, the effect ruined by the bag of sandwiches in one hand. "Cross my heart."

"You sure you can carry me?"

"Why do women always feel the need to ask that? Of course I can carry you. It would be my honor to hold you."

She inhales sharply, and I realize I've come on too strong.

I don't break eye contact. It's true.

"It would be," I add, softer now.

"Okay," she says, her voice so quiet I have to strain to hear her.

Carefully, she scoots across the seat and I reach for her, letting her lead the way. Her hands wrap around my neck and she huffs a laugh when she stops.

"What do you want me to do? Hop and you'll catch me?" Her tone is playful, but her voice is slightly strained.

"I'd love to catch you," I answer, my voice ragged.

"Three, two—" She jumps, and I can't help laughing at the shocked expression on her face as I easily grab onto her.

My laughter dies as she smiles up at me, my body responding to the weight of her body, to the soft curve of her hip against my waist.

Jesus.

Maybe I should have let her walk through my yard barefoot.

"Well?" she asks, her voice lower, huskier now. My eyes half close at it, because if she keeps talking to me like that, I'm going to kiss her. And that was not the plan for tonight.

A hope, yeah, a wish, sure, but not the plan.

I need this woman like I need air.

I'm not going to scare her off by rushing things.

A good quarterback knows when to rush, and when to take their time.

I've learned enough to know the best things in life are worth waiting for, and I'm pretty sure Kelsey Cole is one of those things.

# CHAPTER 8

KELSEY

**D**aniel's home is… magical.

He carries me into his garden like some knight in a fairytale, simply so I don't manage to sprain an ankle in my work heels. The garden itself is fenced with ornate wrought iron, and late autumn roses crawl up an arched gate. I inhale deeply, trying to relax into his arms, trying not to overthink the way his body feels against mine.

Trying not to do anything hasty.

Trying to convince myself that I shouldn't do anything about the way he's making me feel.

"The front of the garden is all flowers, and then around the dining area are all vegetables, though I pulled most of them out already. There are some winter squashes nearly ready to be picked, and I have one tomato plant that's still soldiering on."

I sniff the air delicately. It's like a different world out here. There's no relentless traffic noise, no scent of diesel and garbage and the other scents of the city.

It smells like rosemary and the air is crisp, cool on my flushed cheeks.

"It's beautiful," I tell him, and I mean it. "I think it's awesome that you garden."

"I love it," he says, and damn, his honesty and unpretentiousness are so refreshing after some of the other guys I've dated. "It's really rewarding. Here we go."

He sets me down on a circular paved patio, and the twinkle lights illuminate a table and chairs, enough to seat twelve.

"Do you have dinner out here a lot?"

"Not as much as I'd like to," he admits.

"It's really nice. You should," I tell him. I can see it, a bunch of friends gathered around the table, surrounded by the greenery.

Overhead, stars twinkle brightly in the darkening night sky.

"I forgot how bright the constellations are away from the lights of the city," I marvel. "It's so strange how we're so close and still feel so far away."

"That's why I wanted to be out here. I'm tired of city living. I like it, don't get me wrong… but I wanted something different this time around."

I pick the closest chair and he sits opposite me, handing me a butcher-paper-wrapped sandwich, still warm.

"How many different places have you lived?"

"A lot," he says grimly. "I played with the Denver Mustangs the longest, seven seasons. I liked it up there, too, and it really felt like home. I grew up in Southern California. Played in New York, Florida… and now I'm here," he says. "And I want this to be home."

His eyes hold mine as he says it, and it feels like he's admitted something important.

I don't know what to make of it, so I take a bite of my pork and long hot sandwich, and immediately groan as flavor bursts across my tongue. The meat is succulent and perfect, the bread crusty and fresh, and the long hots —a pepper I didn't even know existed until I moved to Philly— have the perfect amount of spice.

"What about you? Where have you lived?"

"I grew up in West Texas," I tell him. "Small town."

"Football town," he says knowingly.

I nod. "Football and oil," I agree. "I went to school in Dallas and was lucky enough to land on my feet up here with USBC-Philly a couple years after graduating."

Somewhere in the distance, frogs take up singing. We chew in silence and his gaze keeps darting to me, like he wants to ask me more, but doesn't.

"Are your parents in oil, then?" he asks.

I shift on the chair, uncomfortable, the way I always am when someone brings up my parents.

"No."

He watches me carefully, waiting for more. I don't intend to elaborate.

"This sandwich is really good," I say instead.

"Isn't it? Told you Louie's is life-changing."

I laugh through another bite, covering my mouth with one hand. "I'm not sure about life-changing. That might be a bit of a stretch."

"That's okay," he says slowly, grinning at me. "Maybe the company you're with will be."

It's such a bold statement, so flirtatious and out of left field, that I can't help laughing. *Is this guy for real?*

"Oh, is that right?" I finally say, taking another huge bite. Damn, it really is delicious.

"That's right," he says, but this time, there's nothing but seriousness in his eyes.

I grab the bag of chips and rip it open, just to give myself something to do. Is he like this with all women? Maybe this is just his schtick. Make them think they're special, then WHAM! Nothing matters but football.

Didn't he say that himself?

And if I'm so sure, why does that hurt to think about?

"Are you ready to go on the record?" I ask, my voice brisk and business-like.

"Sure," he says, leaning back and licking a finger.

My brain short-circuits.

"What did you want to ask me?" he says, and I suspect he knows *exactly* what he's doing to me.

I clear my throat. My phone is back in the truck, in my purse, but I have no doubt I'll be able to commit this entire thing to memory. I can use these quotes from Daniel Harrison, QB and Wilmington team captain, to get the others to talk to me. He'll add weight to my questions.

This is perfect.

"What is your position on the AFL cheerleaders?"

"They're an important part of the entertainment provided by the AFL."

I squint at him. "As an AFL and Wilmington Beavers employee, do you believe the cheerleaders should be paid more than minimum wage?"

"Absolutely."

"Do you have to pay for your own uniform?"

He blinks at me like this has surprised him. "No. The cheerleaders have to buy their uniforms?"

I nod. It isn't even the tip of the iceberg when it comes to the things the American Football League subjects those women to, but it's a good opener.

"Have you ever received topless photos of cheerleaders from the AFL or team execs?"

His jaw drops. "What? No. I'd... heard rumors, but I thought they were just that. Gossip."

Got him. My hands clench in my lap, but I force myself to remain calm.

I lean forward slightly, not wanting to appear too eager.

"What kind of gossip have you heard?"

He regards me, and I instantly know that I haven't fooled him at all. He knows this is what I want, and I know he knows.

"Exactly the kind you just asked me about," he says carefully. "I thought they were rumors. Guys in suits who wanted to make themselves seem bigger by acting like they had access to the cheerleaders. All kinds of access."

"Off the record?" I ask. He's not going to fold. He's not going to bite the hand that feeds him, and frankly, I get it. The AFL lawyers don't play around.

"Off the record... I think what you're doing is right. I say keep digging, and if I knew more, I would help you."

I sigh, shoulders sagging slightly.

"I'm sorry, Kelsey, but all I know is gossip. They keep the women away from the players, but I know they have all sorts of expectations and appearances tied up in their contracts."

"The things they've told me..." I shake my head and bite my tongue. "I don't know why they keep doing it."

"Oh," he snorts, "that's easy. It's the same reason I keep going out onto that field every day. Because they love it. They love the roar of the crowd. They love to dance. Just like I love the game, even when the game doesn't love me back. We don't get a lot of time in this world to do what we love, not when what we love has an expiration date on it. So you put up with all the bullshit to chase that high of being firmly in the moment."

I settle against the back of the chair. "That was kind of poetic."

"You sound surprised."

"That you're poetic?" Maybe I am.

"You know, I bet we have more in common than you think we do," he says.

"Oh, now you know what I'm thinking?" I laugh, nibbling on a chip.

He shakes a finger at me. "That's not what I meant. Man, you're going to keep me honest, huh?"

I shrug a shoulder, grinning at him over the scattered remains of our sandwiches and crumpled paper.

"I majored in literature in college." He tilts his head at me, waiting for a response.

"I get the feeling you've used that as a pickup line before. Are you about to quote something romantic at me?"

"Do you want me to?" he asks, his eyes sparkling with the challenge.

The look he's giving me... I don't need romantic poetry. He doesn't need that. All he needs is his natural charm, and anyone remotely interested in him would be in a puddle.

"For the record," he continues, his gorgeous smile flashing brighter than all the twinkle lights draped overhead, "I don't use pickup lines."

"I'm not sure I can work that into my piece, but I'll try."

He laughs, rubbing his jaw. "I don't use pickup lines because I've already got the woman I want sitting next to me."

My eyes widen, and he holds my gaze for a fraction of a second, long enough to send heat sliding through my body.

Maybe Cameron's right.

Maybe I should just... have some fun. Why not?

It's not like I have to marry Daniel Harrison or do anything besides enjoy this moment... and maybe the moment after this one, too. The thought makes my face burn.

"Why literature?" I ask again, and the desire building in me passes. Kind of. Mostly.

"I like to read. I thought it would be fun. That was before I had to take a class on Dostoevsky."

The sad thing about Daniel's not-a-pickup-line pickup line is that it's working. I was already attracted to him, furiously so, embarrassingly so... but the idea that he's able to pivot and talk about classic literature at the drop of a hat? It's unexpected. And refreshing.

As long as he doesn't start verbally jerking it to *Catcher in the Rye* or something.

"Favorite book?" I ask, crossing my arms over my chest.

He huffs a laugh. "You know, this has me more stressed out than any of the on-the-record questions you asked."

"It should."

"I have suddenly completely forgotten the name of every book I've ever read."

We both grin at each other, and then he tilts his head up, looking at the velvet expanse of night overhead. I follow his gaze, expecting constellations, only to see a thick haze of clouds. I sniff, and sure enough, the air has that ozone tinge that threatens rain.

"I think it's going to—"

Fat, cold raindrops plop against my upturned face and I exhale, relishing the sensation.

"I love the rain." I hadn't even realized I was going to speak until the words came out of my mouth. Lightning flashes, forking across the sky.

"Beautiful," he says, and at first, I think he's talking about the way the world looks when it rains. Blurred from all the moisture in the air, clean and crisp and refreshed when it stops.

When I glance back at him, he's staring at me intently. Seriously.

"We should head back to the city," I say, but the words are drowned out by a raucous peal of thunder.

And it begins raining in earnest, the friendly, chubby drops turning into a relentless, drenching downpour.

I start to gather up the papers and sandwich remnants, but he beats me to it.

"Let's get inside," he yells, loud enough I can hear him over the sudden storm. I nod my agreement, kicking my heels off and grabbing them with one hand. My jeans are soaked, heavy with moisture, and my blouse sticks to me like a second skin.

Lightning, jagged and vicious, snarls against the clouds and I stare at it, some of the primal terror ancient mankind must have felt when faced with a storm like this turning my lizard brain to mush.

"Come on," Daniel urges, grabbing my hand and pulling me from a standstill into a run behind him.

I've always laughed at inappropriate times. It's a character flaw. And now, with the sky raging around us, thunder so loud it rattles the teeth in my head, laughter flows out of me again. He glances back at me, an incredulous expression on his face, then grins at me again, his whole face lit up with it, brighter than the lightning.

My feet slap against the wet pavestones, and Daniel's sure hand on mine is the only thing that keeps me from stumbling.

Finally, his house looms in front of us and he quickly unlocks the door, ushering me inside first.

It smells like him.

That expensive cologne lingers in the house, the sandalwood and masculine musk, and I close my eyes, savoring it.

The door closes behind me.

"You okay?" he asks.

I turn back to face him, feeling alive. Feeling present in this moment, so rooted to my body that I'm near giddy with it.

"Your suit," I finally say. We're both leaving puddles all around, a river of water marking where we entered. "It's going to be ruined."

Unthinking, I tug at his coat, trying to help him out of it. "We should lay it flat to dry so it's not totally messed up."

He lets me shuck his coat, standing stock still, like he's afraid to move.

It isn't until he's standing in front of me, his dress shirt plastered to his ripped body, that I realize I've started to undress him. My hands are on his chest and I stare up at him, heat rushing across my cheeks.

"Kelsey," he says, leaning down. "I don't care about the suit." His warm breath traces across my lips and I arch my back, needing him with a ferocity I didn't know was in me.

For a moment, we stand like that, our breath mingling, his lips a fraction of an inch from mine, and possibilities unravel between us.

And when I meet him in the middle, my lips colliding against his, gentle, exploratory, soft...

I know there's no going back.

# CHAPTER 9

DANIEL

*uck* taking it slow.

Kelsey's mouth's on mine and I never want her to stop kissing me. Her mouth is teasing, and hesitant, and so fucking sweet I'm half-losing my mind over her.

I don't want to push her.

I've never wanted someone this badly.

"Kelsey," I say again, and her lips brush over mine.

My hands go to her body, her lush curves, and I groan, knowing I should be a gentleman, knowing I should break off this moment and offer her some sweats.

Fuck all that.

Her breath hitches as I curl my hand around the nape of her neck. I want her closer, I want more.

I'm thirty-nine years old, and I can't remember the last time I wanted something as badly as I want Kelsey Cole.

No—I need to do this right.

I break off the kiss, touching my forehead to hers, trying to stop my racing heart, trying to force some of that control back over myself.

"Kelsey, I don't want to take advantage of you," I make myself say. "I need to know you want me to kiss you."

Fingertips brush against my jawline, and I shudder at the butterfly-soft contact.

"Kiss me," she demands.

Never have two words sounded better. When my lips meet hers again, there's no softness left, no room for hesitation or second thoughts. She's tugging at the buttons on my shirt, her hands insistent and so fucking hot.

I would fuck her right here, right now, if she wanted me to.

I help her hands along, breaking away from the mind-melting kiss long enough to speed things along. The wet shirt sticks to me as we pull at it, and she's staring up at me from waterlogged lashes, her hair wet and wild.

For a moment I can't do anything but stare at her, this brown-eyed beauty, sopping wet, her lips red from mine.

"You're beautiful," I say, and my voice is hoarse.

"You are," she says, a shy grin on her face. Her hands trek across my shoulders, mapping the contour of them, the scars that crisscross the one that's needed surgery twice now. Kelsey's fingers tip-tap down my arms and I can't help but flex a little for her.

I want her to need me as badly as I need her.

"What do you want?" I ask, trying to keep my heart out of my throat. Trying to keep some sense in my head.

"Right now?" her voice is breathless and it makes me light-headed with lust.

"Right now. Tomorrow. Forever." I shake my head. I'm coming on too strong.

I don't give a fuck. Why shouldn't I come on strong?

The only game I care about playing anymore is football.

Whatever happens between Kelsey and I won't be a game.

"Right now?" she answers softly, gaze darting between my eyes. "You."

I groan, tilting my chin back and inhaling. My entire body's taut, and then I explode into action, thanking my lucky stars I didn't take that hit last week and ran into her instead.

Because it means it doesn't hurt to throw her over my good shoulder and sprint with her to the bedroom.

I don't think I would feel it even if it did hurt.

# CHAPTER 10

KELSEY

'm laughing so hard by the time Daniel finally stops running, not even winded by the effort, that I'm not sure if tears are streaming down my face or if it's just wet tracks from my hair.

He tosses me on a sumptuous bed, the linens storm cloud grey, the whole bedroom masculine and expensive, and I bounce slightly, the laughter dying on my lips.

I couldn't possibly look at a man like this, half-naked, silver in his hair and fire in his eyes, and laugh.

He's stunning. A thick white scar crosses his shoulder, a smaller one where his arm meets his chest, but it doesn't mar his perfection. He looks like he's seen some shit and only managed to come out the other side stronger.

"Shoulder surgery," he says, noticing where my attention's gone.

I sit up, tracing my finger over the white, unable to stop touching him. My hands are greedy for him, wanting to explore all of him, wanting to make the most of this one night of bad choices.

"Does it bother you?" he asks, and the hesitancy in his voice makes me pause.

"No." I shake my head.

"We should get you out of your soaked clothes," he says, low and husky, and my entire body goes hot and loose all at once.

"I got your bed all wet." I look around in dismay at the damp spot my jeans have left.

"That's exactly what I fucking want you to do."

My eyes go wide, and then his mouth's on mine again, stealing all thoughts save for pure want. He pulls my soft blazer off first.

"Daniel," I murmur, his mouth grazing over the sensitive skin beneath my ear.

His fingers find the hem of my top, the tips of them grazing my stomach as he lifts it. I shudder at the contact, willing him to go faster, willing this moment to never end, this bottomless need, the anticipation ratcheting up until it's all-consuming.

When he pulls my top all the way off, I stare up at him, waiting to see what he'll do next.

"Like unwrapping the best present," he says softly, gaze skating over me.

My soaked jeans and bra press against my skin, and it's too much. They need to come off. I don't take my gaze from him.

I start to unfasten the button of my jeans, but he stops me by circling my wrist with a finger and a thumb, then presses a kiss to my palm.

It shouldn't be so erotic, a simple kiss on the hand, but I swear it sends heat bursting through me.

He kisses it again, and one thing becomes crystal clear.

Daniel Harrison knows exactly what he's doing in bed, and I am about to have a good time. I grin at him, and he smiles back.

A great time.

"Let me," he says, and he carefully, gently begins tugging my jeans off. Well, as gently as he can, considering they're sticking to my body. I lean over, trying to help him, wriggling to pull them loose.

By the time we get them all the way off, we're both laughing again.

His dark eyebrows rise and he holds up the jeans, then bows at the waist with a flourish of his arm before dropping them on the floor. He advances towards me and the laughter dies in my throat.

"Hey," he says quietly, noting my sudden change in expression. "You okay?"

I nod once, feeling vulnerable, wearing only my underwear and bra.

"I need you to say it."

"I'm good," I say, and in fact, my legs are shaking slightly with need.

"Are you cold?" he asks, noticing it and frowning.

"No," I say, and swallow another nervous laugh.

"You're shaking," he says, and lies down beside me on the bed, tucking me into his warm body. He's still wearing his suit pants, and they slide against my bare thighs. "You know, they say body heat is the best way to get warm."

"I've heard that, but I'm not cold."

He props himself up on an elbow, leaning over me. There's not a hint of a smile on his face. "Why are you shaking?"

His hand skates across my thigh. The shivering ratchets up a bit and I bite my lip, sucking in a breath.

"Is it me? Are you afraid?"

"What?" The question explodes out of me. "No, I'm not afraid. I'm so turned on I think I might die." A twinge of embarrassment at my admission makes my lips curl up.

He leans over me, still stroking his big, calloused hand over my legs. Legs I'm now very glad I shaved this morning. Good looking out, past me.

I shiver again and a low moan tears out of me as his fingertips trek further up, to the edge of my underwear at my hip.

"I don't want you to die," he says. "Unless it's the little death that all those old poets loved to write about."

I huff a laugh, but it doesn't last long, his hands wandering all over my body as I lie tucked in tight next to him.

"Take off your pants," I make myself say.

"No," he says easily. "I want you to stop shaking."

"I'm not going to until you get me off," I say, then wish I could will the words back in. "I know. It's weird. But it's adrenaline and tension release, and apparently it's somewhat normal, I promise." I'm rambling and I stop myself, embarrassment growing by the second.

"That's the hottest fucking thing I've ever heard," he growls. He's on me in a flash and I groan into his mouth, his stubble tickling my chin, his tongue insistent. "I love that I have barely touched you and you're already shaking for me."

I moan as his hands go to my breasts, rubbing them gently beneath my bra.

"Tell me I can take this off," he says.

"Please take it off." I'm close to begging and I don't care.

He does so with practiced ease, and once again, all I can think is that Daniel Harrison knows exactly what he's doing.

My bra sails onto the floor and he stops kissing me.

"You're gorgeous, Kelsey Cole." His blue eyes find mine. "Did you know that?"

I don't answer because I don't really know how to. All I know is that he's making me feel good. His mouth covers my nipple and I cry out wordlessly at the intensity of the pressure building inside me.

His hand teases my other breast, and then it drifts down, down to the thin layer of cotton covering my most private parts.

"Please," I whisper, and he raises his head from my breast, a devilish smile on his face.

He kisses me again, lingering over my mouth, so slow and sensuous it's overwhelming.

"Please," I say again.

"Please what?" he finally asks, pulling away from me. "What do you want, Kelsey?"

"Touch me," I beg, my breath coming in short pants.

"Here?" he asks, stroking lightly along my neck.

I shake my head, trembling, trembling with need.

"Here?" he repeats, rolling my nipple between his thumb and finger.

"No," I moan, arching into the touch.

"Mmm, I like that, though," he says, that wicked half-smile firmly in place.

I'm going to die if he doesn't give me what I need soon. "Please touch me," I say, absolutely out of my mind.

"You want me to touch your pussy, Kelsey? Then say it. Tell me what you want."

I moan again, Daniel's dirty talk taking me even higher.

"Please, yes, I want that."

He moves off me, then tugs me closer to the edge of the bed.

"I want you to lick me."

"Is that right? You want me to taste this?" He throws my quaking legs over his shoulders, pulling me towards him, his fingers digging into the soft flesh of my hips.

"Yes," I say. "Please."

"Good girl," he says approvingly, and his mouth closes over my underwear, sending a ripple of pleasure through me. "Lift your hips," he growls, and the feel of his voice, of his lips and stubble through the thin cotton, is obscenely erotic.

My fingers curl into the comforter, every single cell of my body fixated on the way he's licking me, sucking me, through the fabric. The press of it against my most sensitive parts doesn't detract from the feeling at all, adding another layer of friction.

"Can't fucking get enough," he says, and he pulls my underwear to the side.

When the wet heat of his tongue meets my clit, I half-jump off the bed, so freaking close I'm about to come out of my skin.

"You taste so good, Kelsey."

"Daniel," I say on an exhale, losing all control and starting to grind my hips against his mouth, building, building towards release.

"Good girl, that's right," he says, and his voice is full of ferocious pride. He slips a finger inside me and I cry out, clenching around it. His tongue circles, again and again, his finger, now two, pumping in and out of me slowly, so slowly, still not enough.

I'm making wordless noises, beyond caring about anything other than what he's doing, anything other than the pleasure, so fucking close now.

When he finally sucks my clit, the orgasm tears through me, leaving me shaking in earnest, limp and feeling like I'm floating all at once.

Daniel grins at me from between my legs, then stands up, hooking his arms around me and placing me further back on the bed.

"Wow," I say stupidly.

"You know," he says, tugging my underwear off, wet and unusable when he drops them on the floor, "I don't think we got the bed messy enough."

A laugh bubbles out of me. He leans over me, his big body pressing against my bare breasts, pressing a kiss against my lips. It tastes like me, and the reminder of what he just did makes me hot all over again.

"Are you done yet, Kelsey? You're still shaking."

"Take your pants off," I tell him, not caring about the consequences. Not caring about anything other than having more of him. More of this moment, where nothing exists but making each other feel good.

Grinning at me, he complies. "You know, you're a lot less bossy when my mouth's on you. Maybe I should make a habit of it."

"A habit, huh?"

"Yeah, and a good one, too." He pulls his boxer-briefs off, and whatever tart remark I was about to make dies on my lips.

"Damn." All I can do is stare. He's a big guy, easily over six-foot-two, so I don't know why the huge dick is a surprise.

"You can take it," he tells me.

My toes curl and I reach for him.

"Daniel." His name's question and the answer all at once, and he responds with another kiss. It's tender, and sweet, and I sink into it, closing my eyes and letting him guide me. Giving up thinking, giving up any reservations I have.

He made me feel good. He put me first.

We kiss like that until I lose track of time, until it turns to something fiercer, something fast and needy, until my breath's hard to find again.

Daniel reaches between us, his fingers rubbing through my wetness again. "Good," he says. "You're so wet for me."

One hand continues to work me with expert strokes around my clit even as he reaches into a nightstand, pulling out a gold-wrapped condom. I'm hardly aware of it as I work my hips into his fingers, chasing the orgasm starting to build again.

I hear the condom tear, and when my eyes open, Daniel's staring down at me like I'm the best thing he's ever seen.

"Tell me you want me," he says. "Tell me you want this."

"I want you to fuck me," I say, no hesitation at all.

He grins down at me, but the softness in his eyes fades at my blunt words. "Say please."

"Please fuck me," I tell him.

"Then turn around and hold on to the headboard," he grits out.

Oh, yep. This is about to be a real fun time. As if I could say no to that.

I do as he says and I watch him over one shoulder as his cock rubs against my wetness. Groaning, I thrust my hips back, half-feral with need. A small part of me is still saying this is a mistake, that I'm going to regret this, but I shut that down.

This is going to feel so good.

It's going to be worth it.

# CHAPTER 11

DANIEL

**K**elsey is the most fucking beautiful thing I've ever seen. A slight sheen of sweat glistens all over her curvy, deliciously responsive body, so sweet and pretty it makes my heart ache.

When she tells me to fuck her, please, it snaps something inside me. The internal vows I made to romance her, to woo her, to charm her into bed, all shrivel up.

If she wants to be fucked, I'll fuck her. I'll fuck her so good she never wants anyone but me again.

Her fingers curl over the top of my headboard and I drag my dick through her wetness, the sensation tugging a groan through my throat. She's so fucking wet. For me. I did this.

She moans too and looks over her shoulder at me with lust-glazed eyes, her hair drying in unruly waves that make me want to wrap my hands around it.

"Is this what you want?" I ask her, wanting to stretch this moment out. Wanting to give her what she wants.

Wanting to take her slowly, sweetly, make love to her. It's stupid and sentimental, but that's what I want. Still—what I want doesn't matter. What *she* wants matters. It'll feel so damned good either way.

"Yes," she breathes, and that's all I need.

Wrapping one arm around her waist, I hold her still, plunging deep into her. Kelsey cries out, clenching around me, and I grit my teeth, trying to pace myself. Sweat trickles down my temple and I still myself, knowing if I start thrusting into her now, I'll come too soon.

"Want you to come again," I tell her, pressing my mouth and nose into the curve of her shoulder and neck, drinking in her smell, wanting to drown in her.

"Then make me," she says, and I scrape my teeth against her neck.

She makes a small, helpless noise, and I kick her legs wider with my knee, forcing her to sink deeper onto my cock.

"You feel so fucking good, so fucking tight and wet," I tell her and she moans again, goosebumps peppering her skin all over.

Slowly, I pull out, then push back in, nuzzling the nape of her neck. Her knuckles are white on the headboard, her entire body as taut and electric as a live wire.

"I've got you," I tell her, and despite my best intentions to fuck her hard, to do what she asked, I can't. I can't.

I like her too much to make our first time like that.

I smooth one hand over her arm, entwining my fingers with hers on the headboard. Slowly, I pump in and out of her. My release builds, but I want her to come again. I need her to. I want her to remember this night, I want her to remember that I took care of her.

I want her to know I'll put her first. I've fucked that up in the past, and I'll be damned if I'm going to do it again.

My hand reaches around her stomach, down between her spread legs, and I know I've found her clit again when she keens, a high-pitched whine. Heat bursts through me and I make myself move even slower, trying to find the angle that will send her over the edge even as I tease her clit. I drag in and out, our bodies making wet, sloppy noises.

Maybe she's into the dirty talk. Maybe that's what will help.

"You're taking me so good," I say, murmuring it in her ear. She shivers and I smile to myself. "Look at how fucking wet you are for me, Kelsey. I told you you could take me."

I nip at her neck again, the urge primal and unlike me.

I'm moving faster now, unable to slow down, unable to hold back anymore. She's just too perfect, too wet, feels too good.

She arches back against me, making the sexiest noises I've ever heard in my life. She clenches around my cock, her body shaking even harder as she climaxes.

"Fuck, Kelsey," I rasp, holding her up. "I want to see your face," I say, feeling like an idiot.

"Okay," she says dreamily and I pull out, immediately aching with the loss of her around me.

Carefully, I pull her to me, laying her down on my bed, reveling in the soft, sated pleasure on her face, the scent of her.

I can't help kissing her as I push back inside her. Can't stop kissing her as I take her again, thrusting into her warmth until I come hard, so hard, inside her.

I stay like that for a long time, pressed into her body, until she stops shaking, her limbs loose and soft around me.

"Stay with me," I say, and I'm not asking.

I'm also not sure if I mean tonight, or for the weekend, or forever.

"Okay," she says sleepily.

When I go to the bathroom, I keep the door cracked slightly so I can watch her doze in the mirror.

Once with Kelsey Cole won't be enough.

I don't think I'll ever get enough of her.

# CHAPTER 12

KELSEY

I wake up in the pitch black, an alarm going off.

I blink my eyes blearily, trying to figure out where I am.

Adrenaline shoots through me as memories of the previous night tumble through my brain.

Oh my god. I had sex with Daniel Harrison.

"Hey baby," he says softly and I blink, only to see him fully dressed in another suit, looking handsome as hell. "Sleep in. I have to go to work." He gestures next to him and I realize he has a small carry-on-sized suitcase. "Away game."

"I don't have a car," I manage, still groggy. "What time is it?"

"It's four AM. I have to be on a plane in a couple hours to fly out. Stay here."

"Stay here?" I echo, pulling the covers up to my chin. I'm naked. I had sex with Daniel Harrison on a first date, and now I'm naked in his bed.

"Stay at my house for the weekend," he repeats, grinning down at me. "I have food in the fridge, so many streaming services that I don't even know what I have, and a whole roomful of my favorite books. I even have a Nintendo Switch with what-ever games you're into."

"I have to get my car," I say stupidly, trying not to panic.

"You don't like Animal Crossing? Everyone likes Animal Crossing."

"I don't have a toothbrush."

"I keep extras in the guest bathroom," he says, some of the smile fading now. "You don't want to stay?"

He asks the question like he can't quite believe it, can't quite believe a woman wouldn't want to stay in his bed and wait for him to get home from getting beaten and bloodied on the football field.

I close my eyes, biting back what I want to say. That this shouldn't have happened. That I made one choice, and it didn't mean anything. It was nothing but scratching a very sexy itch.

"I can't stay here this weekend," I tell him finally. "I have things I have to do. Work."

"You can borrow my laptop," he says.

"Daniel, you can't be serious. You can't really want me to stay here. You hardly know me. What if I'm a thief? What if I..." I squint my eyes, my brain stumbling over a good reason why he wouldn't want me here. "What if I'm just here because I wanted to nail a football player?"

"If you were a jersey chaser, I would pop a ring on your finger right now and you'd let me lock you down," he answers cheer-fully. "But I can tell from the freaked-out expression on your face that neither of those things are true."

His smile fades and he closes his fingers around my chin. "Stay here. Get some sleep. But first," he dips a hand into his pocket and retrieves the newest iPhone. "Give me your number."

Numb, I take the phone from him, typing in my number.

He squints at me while I do it, like I'm a puzzle he hasn't quite figured out how to put together. Well... that makes two of us.

He takes the phone from me before I can close the screen, tapping the call button.

My phone vibrates across the nightstand, and I notice it's even plugged in.

"I got it from the truck last night while you slept," he explains. "I figured you'd want it. Your clothes are in the dryer. Feel free to steal a pair of sweatpants." He jerks his head towards a door on the other side of the room. "Help yourself to whatever your sticky little fingers want, and when I get back, I'll make it worth your while to stay."

"No," I tell him, even though throwing all my responsibilities in the garbage for one wild weekend shacked up at his house is pretty appealing. "I can't."

Daniel scratches his scruff, which is well past stubble now and on to beard, looking confused.

I wonder if it's the first time he's heard the word from a naked girl in his bed.

"Please?" he asks. "Please stay."

I don't know what to do. Part of me loves the idea of it. Of being here when he gets back, of having sex with him again.

But that part of me isn't rational. It isn't who I am.

"I'll call an Uber."

His face falls, then shutters, and he smiles at me softly. "Okay, if that's what makes you more comfortable. Is it okay if I call you? Text you?"

My heart squeezes, so tight it's uncomfortable, because isn't this what every woman wants to hear after a one-night stand?

That he'll call? That he wants me? That this wasn't just about booty for him, even if it was for me?

"Sure," I say.

He won't call. It's easy enough to say yes when we both know he's lying.

He's Daniel Harrison, revered quarterback, and I'm a nobody upstart reporter from USBC-Philly. I'll probably never see him again, and the only time I'll see his name light up my screen is when I type up his on-the-record remarks for my piece. His quotes probably won't even make it on air.

I'll never taste his name on my mouth again.

So I smile up at him, naked in his bed, and tell him what we're both pretending he wants to hear.

"Of course," I say.

# CHAPTER 13

## DANIEL

In the dim cool of my closet, I can concentrate on finding her a pair of sweatpants. Her jeans are still damp, and she wants to leave now. Already called an Uber, and even managed to miraculously find one out here at this hour.

It shouldn't hurt that she doesn't want to stay here while I'm gone, that she doesn't seem half as affected by our night together as I am. It does, though. It hurts.

I like her. I like what I see in her, her heart and humor, her drive.

I like her a lot.

A muscle in my temple flexes and I pull out a drawer, finding a nondescript pair of sweats that are sure to swallow her whole, along with an old t-shirt—my favorite, actually, from my college days. The college shirt is half her age.

That must be what it is. I'm too old for her, or she thinks so. I know she had a good time last night. At least, I'm pretty damn sure of it.

I know I did.

And I know better than to let a woman like this slip through my fingers. I won't make the same mistakes I've made in the past.

"Hey." Her soft voice filters through the cracked door, and when I look up, she's standing there, the glow of the closet lights illuminating her face, her sandy gold hair. "The Uber says it's five minutes away." She holds up the phone, and sure enough, the ETA is right there, a ticking time bomb.

"I gotcha," I tell her, holding out the sweats like they're the best things I could give her. Fuck, I'd give her half the closet if she'd let me.

Though I'd prefer her naked, the sheet wrapped around her, like she is right now.

Kelsey takes the clothes, clearly self-conscious in the early morning blush of day, not at all like the last woman I took to bed, who wielded her body like a weapon. Though I certainly didn't mind it at the time, Kelsey's sweet. Refreshing.

I could really fucking fall for her.

Fucking AFL, taking me away from her for another stupid game. No wonder my ex-wife left me.

They both deserve better than a man who isn't around.

"What?" she asks, biting her lower lip.

Oh. I've been staring at her like a lovestruck idiot, holding the clothes against my chest.

"You have to promise to give me the shirt back," I say stupidly, looking for any reason to see her again. "It's my favorite."

"You don't have to give me your favorite." A small laugh slides out of her, and god, I want to fucking taste the sound, I want to live on it.

"I want to see you in it," I say gruffly.

Her chocolate eyes go wide, and the pink pout of her mouth curves up in a smile. "Going to be hard for me to wear it if you don't hand it over."

"Just making sure the terms and conditions of my clothing loan were clear." I hold the wad of soft material out to her.

"Crystal," she says. She wraps the sheet around her waist, covering up her small, perfect breasts.

My hands flex at my sides, my mouth gone dry at the reminder of her body beneath mine, at the delicate curves in all the right places.

She puts the shirt over her head, tugging her hair out the neck, and at first, I think maybe she's unaware of the effect she has on me.

Until she looks up at me from beneath her makeup-smudged lashes, heat in her gaze.

I swallow a groan, then smile at her, wide as I can.

"The shirt looks good on you," I rasp.

"The height of couture fashion," she says.

To me, it is. So was the sheet. I want to kiss her so bad I can hardly stand it.

I don't want to scare her away. I don't want to fuck this up any more than I already have.

She shimmies into the pants, the sheet puddling around her bare feet, and I'm transfixed. Fuck. I rake a hand through my hair, sure I've messed up the careful styling I did so I'd be up to travel dress standards, but I don't care.

Better I mess my hair up than mess this up with Kelsey Cole.

"It's going to look great with my work heels."

"I have house shoes you can borrow," I say. "Moccasins. Whatever they're called." I would give her the shoes off my feet.

She huffs a laugh, her eyebrows raising up. God, she's pretty.

"I don't think I'll be able to walk in your shoes."

"It's too late," I say, shaking my head. "You need the complete look. The heels won't work, nope."

Another chuckle trickles out of her, her smile making my heart leap. I tug the shoes off the shelf, then kneel next to her, a fuzzy house shoe in hand.

It's way too big for her, hilariously so, and we're both laughing as she slips her little foot into it. She presses one hand on my shoulder for balance as I slide the other one on.

I glance up at her from my position on the floor, kneeling at her feet.

"My Cinderella in sweatpants," I murmur.

"That would make you my prince." She holds up her foot though, and the shoe slides off. "I think you're looking for someone with bigger feet. Much bigger feet. Much, much bigger."

I stand slowly, and her gaze follows me up.

"Well, you know what they say about big feet." I arch one eyebrow.

She snorts a laugh. "Yeah, I've seen the evidence for myself."

"Excuse you." I arrange my face into faux shock. "I was going to say that I needed big shoes." I wink at her, unable to stop the corny gesture.

To my relief though, she laughs again.

Her phone vibrates in her hand, her expression sobering. "The Uber is here."

The change in her is immediate. Kelsey squares her shoulders, inhaling deeply and knotting my old school shirt up so it shows off her sexy figure... and probably more so because she might trip over the length.

I trail after her as she floats back into my bedroom, where she belongs. I give myself a mental shake. *No, I can't think like that.*

She pauses at the door, a reusable grocery bag filled with the clothes I retrieved from the dryer clutched tight in one hand.

"I don't know where your front door is," she admits.

Begging her to stay again is on the tip of my tongue, but I close my mouth on the words and take her hand instead.

"I'll show you. That way you know your way back here if you change your mind." Fuck. I'm *still* coming on too strong.

"Right." A disgruntled snort punctuates the remark. The look she gives me is slightly frustrated, her nose pinched up like she doesn't believe me. I stare right back down at her as I lead her through my house, quiet in the still dark early morning.

It dawns on me then, why she's acting weird.

She thinks I'm lying.

She thinks I'm playing her. She thinks I'm placating her.

A relieved laugh gusts out of me. It echoes off the hard surfaces of the house, harsher than it should be. Her expression darkens at the sound, her feet shuffling along in the too-large shoes along the distressed wood floor.

"You wanted to know my favorite book," I say, opening the heavy front door. A gold Honda sits in the circular drive in front of my house, the twinkle lights still on in the garden.

She pauses, one foot out the door. "Yeah, I did."

"I can do you one better than telling you. Stay right there."

Her lips purse, but she doesn't refuse, shrugging one shoulder, the collar of my shirt slipping off it, revealing a delicate bra strap.

I stare at it a moment too long, then clear my throat.

"Stay there, I'll be right back," I repeat, then jog to the study directly behind the stairs that spiral down into the entryway. My eyes protest the bright light when I throw the switch and I scan the shelves, trying to find what I'm looking for. Not on the first shelf... no... my eyes dart back and forth until they finally land on it.

There. The book that made me fall in love with reading.

My hands are huge on the tattered paper cover, the pages so dog-eared and the spine so worn I'm almost embarrassed to give it to her.

"Hey, you okay?" Kelsey calls out, her voice loud in the empty house.

I slap the book cover against one hand, smiling to myself as I race back to the front door.

"Here," I say. "This was my favorite book as a kid."

She looks from the book in my hand to my face, then back down again. I tuck it in her bag, and when I glance back at her, she's blinking quickly, as though she's too surprised to comprehend what I'm doing.

I think I like her off-balance.

I think I'm going to have a lot of fun proving her wrong about me, and suddenly, I can't wait to get started.

My chest feels light and tight all at once, happiness cracking it open as I take her small hand in mine, a hand that's thrown a thousand footballs but hasn't ever held anything that felt so right as hers.

I walk her out to the car, my dress shoes loud on the pavestones, her feet making the funniest noise as she shuffles next to me.

"Hey, I know you," the driver says.

Kelsey gives me a bewildered, apologetic look, and I want to wipe that look straight off her face. I don't give a fuck if everyone I run into for the rest of my life knows who I am.

I just want to kiss her.

I lean down, cupping her face between my hands, her lovely, heart-shaped face with melted chocolate eyes. For a second, I only hold her, watching for the moment her pupils dilate, the moment her lips part, and then I brush my lips against hers.

Her body melts into mine, her hand tight round my fingers. I kiss her until I hit the point where if I don't break it off, I'm going to be uncomfortable for the whole flight to Miami. The last place I want blue balls is on a plane full of my teammates.

The Uber driver clears his throat and I grin at him.

"Sorry," I say.

"Sorry," Kelsey echoes, completely breathless. It's a good sound on her.

"I'll call you," I tell her, then greedily press my lips to hers again.

She sits down in the car, clearly out of sorts. Her silence screams how uncertain she is about me still. It shouldn't delight me that she doesn't know what to make of me, that she doesn't know how to feel.

But it does because *I* know how I feel.

I'm grinning like a fool as I wave at the car disappearing down my drive, the light-brown head getting smaller and smaller as it goes.

I can't wait to prove her wrong about me.

The whole flight to Miami, I can't stop thinking about all the ways I'm going to convince Kelsey Cole that she belongs with me, at least long enough to decide how she really feels.

# CHAPTER 14

KELSEY

Our normal Saturday brunch place isn't busy at all, but every time someone looks at me, I feel weird. Like they recognize me.

It's bizarre.

I basically half-dozed in the Uber, fell back asleep on my bed on top of the sheets, and woke up smelling Daniel Harrison all over me, the scent intermingled with his comfy, huge clothes.

And with only fifteen minutes to spare before I was supposed to meet Cameron for our weekly brunch.

My hair's still damp from the fastest shower of my life, and I slapped it back in a tight bun and threw on my favorite caramel-colored jumpsuit and an oversized cream sweater.

Maybe I look like shit. Maybe that's why everyone is staring at me. Wrinkling my nose, I glance down at myself.

I mean, I don't think I look that terrible.

"Well, well, well," Cameron says, a half-smile on her face as I walk over to our usual table. "Look what the cat dragged in."

"Hey, I'm only ten minutes late," I say. "Do I look like crap?" I pat my slicked back hair, cringing at how wet it still is.

"You look as hot as ever, you sexy beast. I already ordered some of our faves," Cameron tells me, sipping a bubbling mimosa. "Speaking of sex and beasts, how was the quarterback last night?"

I stare at her. "What?"

A waitress appears and I try to slow my racing brain.

Maybe she's fishing. How else would she know I had a one-night stand with Daniel Harrison?

"What can I get for you to drink?" The waitress asks smoothly, smiling down at me.

"Water," I say.

"She wants a bottomless mimosa," Cameron tells her.

"That too, and a coffee," I agree.

"But the mimosa first, please. The woman's got gossip to give me."

"Sure thing," the waitress says. "I'll bring the petite almond croissants now, too."

"Thank you," we chorus.

"Spill." Cameron grins, then flexes her hands like a cat, inspecting her sparkling nails. Today, they're a shade of frosty blue, thick holographic flakes glimmering throughout them.

They remind me of Daniel Harrison's eyes. My face turns beet-red as memories of him slide through me.

The candles in the middle of the table gutter as the strength of my sigh batters them.

I stare at Cameron.

She stares at me, one eyebrow raised. Waiting.

It's a gossip standoff. Except she's the only one with a loaded pistol.

"How did you know?" I finally ask. There's no use in pretending like I didn't just have the best sex of my life.

"Well, for one, you have that post-orgasm glow. Or at least you did, before you turned bright red. Really, they should figure out how to bottle it. Illuminating primer my ass, give me good sex any day."

"Illuminating primer's not supposed to go on your ass," I say.

"And two," she continues, grinning at my joke and holding up two fingers. "It's all over BeaverTok. The Hot Dams are going wild with conspiracy theories and fan cuts. Your Uber driver recorded you two kissing. And someone in some deli uploaded a story on Instagram with you two holding hands."

My stomach drops. My heart stops.

I clutch the table.

The waitress reappears, as if summoned at exactly the worst time, as I feel the bottom dropping out of my very soul. Now all I need for the restaurant double whammy is the manager to come over and ask me how my meal is before I've even ordered.

She sets the mimosa down and I sling it back, coughing from the champagne but keeping it down.

The waitress clears her throat. "Okay then. That kind of a morning?"

"Oh yeah, definitely," Cameron says in a sing-song voice.

"I want the house special, please," I manage, curbing a hiccup with the back of my hand. "Eggs over easy, hashbrowns, sourdough, and bacon."

"Fruit or oatmeal?" she asks.

"Fruit. And I want a waffle. Extra syrup."

"You got it."

"Fuck me," I say under my breath.

The waitress gives me a strange look. I'm too upset to apologize.

Cameron rattles off her order. My fingers wrap around her mimosa and I slam it back, too. I press my hand against my mouth, trying not to burp.

They both stare at me.

"BeaverTok thinks I'm having sex with Daniel Harrison," I tell the waitress. "The Hot Dams are after me."

She cringes in sympathy. "I'll be back with another round of mimosas."

The Hot Dams, the fanbase of the Wilmington Beavers, are

notorious. You'd think they would chill the hell out since the Beavers have had a ten-year losing streak. I mean, they've won games here and there, but they haven't made it to the AFL play-offs in over a decade. Things I only know because my dad makes sure to rattle off the stats to me at least once a month.

I'm an expert on football against my will.

The Hot Dams seem to think that the ruder, louder, and more obnoxious they are, the better their beloved team will do.

And now they think I'm fucking Daniel Harrison.

I bury my face in my hands.

"How bad is it?" I moan.

"You haven't checked your socials today, have you?"

"That bad." I collapse onto the table, my gold hoop snagging on my sweater. I sit up, my head tilted, my earring caught, and I'm too freaked out to even bother fixing it.

Cameron reaches over and detangles it from the soft mohair.

Two mimosas land in front of me. I drink one, and half of the other.

Cameron holds out a croissant and I pop the whole thing in my mouth.

"I would say not to gag, but I think we both know that's not a problem," she jokes.

I glare at her.

"Wrong time, wrong time, got it. Sorry."

Another croissant goes down the hatch.

"You can't avoid me with croissants all morning. We need a plan to deal with this. But first, I want to hear all about it. All the dirty details."

"No," I say, and the word surprises us both.

Cameron's face clouds, anger furrowing her brow. Her voice drops, low and serious.

"Do I need to fucking kill him?" she asks. "Because I will make his life hell."

"No," I say, and this time, I can't help but laugh. Maybe that's the champagne getting the best of me. "No, it was all consensual.

And great," I say, a pang of unexpected sadness sending an ache through my chest.

Although that ache could also be from chugging too many mimosas.

"That's a relief," she says. "No need for a little light homicide after all. So… it was good, huh? About time you hooked up with someone."

I press the heels of my hands into my eyes. "Cameron, the last thing I wanted was for a freaking one-night stand to be all over social media."

"Oh please, they have a game tomorrow, right? The last thing the Hot Dams are going to be worrying about as soon as it's game time is whether or not you slept with the quarterback." As soon as she says it, though, she freezes, a croissant halfway to her mouth.

"Fuck," I moan, and this time, I reach for the water, too buzzed from the champagne I stupidly threw down my gullet.

"They're going to blame you for his performance tomorrow, either way. No matter what."

"Gee thanks, Cameron, I can always count on you to bring your sunny perspective."

"You wouldn't be my friend if you didn't like realism, excellent taste, and sarcasm," Cameron replies, not missing a beat.

We stare at each other, though, and I can tell she's worried from the little crease in her forehead.

"What's John going to say?" I tap my nails on the glass of water, biting my lip.

Cameron's forehead wrinkles even more at the mention of our boss.

"He's going to try to figure out an angle to exploit. He'll see it as a way to get an in with the team, or something like that. Honestly, your sex life or lack thereof is none of his damn business, and I am happy to walk us both down to HR and help you file a complaint about his ass."

"You and I both know HR doesn't give a fuck."

I stare at her, Cameron's expression growing darker by the second.

"So you ignore whatever it is he tells you. Besides, you said it was a one-night stand, right? The Hot Dams will have a field day with it for a little while, and then they'll move on to something new next week."

I nod, a miserable knot tightening my stomach. "Right."

"Right," Cameron echoes.

Neither of us sound convinced.

"It *was* a one-night stand, right?" she asks, sipping her mimosa and narrowing her eyes at me over the rim.

"Of course," I squeak out, then clear my throat. "Of course it was a one-night stand."

Cameron snorts, her eyebrows raised.

I grab the mimosa again, and a flurry of bubbles pop to the surface through the orange liquid.

"He asked me to stay at his house for the weekend, while he's gone." The knot in my stomach gets tighter and I drop my hand to my lap, folding and unfolding the cloth napkin.

Her nostrils flare as she inhales, tipping her chin up and staring at the restaurant ceiling.

"He was just being nice." Wasn't he? "You know how I feel about football. The last thing I want to do is get involved with a football player."

"That ship has fucking sailed, friend," Cameron says, refocusing on me.

"There's no way I am going to put myself through a football wife lifestyle," I say. "You know how hard things are for my dad. You know how I feel about the AFL."

"It sounds an awful lot like you're trying to convince yourself."

The waitress reappears and we both snap our mouths shut, then thank her as she sets plate after plate in front of us. I don't even want to eat anymore. I'm in the middle of a freakout.

Cameron picks up her fork, then puts it back down with an enormous sigh.

She leans across the food, pitching her voice low.

"I know the AFL screwed your dad over. I know he's struggling, but he played decades ago."

I squeeze my eyes shut, but that doesn't stop her from plowing forward.

"They've changed concussion protocols since then."

"Stop," I tell her. "Just stop."

I make myself cut a bite of waffle. The fork and knife make a sharp, unpleasant ping against the plate. Despite the blueberry syrup, it tastes like ash in my mouth.

But Cameron's Cameron, and one of the reasons she's a great reporter is because once she has an idea in her head, she doesn't let it go.

"Do you like him? Because if he's inviting you to stay at his house, it doesn't sound like he thinks it was a one-night stand." Her face pinches then clears, as though she's realized something. "Didn't you tell me he called you his future girlfriend?"

"He did," I say, my voice all high and funny. It's not the mimosas' fault, either.

"Eat," Cameron commands. "Eat, and think about swallowing the idea that maybe he doesn't think he's a one-night stand. And leave the mess of your dad out of it too, and think about whether or not you want Daniel Harrison to be more than a one-night stand."

I glare at Cameron but do as she says, forcing another forkful into my mouth. Cameron grins at me.

"You know, if you weren't such a good friend, I don't think I'd like you," I grouch at her.

"That's fine. I don't have the desire to be universally liked," she says. A flicker of something like annoyance passes through her eyes before she's grinning at me again.

The waitress reappears, topping off the mimosas.

I don't touch mine again, feeling half-drunk emotionally and physically.

Not a one-night stand? I feel like an idiot. Maybe he did mean it.

"He hasn't texted me," I say. "If he really was into me, wouldn't he have texted me?"

"How old is he? Forty-five?"

"Thirty-nine," I say. My cheeks immediately heat. Stupid alcohol. I take another sip.

"For someone who doesn't follow football, you sure know a lot about this quarterback. For someone who says it was a one-night stand, you sure were quick with that."

"Ugh," I say, pressing the cool mimosa against my steaming cheeks.

"I mean, maybe he does the three-day rule. That's an old-school thing. So you guys are what, fourteen years apart? I could see it working."

"Stop," I tell her.

"I mean it." She shrugs, then takes another bite, chewing thoughtfully.

My waffle stares up at me forlornly, begging me to eat some more, but I move on to the bacon. The waffle's too sweet for how I'm feeling. Salty sounds right.

Maybe some bitter black coffee, too.

"Three-day rule? Like three days to text, right?"

My phone vibrates in my purse next to me and I take it out, expecting it to be my dad.

I freeze.

I take the mimosa and drain it.

"Is it him?" Cameron scream whispers, reaching for the phone. "It's him, isn't it? Oh shit, he is into you. I fucking knew it. I knew it from the way he was holding your face in that viral TikTok."

"Viral?" I yelp.

Half the restaurant goes quiet, their attention firmly on me.

"You didn't tell me it went *viral*," I hiss.

"Oh yeah, well, I didn't think you needed to hear all the details."

The phone vibrates in my palm again, and my heart beats a mile a minute.

"Answer it," Cameron urges. "You said the sex was good, right? Who cares about long-term. If the sex is good and he's nice, then see where it goes."

I glance at the mimosa, but the damn bottomless thing has bottomed out. It's empty.

"I don't want to be rude to you," I tell her.

"If you don't answer it, I will, in fact, be upset," Cameron promises. "It would be rude of you to not answer."

Fine.

I hit the green call button and hold the phone to my ear, trying to slow my racing heart.

"Hello?" I say, like I have no idea who's calling. I grimace.

"Kelsey Cole," Daniel's smooth, low voice, as rich as black coffee, fills my ear. Goosebumps spread across my skin. "For a second there, I thought you were going to screen my call. I have to say, it's good to hear your pretty voice."

"Hi," I say.

Cameron rolls her eyes, laughing at me across the table.

"I can't talk long, but I wanted to let you know we just touched down in Florida."

"That's good," I say, and the knot in my stomach loosens slightly, replaced by a warm, intoxicated feeling. "I'm glad you got there safely," I add, and I'm surprised to find I mean the platitude.

"Makes me smile to hear you say that," Daniel says, and I can hear the grin in his voice. The warmth explodes into butterflies, and I'm smiling right back at the phone, like he can see me.

"I wanted to know your address, if that's okay. I have something I want to send you," he says. "If that's alright. I know… you didn't seem sure about me this morning. So if you say no, I understand—"

"I'd like that," I interrupt. "I would like that."

Cameron's clapping her hands in excitement, only witnessing one side of this awkward conversation. I point at her, then draw a slow, meaningful line across my throat.

"You want to text it to me? I have to get off the phone, but I promise I'll make it worth your while." His voice turns low and suggestive, and I fan my face.

"Yeah, I can do that," I say.

"I'll text you tonight, if that's okay."

God, I love how sweet he's being. I love how he's asking for permission with every single thing he does. It makes me feel good. It makes me feel safe.

Maybe I *should* just let Daniel make me feel good for a little while, without worrying about all the what-ifs.

Cameron's right. Talking to him, hanging out with him doesn't mean I have to expect anything else.

"I would like that," I finally answer.

Cameron squeals, doing a little shimmy in her chair.

Guess I'm not the only one feeling the effect of the bottomless brunch mimosas.

"That makes me happy, Kelsey Cole," he says after a beat, and I believe him. "I gotta go, but text me your address. I'll talk to you tonight."

"Okay. Tonight. It's a date."

"A date." He laughs. "I like that. Bye, Kelsey."

"Bye."

The call ends and I stare at my phone for a second, in a state of slight shock.

"What did he say? What did he say?" Cameron chirps, and I realize with a start my mimosa has magically refilled itself.

The phone lights up again, and it's Daniel.

> Address please? I promise it will be worth it

I tap out my address, then put the phone face down.

It vibrates against the table and Cameron grabs it, staring at the screen.

"He just sent you a bunch of flower emojis. What did he say? You're killing me. Let me live through you. Tell me. Everything." Cameron's holding her butter knife in one hand, her phone in the other, a menacing expression on her face.

"He wanted to send me something. And to talk tonight." I shrug one shoulder, like hot, sexy guys who know how to use their mouths send me things all the time.

"He liiiiiikes you," Cameron sings, handing back my phone.

Sure enough, there are a dozen flower emojis. "Want to bet he's sending flowers?"

"So cute. Overdone, sure, but cute all the same."

"He's a gardener," I tell her. "His house is… amazing."

"Awwww," Cameron's nose scrunches up as she smiles. "I'm super happy for you. This is exciting. Now tell me about the sex."

"Don't be gross. I'm not telling you anything." A slow smile creeps across my face and I raise one eyebrow. "Other than it was good. Really good. Great, even. He's… he seems like a really nice guy."

A guy who plays football. But still. I am not going to read into anything. For once, I'll just live in the moment. It'll be fine.

"Living the dream," Oliva says on a sigh. "Good for you, Kelsey."

I return to my food, eating with more gusto, enjoying it.

Enjoying the idea of there being flowers waiting for me at my apartment from a man I like.

I can't stop smiling.

# CHAPTER 15

## DANIEL

I feel really good. Sure, I have the same pain in my bad knee, the same ache in my messed up shoulder, but it's not bugging me like it normally does.

Darius, one of the few men I've played with before we were both traded to the Wilmington Beavers, gives me a once-over.

"New girl?" he asks.

"Why do you say that?"

"I've been married for ten years, man. Trust me, you either learn to read people by then, or at least your partner, or things get shitty fast. Also, you keep checking your phone. Dead giveaway."

I laugh. "You got me. How's your wife and kids?"

"Good, man, they're good. I gotta say, as much as I love the game..." He drifts off, then closes the space between us. Darius is a massive guy, one of the biggest linebackers on the team. He hits like a fucking wrecking ball, too, but he lowers his voice to say, "I'm getting real tired of being away so much, ya know? Wears on me."

Darius squints at me. "You don't have to answer. I know you feel the same. I can see it in the way you play. Having a woman will be good for you, man." He claps a hand on my shoulder, then strides away to the room where the defensive line sits with their coaches, about to watch tape.

"Dude, you went viral." Ty Matthews comes up beside me, his brother next to him as we all walk to our offensive team meeting. "Nice."

"What?" I ask. "For what?"

"I swear to god, I get a gray hair every time you open your mouth," Ty says, and his brother laughs.

I arch an eyebrow at him.

"BeaverTok blew you up. There's all kinds of fan cuts of you running into that hot girl from last week's game." He frames his hands like a camera and his brother mimes sacking someone. They both laugh. "Then it cuts to you kneeling next to her, and then holding her hand, and then you guys are making out." He shakes his head, incredulous. "The Hot Dams are out of their damned minds, if you ask me."

"Fuck," I rake my hands through my hair.

"Nah, man, no footage of that. Yet," Ty's brother, Jacob, adds.

I glare at him and he holds his hands up.

"You're not going to let it affect your game, right?" Ty asks, not bothering to beat around the bush.

His brother shoves him, giving him a meaningful look, but the rookie receiver just laughs it off. "What? I'm not allowed to ask?"

"Shut up," Jacob says. "Sorry, Daniel. We won't talk about it again."

"Tell the coaches I'll be right there," I say and pull my phone back out. I should text Kelsey, see if she's okay.

My finger hovers over her number. I'm about to call her again, even though I know that's coming on too strong. I don't want to push her. I've already pushed her pretty far, and I don't want to scare her away.

The phone lights up before I have a chance to call Kelsey, though, and it's my agent.

"Hey Brent," I answer, squeezing my eyes shut.

"Daniel, have you seen social media? You went viral with some woman."

"I know," I grit out.

"Listen, man, I know you like to keep your private life private, but this is some damn good PR. Lots of people out there rooting for you to be some kind of fucking romance hero to this woman. She's good-looking too, which helps."

I ball my fists. I don't like Brent commenting on how Kelsey looks. I don't like it at all.

"I think you need to work this angle. I think this is a good look for you, especially to help line up some positive public sentiment towards you as you… start to transition off the field."

"You realize I have a game to play tomorrow, right, Brent?"

"I know, Daniel, I know. Just trying to think ahead."

Think ahead to when I finally announce my retirement and Brent tries to hang on to the oldest cash cow in his stable. I like Brent, but sometimes he annoys the fuck out of me.

"I just wanted to say keep it up. TikTok loves you two together. The more public you can make this, the better. This is the perfect move right now."

"That's not why—"

"The why never matters, Daniel. Just the result. Try to make it work with this one."

"That's what worries me, Brent," I say quietly. "I want to make it work with this one."

"Then it shouldn't be hard for you, should it? Better and better. Anything I can do to help. Tickets to shows, dinner reservations, whatever."

"I already sent her flowers," I tell him. "I don't need dating advice from you."

"Hey, just because I'm on wife number five doesn't mean I don't know how to treat a woman."

"Right." I start to roll my eyes and hang up but stop myself.

Next week is bye week. Next week, I'll be home, no game.

"You know what, Brent?" I ask slowly. "I may just take you up on that. You organize the dates."

"My assistant will organize them," he corrects me, and this time, I do roll my eyes. "What else for my favorite quarterback?"

A small, possessive grin unfurls on my face. "I want to send her merch. As much Wilmington and Daniel Harrison merch as possible. Courier it over today, so she has it for the game tomorrow. And write her a note."

"That's easy enough. What do you want the note to say?"

When I tell him, he's silent for a second.

"I take it back, man. I think you might not need my help after all."

"Just make sure she gets it. I'll forward you the address."

"You got it. Now go get to work and try to win, huh?"

"Always do, Brent."

I turn the phone off. I can't wait to hear Kelsey's reaction to what's coming her way.

I can't wait to see her in my number.

# CHAPTER 16

KELSEY

'm half hungover when the second knock of the day raps against my door. There's already a huge bouquet of fuchsia roses on the counter, and a fresh surge of happiness courses through me as I glance at them.

A quick look out the peephole shows a guy in a navy polo holding a huge box with a navy bow wrapped around it.

"Delivery for Kelsey Cole," the man says in a bored voice.

I throw the latch on the top of my apartment door, then the bolt, and open it.

"Hi, I'm Kelsey," I say, confused and still slightly drunk from all the mimosas at brunch. The buzz didn't help me write any more notes on my story, and the building headache won't either. So much for my responsibilities today.

"Sign here," the guy says, thrusting a clipboard at me.

I do as he asks, signing across the dotted line. He sets the package down in front of my door and I stare at it, then at the logo across the top of the paperwork.

"It's from the Wilmington Beavers?" I ask, confused.

"Nah, it's from Daniel Harrison. I'm just the courier for the Beavers. Want me to take it inside?"

"No," I say quickly. "I got it."

"Cool. Have a good day," he says, then takes the clipboard, leaving me with the cardboard box and bow.

I lean down, using my shoulder to keep the door open, and heft the box into my arms.

"Oof," I say. It's heavier than I thought it would be. The door closes softly behind me. I juggle the package for a second with my knee and one arm as I click the lock into place. The weight of the loaded box makes me shuffle slowly forward, the huge bow tickling my nose. How the courier got this upstairs without pulling a muscle, I have no idea.

I bite my cheeks in excitement, placing the box down on my teensy kitchen table.

"Well, Daniel Harrison, you sure are raising the bar for every dude that comes after you," I mutter.

I glance at my phone charging on the polished kitchen counter, the social media notifications now so daunting that I'm afraid to even open the apps. I don't know if I want to see Daniel and myself through BeaverTok's eyes. And if there's one thing I know about social media… it's that there are going to be a ton of nasty comments along with the nice.

Maybe I should just delete all the apps.

Daniel hasn't texted, not even after I sent him a pic of the roses with a heartfelt thank you.

He's probably just busy.

Not too busy to send this, whatever it is. I cross my arms, staring at the box.

I grab my phone and make a gut decision. I need reinforcements.

Cameron's face fills the screen in the next second.

"What's wrong?"

I turn the phone around and show her the huge, fluffy-bowed box.

"What's that? I'm too hungover for this."

"Same," I say. "And I don't know. It's a box with a bow."

She frowns. "Why are you showing me a box with a bow?"

"Daniel had it couriered over."

"Shut UP," she screeches. "That's so fucking cute. I'm dead. I'm screaming. Dead and screaming."

"I think you're still drunk from brunch."

"Mood," she says and the camera tilts as she sits up, her hair falling all over her face. The sudden movement makes my stomach swim. "What's in the box?"

I bite my lip. "I don't know yet."

"What are you waiting for, an engraved invitation? Open it."

"Fine." I glance back at the package, then at Cameron's face. She's not paying attention to me but fixing her eyebrow in the front-facing camera.

I put the phone up on the bar-top counter so Cameron can watch.

"I like the bow. It's a nice touch. Oooh," she says suddenly, and my fingers freeze on the knotted ribbon. "What if it's kinky sex shit?"

"What? Why would you say that?"

"Maybe he's into some weird shit. Maybe this is your fifty shades of football moment. Maybe it's a bunch of sex toys and an NDA."

"The Beavers courier brought it here. It's not going to be sex toys," I tell her. God, that would be weird to open up with my friend on Facetime. Hilarious, though.

"A girl can dream," Cameron says.

"I honestly don't know what to say to that," I tell her, suppressing a laugh. The bow finally unknots.

"Hmm." The box is taped shut, and I have no idea where my scissors are. After a second, I fish a pen from my purse and wrench it through the clear plastic packing tape.

"There's a note on top," I tell Cameron.

"You better read it out loud."

"What if it's private?"

"You better read it even louder if it's private," Cameron says, and I snort at her wiggling eyebrows.

The creamy envelope is heavy, the kind of expensive stationery I drool over in stores, and I run my fingertips over it slowly before pulling out the card inside.

It's embossed with the Beavers logo, too, and I grin at it for a second. Something about the idea of a beaver being the AFL's idea of a terror-inducing mascot never fails to amuse me.

"Kelsey," I read out loud. "I wanted to send you all the things you might want to wear tomorrow for the game."

My eyes widen at the next line, and I fall silent.

"What? What? Don't stop now, I can tell you got to the good part."

I clear my throat and set the note down.

Sure enough, beneath the orange tissue paper is a plastic-wrapped jersey, navy with gold print. The name Harrison screams across the back, along with his number.

"He sent you his jersey? That's so fucking cuuuuuute, Kelsey, I cannot even. I can't. That means he's serious."

I riffle through the rest of the package. It's all Beavers merchandise. A coffee mug. A huge tumbler. More shirts, so many shirts. Sweatpants emblazoned with the beaver on the hip.

I hold them up to Cameron and she laughs.

"God, like we need to put a beaver face next to our crotches. Who designs this shit?"

I pull the jersey out of the plastic, surprised how wildly my heart's beating.

"You look weird. Tell me what else the note said," Cameron insists, but I can't. Instead, I hold the note up to the phone camera so she can read it herself.

"Wear my jersey tomorrow, so no one forgets who you're with —me," Cameron reads, then squeals. "Whoo, that is hot."

I hold the jersey up to myself.

Daniel Harrison has all the subtlety of the beaver logo on the sweatpants.

I'm not sure I mind.

# CHAPTER 17

DANIEL

The hotel room is familiar and foreign all at once. The air conditioner clicks on, and I sit on the edge of the king-sized bed listening to it whir, too loud in the silence of the room.

I've spent too many nights alone in hotels just like this, breathing in the recycled, stale air, my muscles in various states of soreness, trying to sleep alone the night before a game.

I'm so fucking tired of sleeping alone.

I miss my bed. I miss my house, deep in the woods in South Jersey, my garden.

And I shouldn't because it's too fucking new, but I miss Kelsey.

As soon as I think of her, desire kicks into overdrive.

My fingers are dialing her number before my brain has time to think better of it. At least we're in the same time zone—makes it a hell of a lot easier.

She picks up on the third ring, sounding sleepy.

"Hello?" she asks, and her voice sends a shiver of pleasure through me.

"Kelsey Cole," I say, my voice a low growl. Fuck, I want her again. I wish she were here. "What are you doing?"

"Honestly?" she laughs, and I close my eyes, drinking in the sound. "I know it's only nine-thirty, but I'm going to bed. I had too much to drink at brunch with Cameron, and I've had a killer hangover all day."

"Sounds like you did have a lot of responsibilities today," I say, laughing. "That sounds more fun than my day, that's for sure."

"Well, I got a little work done, too," her tone is slightly prickly, and I instantly regret my gentle teasing.

"No, I think it's awesome that you went out with your friend. Just laughing, sorry. Been a long day of training and discussing the game plan for tomorrow."

"Thank you for the flowers," she says after a beat. "They're beautiful. They've made my whole apartment smell amazing."

She doesn't mention the other package, the one full of Beavers merch. Or the note.

"Did you get the other thing?" I lie down on the bed, keeping my eyes closed, imagining she's in bed next to me and not miles away in her apartment in Philadelphia.

"I sure did," she says, and to my relief, there's a note of amusement in her voice. "You know, you're pretty full of yourself, Daniel Harrison, quarterback."

"I'd rather you were full of me," I say without thinking. Dammit.

She sucks in a breath, though, and my body goes tight with desire.

"Is that why you called me tonight? To dirty talk?"

My eyes fly open at the husky note in her voice.

"Why, is that what you want me to do?" I ask. I didn't plan on that, no, but hell, if she wants me to talk dirty to her over the phone, there's no way in hell I'm going to say no.

"Just curious," she says.

Now that she's mentioned it, though, I'm not going to let her off that easy. No fucking way. Shit. Now it's all I can think about.

"Are you going to wear my jersey tomorrow, Kelsey?" I ask, my voice a low rumble.

"Are you going to ask me nicely?"

I grin. "Kelsey, please wear my jersey tomorrow."

"Okay," she agrees, her voice soft. Fuck, but I like when she sounds like that.

"Kelsey… why don't you go put on that jersey? I'd love to see you in it. Please."

My free hand fists around the sheets. My cock's hard as can be, but I'm not going to touch myself. Not the night before a game. Maybe I'm old-fashioned, maybe it's a myth, but there's no way I'm doing that.

I might just be about to drive myself crazy over Kelsey, though.

"K." The phone goes dead and I'm left staring at it, seconds sliding together.

The phone dings quietly in my hand and I tap the screen, enlarging the picture she's sent.

"Fuck," I grit out.

She's wearing my jersey, alright.

A full-length mirror leans up against a wall. Kelsey's centered in the frame, holding the navy jersey down with one hand. Bare legs stretch up into it, the jersey hiding the rest of her. Tousled sandy-blonde hair hangs low over one shoulder, partially obscuring my number. White teeth bite her bottom lip, and her brown eyes are just as beautiful as I remember.

For the first time in my life, I'm regretting my no-masturbation-before-game-day rule.

I'm hard as a rock.

Another picture chimes through, and I groan as I devour the image. Kelsey, the phone aimed over one shoulder, a flirtatious look on her face. This time, though, it's from the back, the camera aimed over one shoulder.

"Fuck me," I repeat.

My name's fully visible, and so is the bottom of her curvy ass.

This woman is going to drive me crazy, and I'm going to love every minute of it.

I call her again.

"What do you think?" she asks, and I laugh.

"I think you're fucking gorgeous," I tell her. "You make my name look good."

"Is that right?" she asks, and the weight of my words hang heavy in the distance between us.

"The jersey looks fantastic on you. I like how you're wearing it," I quickly add, because why the fuck did I have to say that about my name?

"Oh yeah? You like the no pants look?"

"I fucking love the no pants look. I don't think I can pull it off like you can, though."

She laughs, and the sound makes me smile.

"What if I told you what else I'm wearing?"

I go silent, still, wishing like hell I wasn't in Miami. "I would like that," I finally answer.

"I'm wearing your jersey," she says. "And..."

"And?" I prompt, my voice hoarse.

"And nothing else," she finally finishes. The humor's gone from her voice, replaced by a husky note that has my entire body sitting up and taking notice.

"Nothing else. Fuck, Kelsey."

"Isn't this why you called?"

"I mean, it's a bonus, but I just called because I wanted to talk to you. Now I'm more interested in what you're doing right now, on the phone, in your apartment, by yourself with nothing on but my jersey."

"You just wanted to talk?" she says, and I hate the confusion in her voice.

"Kelsey, trust me, I would love to have phone sex with you. If you want to talk dirty to me right now, I am happy to participate in that. But I... yeah." I rub the scruff on my jawline. "I just called because I wanted to hear your voice. Hear how your day was. Hear if you liked the flowers."

"Oh," she says, and her voice is small. "I feel stupid."

"Jesus, no, don't." I could slap myself. "Please, if you want to get off with me on the phone, I'll help you. I'd fucking love to help you."

"I'm embarrassed now."

"We can't have that," I tell her, mentally kicking myself. "How about this. You go lie down in your bed, wearing my name, my jersey, on your naked body, and you tell me exactly what you want to do to yourself."

"Okay." She still sounds unsure. "Are you going to…"

"I don't touch myself the day before a game. Maybe it's superstition, but I swear it keeps me clear-headed. Aggressive."

"We can just talk," she says, but I hear the disappointment.

"Fuck that," I say, laughing slightly, even though this isn't funny, not really. "You be a good girl and do as I say." The words come out sharper than I intended, but she lets out a little whine that tells me she likes it.

"Okay," she says, her breath hitching on the word.

"Are you going to use a toy? A vibrator?" I ask. My cock strains against my pants, but I ignore it, focusing on her.

"Do you want me to?"

"I want you to get off," I growl into the phone. "I wish I was there to spread those pretty thighs and feast on you."

A moan is my reward and I memorize the sound, wanting more of them, wanting to hoard all her little noises.

"I have my vibrator," she says, and sure enough, a hum starts in the background.

"Are you wet?" I ask her, my voice a rasp.

"Not as much as I was last night."

I grit my teeth. "You were so fucking wet and tight. I want you to get wet for me again. I want you to think about my tongue between your legs, on that perfect pussy."

"Yes, Daniel," she moans.

"Good girl," I say. "Now tell me what you're doing."

"I'm using the vibrator on my clit," she says, and from the way her voice trips over the words, I wonder if she's new to this, to having phone sex. It seems like she might be. It's one more sign of how much more experienced I am than her, and it could be a turn off… but damn, I like it. I like the idea of showing her how good it can be.

My jaw clenches. "Why don't you let me tell you what to do instead?"

"I like that idea."

Her voice is soft, and high, and needy, and I've never heard anything better.

"Make little circles all around that pretty clit."

"Oh god," she says. "Feels so good."

"Good. I want you to feel good. Say my name." The demand leaves my mouth before I have time to think on it.

"Daniel, it feels so good. Daniel." Her voice is pleading, sweet and so needy.

"You're getting close now," I continue, relentless, needing release so badly but wanting her to find hers even more. Wanting my name to be on her lips when she does.

"Yes," she says.

Fuck, I want to touch her. I want to lift her thick hips and plunge deep into her warmth.

"I want you to reach up under my jersey and touch your breasts."

She makes a needy noise and I wet my lips.

"I'm close," she says.

"Good. Come for me. Say my name when you come, like a good girl."

"Daniel, Daniel," she pants and my cock twitches, so hard it aches. A low moan reverberates in my ear and I close my eyes, remembering the way she tasted. Her scent.

The vibrator shuts off and she sighs, a sound that would be twice as sweet if I was there to feel it against my skin.

"How do you feel?"

"Like I want to cuddle."

My eyes go wide and I stare at the ugly popcorn ceiling in surprise before my lips stretch in a smile.

"I want that too, Kelsey Cole. I would love to feel you against me right now."

She's silent for a long time and her breathing evens out, and after a couple minutes, it becomes clear she's fallen asleep on the phone.

It makes me laugh, a chuckle rolling out of me.

"Goodnight, Kelsey. I'll see you when I get back tomorrow."

She doesn't answer, and I don't expect her to.

I lie awake that night for a long time, thinking about how much I wish I was anywhere but this hotel room, as long as I wasn't alone.

# CHAPTER 18

KELSEY

When I woke up this morning, I was still wearing Daniel's jersey. My jersey, really, considering it's brand-new—but his all the same. His name on the back.

*I like you wearing my name.*

His voice echoes in my ear, his praise still in the back of my mind. I don't know what it says about me that I liked it so much, that I want him to say it again.

I swallow hard, not believing that the woman in the mirror is the same one who was horny enough to send a half-naked selfie to him last night. I raise my chin at my reflection. He made me feel good. Twice now.

I'm wearing his jersey again. I washed it this morning while I worked on a few pieces for work, following up with leads and tweaking paragraphs.

It smells like my laundry.

I close my eyes. I wish it smelled like him.

I tug my phone out of my back pocket, my mouth screwed to the side as I try to figure out if I should even text him.

It's been so long since I've been in a relationship, and even though I'm not sure what he and I are, it sure feels like I need some kind of rulebook.

I haven't had a serious boyfriend since college, since four or five years ago, now.

I'm going to text him.

I type something out, then delete it. Type something else, delete it. Daniel beats me to it.

> I see you trying to type something

> good luck today

My message comes less than half a second after his, and I twist my lips to the side in amusement.

> I don't need luck.

> sorry! You're right. Go kick ass

> no, you misunderstand

> I don't need luck because I have you, wearing my jersey

> That's all the luck I need

I stare at my phone because there's something ridiculously romantic about seeing that written out on my screen. My chest feels tight and happy, about to burst.

> you are being good and wearing it, right?

My cheeks get hot at the reminder of him calling me his good girl last night, and my entire lower half clenches.

Oh yeah, there's chemistry, alright. Enough to set my entire apartment complex on fire.

> I'm wearing it

> I would ask to see a selfie, but I'm in a locker room full of guys and I can't stand the thought of them seeing your bare legs.

> I'll see you tonight

I reread his last message, letting it wash over me.

"He'll see me tonight?" I say it out loud, but my reflection in the mirror doesn't answer.

I'm halfway out the door when my phone vibrates again. My keys jangle in the lock and I pull my phone to my ear without looking at the caller ID.

"Hi," I say, expecting Daniel. Grinning.

"Hey honey."

"Dad," I say, gripping the keys so tight they start to hurt my palm.

"How are you, sweetheart?"

"I'm uh, I'm really good, Dad. How are you?" I squeeze my eyes shut, leaning my forehead against my locked apartment door. The fluorescent hall lights hum overhead, a high-pitched whine that sets my teeth on edge.

"Oh, you know," he says. "Same old, same old."

I choke back a sigh, because I do know.

"Is it your head? Is it bothering you again? Did you try that new doctor I told you about?"

"Kelsey, honey, you know I don't like it when you worry about me."

"That's my job, Dad. I'm your kid. I love you, of course I'm going to worry about you." If I've said it once, I've said it a million times.

"That new doctor's expensive, and he's not going to tell me anything we don't already know. I don't need to spend a couple hundred bucks just to hear the same thing."

"Dad, they have all kinds of new therapies and treatments—"

"Kelsey, I didn't call you so you could try and persuade me to go to the doctor."

I bite my cheeks, turning around so I'm facing the hallway instead of talking to the door. A stain discolors the ceiling, and I squint at it. A rabbit, I decide. That's what it looks like.

"Why'd you call, Dad?" I finally ask, the phone silent besides his breathing.

"I heard you were dating Daniel Harrison."

I ball my fist up and smack my door with it.

"I think that's great, honey. You know he played for the Denver Mustangs, right?"

"Mmhmm," I say, tucking my coat tighter around myself. God, has he been on BeaverTok? The thought of my father watching Daniel make out with me in some weirdo fan CapCut treatment makes me slightly nauseated.

My dad continues rattling off Daniel's stats as I make my way down the stairs, through the parking lot, and to my car. It's turned colder, the air more frigid than crisp, a sign that winter's waiting in the wings.

"He's a little old for you, though, isn't he?" my dad finally stops his monologue about completed pass rates and yards, and I tune back in.

"He's thirty-nine." I unlock the car and slide into the front seat. The engine turns over, and heat floods the car. The phone skips, connecting to the Bluetooth.

"And you're twenty-nine. Ten years isn't so bad."

My stomach drops. On the wheel, my knuckles are white, my fingertips cold on the plastic.

"No, Dad," I say softly. "I'm twenty-five."

I want to cry. I lean over the steering wheel, embracing it like a lover, like the airbag inside will somehow protect me from the truth.

The head injury my dad sustained playing in the AFL when I was little is only getting worse, and this is why I swore I would never have anything to do with the AFL or football or anyone who bought into a game that uses athletes up until there's nothing left.

"I knew that, sweetie," he laughs, but there's no humor in the sound. "Hey, you know what, why don't ya send me the info for that doctor again, if it means that much to you."

"Sure thing, Dad."

"You watching the game tonight?"

"Yeah, I'm headed out to pick up my friend Cameron. Do you remember her? We're headed to Wilmington to watch it right now, actually."

"Okay, Kelsey. Makes me happy to hear you're watching my favorite thing in the world again. Have fun, honey."

"I will," I say, and it tastes bitter, like a lie. "Have a good night, Dad."

The line goes dead and I stare at my phone long after the screen's turned dark. The car's become uncomfortably hot.

I put the car in reverse, making myself drive to the bar to watch the man I'm dating put his body on the line to play a game I hate.

# CHAPTER 19

## DANIEL

F uck, I love this.

I soak it in. Despite the time of year, Miami's balmy as ever, the night sky clear and the air thick on the field. The grass seems greener against the white stripes, my senses heightened.

We're playing great. The Miami Reef Sharks are too, but we have an edge we haven't had all season. Every fucking pass feels like gold, the football an extension of my body.

The Matthews brothers are on point too, sticky hands and somehow always finding the perfect opening in the sea of orange and teal uniforms.

It's the fourth quarter and adrenaline still rages through me, beating out exhaustion and even pain from a hit in the first minute of the second quarter. We're down by three, but the guys aren't quitting yet. The clock's running down and we're in possession. Their hope's palpable, radiating from each of them, evident in the brightness that's more than the reflected stadium lights.

They think we could still win.

Our first win of the season.

I can fucking taste it, too, and damn, it is sweet.

This is the reason why I do this. This feeling is why I throw myself into a sea of muscle and bone to get chewed up under the lights and the scrutiny of millions of people who wish they could be in my cleats. Because of moments like this, fleeting moments that no one will remember but me, where the men on my team look at me like we're about to make fucking history.

Inhale. Exhale.

The defense repositions itself, and the x's and o's of the playbook flash through my mind. The play the coach called isn't going to work.

"Fuck," I mutter, the word somewhat garbled by my mouthguard.

They're doubling up defense on Ty. Jacob is on the sidelines, icing the fuck out of a nasty ankle injury.

One look to my right tells me they've doubled up defense on the other wide receivers too, and my tight ends look locked the fuck down. A second slides by, sweat dripping down my neck in the hot Florida air.

Miami's made a mistake, though.

They've left me open, save for one lineman who looks more interested in number forty-nine than me.

It's obvious why they've done it. They think I'm too old to run it into the end zone.

They saw me avoid the hit last week, must have watched the tape over and over again when I careened into Kelsey.

I smile into my helmet, and it's a fucking ugly one. They're going to regret assuming shit about me.

I call the audible, the word slamming from my mouth with an intensity that rattles my teeth. Forty-nine flicks his head towards me, and I see the doubt turn into determination as he rolls his shoulders, ready to pull attention to himself. Ready to take the heat from Miami's defense.

I don't want to yell hike, I don't want to draw any attention to myself. Our center's holding the ball, ready to snap it to me.

Chances are with the sound of the Miami crowd, he wouldn't hear me, anyway.

I lift my foot for the leg cadence, and the world slows. The ball snaps back, and the sound it makes on my hands is fucking glorious. Defense is firmly focused on everyone else, and I see the opening like it's happening at half-speed. I tear through the line of orange and blue, their helmets whipping towards me as they belatedly realize what's happening.

I don't spare a thought for them, gunning as fast as I can for the end zone. I don't have the speed I used to, but I'm still fast enough. I'm eating up the ground, yard lines blurring past me, the lactic acid in my thighs burning as I turn it up, faster now.

And I think of Kelsey, wearing my jersey, watching me run for the end zone, a thousand miles away.

When I cross the goal line, my smile isn't ugly anymore.

I feel fantastic.

A glance up tells me there's still twenty-seven seconds left in the game, but it's not enough time for Miami to do shit. We've fucking won.

I can't wait to see Kelsey tonight. I can't wait to celebrate.

I turn, watching the refs put their arms up to signal the TD.

A second later, I'm flying through the air, a massive orange-and-teal-clad player on top of me.

It stuns me. A yellow flag floats into my periphery, landing somewhere next to me.

"Go home, old man," the player on top of me says, kneeing me in the hip.

"Get the fuck off him," someone shouts, pulling the Miami player off me. Ty Matthews.

"Unnecessary roughness," a voice booms through the stadium.

I'm dazed, trying to shake it off. Trying to shake it off, but it's taking longer than it should.

# CHAPTER 20

## KELSEY

I never thought I'd actually enjoy watching a football game.

The Beaver Trap, the local bar for the wildest fans, the one Cameron likes to go to for Beavers games, is packed. The energy is wild, the whole bar on edge, living for the seconds ticking down on a clock a thousand miles away.

Daniel is magnificent, and I can't keep the smile off my face as he squares off with a minute left on the clock. I know enough from watching with my dad growing up to follow the action, know enough to scream for him to go, go, as he sprints toward the end zone.

But I know too much, too, and when he gets tackled, flying through the air, my hand covers my mouth. He bounces, the Miami player pinning him down as his head snaps back.

Then he lies still.

Horror fills me. The cold chill of it trickles down my spine, and I can't breathe. I can't breathe.

A Wilmington player pulls the asshole off Daniel, and still, he lies there. Not moving.

I rake a hand through my hair, and a sob leaves my throat.

I can't watch this. I can't.

"Kelsey?" Cameron's voice is low and worried, and her hand lands on my wrist.

I shake my head, tearing my gaze away from the huge screen behind the bar. Everyone's celebrating. Everyone's cheering.

He's not getting up.

"I can't," I tell her. "I can't."

I push past her, through the swell of the navy-and-gold crowd. I can't breathe.

He's hurt, he's hurt, and I knew this would happen, I knew I shouldn't have enjoyed watching the game.

I shouldn't have gotten mixed up with a football player.

My hands shake as I push the black bathroom door open. A huge mural of a beaver in a pink dress and an inexplicable coconut bra fills the space behind the sinks.

I stare at it, bracing my hands on the counter, trying to breathe.

I barely know Daniel Harrison. We've had a couple of fun times, yeah.

A cheer goes up outside, the Hot Dams filling the bar chanting Daniel's name.

I am sick at the thought of him being hurt.

I pull my phone out of my back pocket, and before I can think better of it, I'm dialing his number, the taste of beer sour in my mouth.

It clicks through to voicemail.

"Daniel, it's Kelsey," I say, then pause. "I… you… I hope you're okay. God, Daniel, I hope you're okay."

Cameron appears in the mirror next to me and she takes the phone from me, pressing the button to end the call.

"Babe," she says, and I fling my arms around her, sobbing into her shoulder. "He's okay, Kelsey. He got up."

"That guy hurt him," I say. "He hurt him on purpose, and for no reason."

"Yeah, everyone knows Rhett Edwards is the biggest asshole

in the league. Daniel's okay though, Kels, he walked it off. He's okay."

I scrub the tears off my cheeks with the palm of my hand, and Cameron gives my shoulders a tiny shake.

"You really like him, huh?"

"It's stupid," I sniff a little and Cameron huffs a laugh, then pulls me in for a hug.

"How you feel isn't stupid, Kels."

"I hate football."

"No," she says on a sigh. "You don't hate football. You looked like you were having fun tonight. You were having fun tonight. You hate what football took from your dad. You hate that the league didn't help him like they should have."

"Are you trying to make me cry?" I ask.

"Do you want me to be mean to you instead?" Cameron asks, squinting at me. "I could slap you if you want." She raises her palm, wiggling her eyebrows and giving me a smile that's pure evil.

"I barely know him," I tell her, leaning my butt against the sink. And immediately regret it, cold water seeping through my jeans.

"You don't have to be in love with someone to be worried when they get tackled like he did." Cameron's still scrutinizing me. "Especially with what your dad's been through."

I peek in the mirror, fixing some of the mascara currently migrating from my eyelashes.

"Kelsey, he's okay. He was slow getting up, but he got up."

"I just… I just don't know if I can watch him get hurt," I confess.

The bathroom door swings open and Cameron huddles close to me as a crew of half-drunk women push into the space.

"Are you guys waiting to go?" one says. Her friend grabs her wrist, her Hot Dam t-shirt tied up tight around her waist.

"Oh my god," she says in a hushed whisper. "You're that girl. From BeaverTok."

"You guys," the first girl screams. "It's the girl that managed to get her claws in Daniel Harrison!"

"Good job, lady," another says, holding her hand up for a high-five.

Bewildered, I meet her halfway, because who the hell leaves someone hanging for a high-five?

"Good job?" I repeat.

"Hell yeah, good job! You must have a magic beaver. He hasn't played that well in years."

All the women around her start laughing, one doubling over as she races into an open stall.

"What?" I ask, my eyes wide.

"Your cho-cha. Your pussy. The poonanny. The pink taco. You must have cast some kind of spell on him." She wriggles her fingers at me. "Good work."

Oh. My. God.

Cameron pulls me by the elbow, towing me from the restroom and the Hot Dams, who are snapping photos of me and the coconut-bra-wearing beaver like their lives depend on it.

"Keep it up with the magical beav," one yells after me. "We need to win!"

"What the fuck," Cameron says under her breath. "This is wild."

"Magical beav," I repeat, and then I bite my cheeks. It doesn't stop the laughter from spilling out. "Magical beav? The *pink taco*?!"

"Listen, of all the things I thought I would be thankful for, a rando Hot Dam telling my bff she has a magical beav didn't even rank on the list. But hey, laughing is better than crying, right?"

I nod, the sting of tears threatening again.

"Come on," Cameron says softly, barely audible over all the celebrating fans. "I'll drive your car home."

———

I wake up to a soft knock, my eyes swollen. Blearily, I glance at my phone on my bedside table—there are five missed messages from Daniel, and it's just after one.

My heart leaps.

He came. He did what he said he would, and he's here now.

Despite all my misgivings, there's no fighting the smile blooming across my face. My slippers slide onto my feet, and I pad across the floor of my room, half-awake. I peek through the peephole, and sure enough, there's Daniel.

A sigh leaves my lips.

He's so handsome, even at 1:20 in the morning. I unlock the door and his whole face lights up as I open it.

"Hi," I say quietly. "You're okay."

"I got your voicemail." He raises one eyebrow. "Can I come in?"

"Yeah, please." I push my hair out of my eyes, realizing I probably look like death warmed over.

His hand follows mine, tucking my hair firmly behind one ear. I swallow hard, coming more fully awake.

"We need to talk. Well, I need to talk. I need to talk to you." My nose scrunches up.

"Okay," he says quietly. "Do you want to talk in the doorway, or…" He trails off, leaving the question hanging in the air, his hand still on my cheek. I lean into it, half-closing my eyes.

"Come with me," I tell him, and I put my palm over his hand, tugging him behind me. "I wasn't sure if you were really going to show up." I pick at the hem of the scraggly old shirt I wore to bed, awake enough to be self-conscious.

"I can go if you don't want me here, Kelsey Cole." Daniel's fingers give mine a little squeeze.

He's so sweet and concerned that it makes me feel… even worse about what I have to tell him.

I pull him onto the couch next to me. When he moves to pull me into his lap, I grab one of my fluffy throw pillows and hold onto it instead.

"I need you to just… I need you to just listen for a minute, and if you start touching me, I'm not going to be able to tell you what I need to tell you."

He holds his hands up in the universal sign for surrender, blinking at me.

I study him, the dark circles beneath his eyes, the start of crow's feet at the corners, a slight tan across the bridge of his nose and cheekbones. He's too big for my couch, my apartment, larger than life and mismatched with my oyster-cream walls and girly gold accents.

I clear my throat, and a frown pulls the corners of his lips down.

"You're scaring me, Kelsey. If you don't want me around, then just say it. Just tell me."

"That's the problem, Daniel." My throat gets tight. "I do want you around. I like you."

He shakes his head. "I don't understand. How is that a problem? I want to be around you. I like you, too. A lot. A whole helluva lot, considering the little time we've spent together."

"Daniel…" I try to form the words, try to tell him what I'm thinking, but I just stare at him instead.

He runs his knuckles across my cheek and I suck in a breath, my body coming alive at the gentle touch.

"Daniel," I say again.

"Fuck, Kelsey, I like hearing you say my name."

I scoot back on the couch, putting more distance between us. "My dad's name is Warner. Warner Cole."

Confusion mars the heat in his eyes, and he leans back against the couch too, draping one huge arm across the back. "Okay. Do you want me to meet him?"

I pull my knees into my chest. "Warner Cole played for the Texas Oilmen when I was a baby, then a toddler. Some of my earliest memories are of being at the games."

"Your dad was a pro footballer?"

"Yes." My hands knot against each other. "I rehearsed this speech the whole way home from the bar last night."

Silence, and then he makes a small, comforting noise.

"Whatever it is you're trying to tell me, I can handle it, Kelsey. Put it on me. I'm tougher than I look." He leans forward now, focused on me, his elbows on his knees.

"Warner Cole played for three seasons, until an injury made it so he couldn't play anymore. A head injury. The Oilmen cut him, the AFL didn't care. My mom was a nurse, she worked so hard to pay the bills, and it was a good thing she was a nurse because my dad needed all the help he could get. He still does."

I take a deep breath, closing my eyes, trying to get all the words out before I lose the will.

"Watching you get hit like that today, watching you lie on the ground after… I nearly lost it. I had to run to the bathroom. It freaked me out. My dad… he doesn't remember things. He doesn't remember how old I am, where I live. He can't hold a job, and the AFL couldn't give two shits about what happened to him. I hate football, and I hate the AFL. And I, and I… I just thought you should know that." My hands are cramping from how tight I'm holding them, and a muscle twitches in his jaw.

"Kelsey." He scrubs a hand over his face, then takes one of mine, squeezing it. "Thank you for telling me that. Thank you for sharing that part of yourself with me."

It could have sounded patronizing, but it grates out of him, full of emotion, and I bite my lips, trying not to cry.

"I worry about my dad every day. I worry about him, and it makes me so tired. And now I worry about you. I told myself I would never, ever… get involved with a football player, and here you are, in my living room, and in my life."

"I feel honored to be in both your living room and your life," he says, quietly. Sincerely. Slowly, he pulls my hand from the pillow, drawing it to his mouth, where he presses a kiss against my knuckles. "I feel honored that you feel safe enough with me to share that about your dad." A long sigh rips out of him and he rubs his thumb over the back of my hand.

He quirks an eyebrow at me and I stay silent. It feels good, though, the kind of companionable silence I've only ever had with a handful of people. I also feel empty, emotionally spent, after everything I've just told him. Deflated, even.

"Kelsey, I'm sorry about what happened to your dad. That's... every athlete's nightmare, I think. And their families'. We all pretend like we're invincible, you know? We strap on the pads and helmets like it's armor for battle, and the whole time, we know this time on the field could be the last. But we push it down, and we push through, because we love the game." He gives his head a little shake, like he's surprised at what he's just said.

"Do you love it? Still?"

"I do," he says, holding my gaze. "I love football, and I'm sorry that you don't. I'm sorry for everything you just told me. But I'm so fucking glad you told it to me, because now I know even more about you. I want to know you, Kelsey Cole, the good, the bad." He purses his lips, then grins at me. "Maybe not the ugly, but I'll take it, too. I'll take it all. Whatever you want to give me."

I don't think, I just launch myself at him. I wrap my arms around his neck, breathing in his scent, already familiar, already comforting. Safe, it says, and I inhale deeply.

He grunts and I go stiff. "Shit, I'm sorry, did I hurt you? Are you hurt?"

"Just sore," he says. A big hand curls around the nape of my neck and I'm in his lap, staring up at his jawline, the smile on his lips, the smile in his eyes. "Do you think your dad would like me?"

I laugh, and then cock my head at him. "Oh, don't worry, he's already planning our wedding, I'm sure. He heard about us somehow. He's worried about the age difference—" The smile slides from my face as I remember he forgot how old I am.

Daniel's eyes are wide and I blink, trying to backtrack. "That was a joke. He's not actually planning our wedding. I just meant he's already in the Daniel Harrison fan club. There's no wedding."

I yawn, trying to cover my discomfort with it until it turns into a real one, embarrassingly long.

"Can I stay here? Tonight?" Daniel's question, especially after I awkwardly brought up our fictional wedding, takes me by surprise.

"Don't you have to work tomorrow?" I ask. "It's going to be a shitty drive from Philly to Wilmington."

"Some things are worth sitting in traffic for." He touches the tip of my nose. "Come on, you have work, too." He stands, still holding me, opening a door and carrying me… into the teensy coat closet.

"This is where I sleep," I tell him, biting back a laugh. "I like to cuddle with my jackets. The down one is especially nice."

He barks a laugh. "I see the appeal."

I squirm in his arms, pointing to the door to our right. "That's my bedroom."

A soft groan creeps out of his mouth and I go still. "You're hurt. Put me down."

"Kelsey, no. I'm not. Not really."

"Then why did you make that sound?"

"Because as soon as you say bedroom, all I can think about is fucking you."

My mouth goes round with surprise. "Oh. What if I told you… I think I'm too tired?" I'm not, but a mean, nasty part of my brain keeps telling me that's why he's here. That I'm a booty call. That I was close to the Philly airport and he stopped off here because it was easy.

"Then I would say let me hold you while you sleep," he presses a kiss against my temple, and my heart does a little happy flip inside my chest.

I yawn again and he grins down at me, then places me gently on the bed. He pulls off his grey sweatpants, then climbs in next to me. My old queen-sized bed groans in protest, and I snort in amusement.

"Do you fit?" I ask.

"Oh, babe, I will make it fit," he says, and then we both laugh as he pulls me into his warm body, spooning me.

At first, I think there's no way I'll fall asleep with him here, my thoughts still racing a mile a minute. He rubs his hand gently, so gently, across the curve of my waist, his breathing deep and even.

I snuggle deeper into his big body, loving the way his hand feels on my hip, the way I fit across his arm just right.

I'm asleep before I know it.

# CHAPTER 21

## DANIEL

The alarm going off isn't mine.

It takes me a second to realize where I am, that the warm shape I'm wrapped around isn't a pillow.

*Kelsey.*

I tug her to me and she squirms, making a slight squeak. Damn, she's so fucking cute.

"Good morning," I say into her hair, her hair that smells so good.

"Hi," she says. "I've got to get ready for work."

I clamp my arm tighter around her waist and she makes another small squeak. I grin.

"Stay home. Stay with me."

"You have to work, too," she protests, turning towards me. I loosen my grip slightly so she can. Her oversized shirt's slipped off one shoulder, and I groan at the sight of her bare skin, her sleepy eyes and lips.

"I can think of so many better things to do than going to work today," I say, nipping at her shoulder.

"I have too many things to do to call in."

"I know, I know," I say, even though I don't, not really. I squint at her. "Like what?"

"Like I'm still pulling together the investigative piece on the AFL cheer teams. Like a piece I need to follow up on about the downtown farmer's market."

"I like that," I tell her.

She raises an eyebrow. "Like what?" She squirms slightly, her hands on my bare chest. It makes me hard. Not like it takes a lot, not with Kelsey half-dressed in my arms.

"I like that you're a badass. An investigative reporter."

"Thanks," she says slowly, a smile dawning on her mouth, better than the sun slowly rising out the window.

"I wish you could like what I do, too."

Her expression darkens, and I immediately regret the words.

"Wait, not like that. I didn't mean it like that. I meant I wish things had been different for your dad."

"So do I," she says, her voice so soft I have to strain to hear it.

She slides out of my arms and I roll onto my back, sitting up, watching her collect items from a tiny reach-in closet.

"Kelsey, I didn't mean to upset you."

"I know," she says.

"Can I take you out tonight?" If this was the monthly poker night with my friends, all my cards would be on the table. All my chips would be in the pot, likely along with the keys to my truck.

I'm all fucking in with Kelsey Cole, and she doesn't have a clue.

I'm having way too much fun trying to get her to bet on us, too.

I cross my arms behind my head, knowing it makes them look bigger. She glances over at me, a suit jacket in her hands, and her gaze drops to my pecs. I flex them, ignoring the sting of pain from where I was hit last night.

"Where?" she asks, a ghost of a smile on her lips.

I think back to the email my agent sent me with a list of events and reservations and tickets he managed to get me for this week. For me and Kelsey, a PR blitz, the email had said.

"It's a surprise," I say.

"Okay, and what do I wear to this surprise?" she asks, voice muffled as she shuffles through her closet.

"A dress." It won't matter, not really, but I want to see her in a dress. I want to think about her in a dress today. I want to bend her over my bed and fuck her while she wears a dress.

"One like this?" Kelsey holds up a cream sweater dress, and the color and shape of the dress in my little fantasy shifts.

I'll be thinking about it all day.

"That looks fucking perfect." My voice comes out husky. "How about being late to work?"

She laughs, arching a brow at me, then sobers, biting her lower lip. It's not a sexy look, but one that makes me sit all the way up.

"What's wrong?"

"Is this…" She gestures between us with the sweater dress in her hand. It flaps wildly, and I look from her to it and back again. "Is this thing between us, is this just about sex?"

"What?" I'm taken aback. Completely. Wildly. "Shit, Kelsey, no. No. Did I make you think that? No." I shake my head emphatically.

"I mean, we had one date. Then we had sex. Then we had phone sex. Then you show up in the middle of the night…"

Fuck.

"Kelsey, no." I get out of bed, unable to keep my distance from her, even though maybe I should. Maybe I shouldn't be running to hold her, running to comfort her, to dissuade her from this notion. "This is not about sex for me. Though, honestly, that was amazing, and I would very, very much like to do it again."

She stares up at me with big brown eyes, her hair waving around her face, half of it still up in a bun, half of it falling out everywhere. It's messy and perfect and I want to mess it up even more.

"Kelsey, I can have sex with anyone."

"Is that right?" She juts her chin out, the hand with the dress in it on her hip now.

"That didn't come out right," I backtrack. "To answer your question, no. This isn't about sex. I like you. I want to get to know you. I liked... learning more about you last night. I liked holding you last night, feeling you fall asleep in my arms. I loved waking up to you this morning."

The frosty expression on her face warms slightly. "Yeah?"

"Hell yeah," I say. My lips quirk to the side and I rub the stubble on my jaw. "I tell you what. I want to see you tonight. I want to see you all week. I want to spend time with you." I pause, then ask the question I've hung all my hopes on. "Do you want to spend time with me?"

She glances down, and my heart drops.

But when she looks up at me, that ghost of a smile has turned into a full-fledged grin. "Yeah. Yeah, I would like that."

"Okay. So we won't have sex this week." My balls are already pissed about this plan, but fuck it. "We won't have sex until I've convinced you that I'm here for you. I won't have sex with you again until you're begging me to touch you."

Her throat bobs, pupils dilating.

"What if I want to have sex tonight?"

I swallow a groan because fuck, please, I want that, too.

"If that's what you want." I shrug one shoulder. Bad idea. That hurt.

"What if I don't want to have sex for three months?"

"Then I will be masturbating to my memories of you for three months," I say bluntly. "But I will respect what you want, for however long you want. We didn't start this off... traditionally, I guess. That doesn't mean I don't want it to... be that." I almost said end traditionally. Because dammit, ever since she joked about planning a wedding last night, then apologized for it, I haven't been able to get the idea out of my head.

I've never been the type of guy to date around. Serial monogamist, a former girlfriend called me.

With Kelsey, though, not only do I not see anyone else… I also see a future.

And the future looks good.

"Whatever you want, for as long as you want it," I tell her, placing my hands on her hips, unable to not touch her, at the very least.

"Sounds kinky," she says, then laughs.

"If that's what you're into." God, I hope it's not three months. My balls are going to shrivel up into tiny little raisins. RIP my balls.

"Okay," she finally agrees. "Tonight. Surprise date, no sexpectations."

"Okay?"

"Okay." She laughs, and I tug her into me for a hug. I'm hard as a rock, though, and my dick pokes her in the stomach.

"Sorry," I mutter, running my hands up and down her back. Three months might kill me, but damn, it will be worth it.

"I gotta go get ready." Kelsey holds up the dress, and I lick my lips. "When do you need to leave?"

I glance at the clock on her bedside.

"Soon," I admit. "Now, probably."

"Do you want food? I have… cereal and yogurt."

"Nah, they have food at the facility."

She's staring up at me, and I can't stop looking at her. She's so pretty, with her hair all wild around her head, in a ragged old t-shirt.

"I never told you congratulations for yesterday," she says slowly, and the words take me by surprise. "You scared the hell out of me at the end of the game… but I have to admit, I was surprised."

"Surprised I ran it in for the TD?"

She hits my shoulder playfully, the hanger bouncing off me. "No, surprised how much I actually enjoyed watching you play. I never thought I'd watch football and actually like it. I know most people do, Cameron loves it. But watching you play last night… it was fun. You looked like *you* were having fun."

"Fuck." The word explodes out of me, my fingers tightening on her hips.

"What?"

"I agreed to take sex off the table and then you hit me with the dirty talk."

She laughs, then her arms circle around my waist and I pull her in tight for a hug. I kiss the top of her head, reveling in the newness of this thing between us, the way it feels easy and comfortable and familiar. The way she feels exciting and new and so right, all at once.

I haven't felt so excited about anything in a long, long time.

"Go to work," she says, then smacks my ass.

"What was that for?"

"I thought that's what football players did. Spank each other on the butt."

"Does this mean I get to spank you?" My smile turns devilish and I pull her closer, until she has to fully tilt her chin to look up at me.

"Depends on how the next six months go, I guess." She flutters her eyelashes at me.

I laugh. "Six months? I thought you decided on three?"

"We'll see."

I glance over my shoulder at the clock again and sigh. "I gotta go."

"Me too."

I lean down, kissing her forehead, her nose, and then her mouth.

"I'll pick you up at seven."

"It's a date. A no-spanking, sexless date," she says.

"Why do I get the feeling you're going to make me regret this?"

"Oh, come on… it'll be fun." Her grin's just as wicked as mine, and when she squeezes my butt, I laugh again.

Her hands migrate up to my shoulders, the smile fading. "Thank you. Thank you for listening. It means a lot to me."

"Always," I tell her, drinking her in. "Who have you been dating that hasn't wanted to listen to you?" It's a rhetorical question. I don't want to know who she's dated. That way I can't be jealous of them.

"Not you. I wasn't dating you," she replies, and I cut off whatever else she's going to say with a kiss against her lips.

"I'll see you tonight," I promise, finally pulling away long enough to collect my sweats and shirt, pulling them on slowly, my shoulder and hip still bothering me.

"Tonight," she agrees, and I hold her hand as I walk to the front door, where I slip my shoes on.

I give her one last quick kiss before leaving.

The door closes behind me, and I've never wanted to go back inside an apartment so badly.

# CHAPTER 22

## KELSEY

The morning passes by faster than I imagined, and even though I would have loved to skip work today to snuggle with Daniel, I'm glad I didn't.

I'm slammed.

From sources reaching out to verifying information and prepping for the next time I'm on camera with a segment, the hours fly by.

When Cameron stops by with a brown paper bag and a coffee for me, I finally look up, blinking blearily at her.

"You need to take a break," she says. "You've been on DND all day, and when I came to check on you earlier, you looked so into what you were doing I didn't want to interrupt. Now you're taking a break with me."

I yawn, glancing at my minimized internal chat. Sure enough, I've missed at least ten messages from her, and dozens from others.

"Why are you so tired?" she asks, pitching her voice low. "Did… something exciting happen last night?"

"Cameron, please." I wrinkle my nose, taking the bag from her. "What's in here?"

"Bacon cheeseburger."

"My favorite."

"I know. Take a walk with me. You need some fresh air. You look like you're about to crash."

"I'll try restarting myself," I say.

Cameron groans. "That was literally the worst joke I've ever heard."

I stand up slowly, then stretch, cracking my neck. "You're right. I feel like I've been sitting all day."

"You have been. Come on. Lap around the building while you eat."

"Thanks Cammy-boo."

Her lip curls in disgust at the nickname. "Don't."

I snort. "Sorry. Okay. Yes. Lap around the building, bacon cheeseburger, and I need to talk."

Cameron fist-pumps, then pulls her dark, near-black hair back into a ponytail. "Hell yeah. You know I want the hot goss."

"If I can't call you Cammy-boo you can't say hot goss."

"Deal," she says instantly. "Now give me that steaming goss."

I laugh, filling her in between bites, glad I wore my flats today.

By the time I finish telling her about how Daniel came over last night, about how we're going to slow things down, she's looking at me starry-eyed.

"What?"

"It's really cute, that's all."

"What is? How I freaked out when he got hit? Or the fact we decided not to have sex for a little while?"

"All of it. But mostly, the way you talk about him. You seem happy. Are you happy?"

"I'm..." I pause, because I don't know how I feel yet. "When I'm with him, I feel good. He feels good. We fit together nicely. I don't know. It's so new." I shrug, crumpling up the white paper wrapper. Watery fall sun washes over my face, the temperature warmer today.

I don't tell her that I'm worried. I don't tell her that I threw myself into work today so I wouldn't replay him getting tackled in the end zone over and over again in my head. I don't want to tell Cameron that his job freaks me out.

Daniel's more than his job, more than the quarterback for Wilmington. He's a man, and I want to know the man, not the quarterback.

"You have a weird look on your face."

"The football stuff freaks me out. I don't love it."

"Then just take it one day at a time. You said you're going to slow down," she pauses long enough to do a shimmy, "sexually, so just slow down. Have fun. Don't worry so much."

"What about you?" I ask, squinting at her. We've made our lap around the block, the building entrance looming in front of us.

"What do you mean, what about me?"

"For someone that's so into my personal life, you don't seem to have a lot to add to the conversation."

"Nailed it." She mimes hammering, but I don't laugh.

Crossing my arms over my chest, I raise an eyebrow and wait.

"Ugh. Okay, well. If I had details to share, I would share them. Until then, I will scrounge for the scraps of your romantic life."

"Hmm," I say, not sure I believe her. Cameron's gorgeous, she gets asked out all the time, but aside from a few dates that went nowhere, she doesn't talk about her own love life. Ever.

"Hmmm," she echoes, then grins. "Hey, did you know that our boss wants us to go to the Beaver Ball?"

"The Beaver Ball? Seriously?"

"Yeah. God. I just think the whole thing is so hilarious." She grins, biting her cheeks. "To go from having a live beaver mascot, to then enduring animal rights protests, to dumping the mascot and starting a foundation to preserve native beaver habitats... I mean, the whole thing is a joke."

"It's for a good cause."

"Anyway, the Wilmington Beavers sent over tickets, and he thought it would be a good idea to send the two of us to cover it. Nice and fluffy."

"Are you asking me out, Cameron?"

"Yes. As my work date to the Beaver Ball. It's not an invitation to use your magic beav on me." She bats her eyelashes and I snort.

She laughs once, but it dies quickly. "To be honest, Kels, I need you as back-up."

"Back-up?"

Cameron takes a deep breath, her face more serious than I've seen in a while. "I'm going to tell you something, but I don't want to talk about it."

"You have my complete attention. And my silence." I mime zipping my lips, locking them up and throwing away the key.

Cameron doesn't smile. "My ex-boyfriend plays for the Beavers. And things ended badly between us."

"Whaaaa—"

She silences me with a deadly look. "I don't want to talk about it, remember? I just... I need you to run interference. Keep dudes away from me."

"You want me to be the anti-wingwoman. Got it." I nod.

"I mean it," Cameron says, and there's an ache in her voice I haven't heard before. "Wait, Daniel didn't ask you to go with him, did he?"

I frown, shaking my head. "No. When is it?"

"It's in four weeks. If he asks you, you can't ditch me for him."

"It's a month away, Cameron. By then, we could both be dodging exes." I laugh, but it's a hollow noise, and it doesn't feel funny.

The thought of not having Daniel around in four weeks... it stings.

"Mmm," Cameron says. "Listen." She shakes a finger at me. "Feel free to let him hang with us at the ball, but don't you dare leave me alone there for a minute."

"Is your ex dangerous?" I ask her, confused.

"No." Her expression turns grim. "But I'm pretty sure he's still in love with me."

"And you don't want to talk about it."

She nods her head fervently.

"But you want to hear all about my love life," I continue, crossing my arms.

"I'll tell you one day. But that day is not today, won't you look at the time? Lunch break is over!" She opens the door and I follow her into the lobby.

I squint at her retreating back.

Cameron's fearless, more so than I've ever tried to be. If she's afraid this guy still has feelings for her, and if she wants me to run interference for her... I'm pretty sure that means she might still have feelings for him, too.

The reporter in me wants to dig. As her friend, though, I won't.

I sigh. Besides, I have enough work to do that doesn't involve Cameron. For one, I need to follow up on something I found in my notes on one of the Beavers cheerleaders.

# CHAPTER 23

## DANIEL

After reviewing tape all morning, I'm looking forward to lifting and then meeting with the team doc for another eval. I might love playing the game, but after so many years watching tape the day after, it's gotten a little stale.

The rest of the offensive line's with me in the weight room, the Matthews brothers joking and one-upping each other, when a huge dude walks through the door, followed by one of the defensive line coaches.

I keep lifting, finishing out my reps, enjoying the familiar burn in my legs.

"Guys, I'd like you to meet the newest member of the Wilmington Beavers, Rhett Edwards. He'll be joining us as a linebacker."

The name makes me look up, taking in the newcomer.

Instead of the usual lukewarm greetings, the good-natured banter of the weight room falls silent.

"Well, I can't say I didn't expect that," Rhett mutters.

"What the fuck?" Ty Matthews asks.

The last thing I want to do is the right thing. In fact, I'd like to be anything but nice. Rhett Edwards is the linebacker who fouled me last night, throwing me down in the end zone and then kneeing me in the gut.

Before telling me to go home.

Before calling me an old man.

I make myself stand up, taking my time. Wiping my hands on my sweats and making my way to where Rhett and the defensive line coach stand, taking in the scene of belligerent athletes.

"Rhett Edwards," I drawl, holding out a hand for him to shake. "Welcome to *my* home."

His hazel eyes heat, his mouth turning down into a scowl, but he takes my hand.

"If you hit that hard all the time," I continue, "then we'll be glad to have you on our side."

"He should apologize," Ty says.

"It's in the past," I say, and I force myself to let Rhett's hand go. "We're good."

The look Rhett gives me is calculating, but not ill-natured.

That's right. You're on my turf now.

"As long as he doesn't pull that shit again," I say, nodding at the coach next to him.

Rhett makes a low noise in his throat but doesn't say anything else. Guys like that, with more anger than good sense, won't last much longer in the AFL. Anger is a tool, like anything else on the field, but unchecked, it's a disaster. Teams have to work well together.

Rhett turns, shouldering past the coach, who throws me a reproving look before nodding to the rest of the guys in the weight room.

"Fucker," Ty says. "I can't believe they traded him to us."

"We're the lowest ranked team in the league. They'll send us whoever they want, and we'll tell them thank you," I say. "Guy might be an asshole, but he's an asshole who knows how to throw his weight around. That was a good hit. Illegal hit, sure, but it was a good hit. If we can use him, then we'll fucking use him."

I'm ready for this day to be over, I decide.

I want to see Kelsey. I don't want to make the guys feel better about this new asshole on our team. But this is how the sausage is made. Men get traded in and out. One day one guy's wearing a jersey, a part of the team, and the next he's replaced by a new face.

We're all expendable, each of us a combination of stats weighed against a stack of papers detailing every injury we've ever had in the name of the game. And one day, for all of us, those injuries will outweigh everything else, and then we'll be done.

For most of us, it's worth it. For most of us, we've breathed, dreamed, lived football our whole lives.

The familiar spiral of my thoughts has a new coloring to it, a new name.

Warner Cole, Kelsey's dad. Across the training room, someone drops their weights, the noise echoing across the expanse of mirrored walls. Sweat drips down my neck and I grit my teeth, inhaling through the required reps.

*Fuck.*

I shouldn't want her as much as I do.

It's selfish. I homed in on the one woman who has a great reason to stay far the fuck away from me, and I don't want to let her go. A better man for her would be younger, wouldn't have an ex-wife he didn't deserve, wouldn't have had more serious injuries than she's had birthdays.

But none of those men would treat her the way I will. Someone closer to her age might have more in common with her… hell, even someone who isn't addicted to the sport she hates might be better for her.

I hate the idea of it. Can't stand it.

I strain, putting more weight on, until my muscles are shaking and fatigued.

I don't want to let Kelsey Cole out of my grasp.

I just need to be the man she deserves and hope it's enough.

# CHAPTER 24

## BEAVERTOK COMMENTS

Image description: Daniel Harrison running off the field, into a reporter on the sidelines. The video changes, moving in slow motion as he gets off of her, the camera zooming in on the moment their eyes meet. He smiles. The image changes to a photo of him taking her hand in his. The photo zooms in on the soft smile on her face. The TikTok goes dark, then a video appears of him taking her cheeks in his hands, kissing her outside a car. The footage changes again, to Daniel Harrison running in the ball for a touchdown.

Text over the video reads: SHE MAKES DH YOUNG AGAIN

Comments:

> @wilmbeavs4ever: bestie this is so cute I cannot even

> @realbeaverfan: they're my life now

> @hotdamyesmaam: how does it feel to live my dream

@beaversfirst: he's too old for her- he's one fall away from breaking a hip

@phillygir1111: she's ugly

@beavercheeraddict: what do I have to do to get tackled by a football player in my end zone

@theREALbeavercheeraddict: what do I gotta do to put him in MY pocket

@be@v3rsarelife: I would let that man ruin my life PLZ

@eatmybeavdaniel: I would let him snap my back in half like a glow stick

# CHAPTER 25

## KELSEY

Savannah answers my call right away, her voice bright and bubbly like it always is. Getting to know the cheerleaders has been an unexpected bonus for this piece. They're awesome.

"Hey Kelsey, how's it going?"

"Hey Savannah! Good, good. I had a few more questions for you about something you mentioned the last time we spoke. I was wondering if you had time to follow up?"

"Actually, you caught me at the perfect time. I'm just getting off work and driving to dance practice now."

I check the clock on my computer. Shit, it's after five. How the hell did it get that late?

"Don't worry." Savannah laughs nervously. "I have you on Bluetooth, not breaking any laws!"

I laugh too, trying to put her at ease. Savannah's slightly high-strung, but so sweet that it comes off quirky and adorable. "That's good, that's good. Well, I was looking through my notes, and I wrote down that you mentioned you all weren't allowed to have any contact with the football players, to the point that if you even followed them on social media, you'd be forced to forfeit your position as a Beaver cheerleader."

The line is silent. I frown, doodling in my legal pad.

"Savannah?" I ask. "Did I lose you?"

"Did someone say something to you?" Her voice is higher than normal, and my instincts sit up and take notice. I stand abruptly, trying to make my own voice normal.

"Why would you ask me that?" I smile, trying to sound friendly. Trying not to sound like I've just scented blood in the water. "You okay?"

She laughs, and the sound is weird.

Oh yeah, there's something going on.

"Savannah?" I press. "Is there something you want to tell me?" I pace my cube, an easy task, considering it's about three steps wide.

"It's against the rules for a cheerleader to be involved with a player at all. From social media to, well, anything else. No fraternizing, no ma'am!" She giggles again, then lets out a long exhalation.

*She's seeing one of them.* And worse, she's a bad liar.

"Savannah, how would a player and a cheerleader be able to avoid each other that well?"

"Well, it's pretty easy. You just ignore them, even at, you know, appearances. Polite but cold, that's what our directors tell us. Just ignore them, even if you're both in Vegas at the same time and don't recognize each other."

My eyes get round, and I try to process that statement. "In Vegas at the same time?"

"Oh you know, hypothetically."

I crash back down in my chair, holding my cell phone between my jaw and shoulder, typing furiously into the search engine.

*Beaver cheerleaders in Vegas*

A dozen articles from the summer pop up, showing the gorgeous women smiling and posing, apparently there for a dance camp at UNLV.

I shake my head. This is her personal life. But... if it were to play out?

Sometimes, being a good reporter makes me feel like an asshole.

"Savannah, if you knew of someone being unfairly disciplined for fraternizing with a player that they didn't know was a player at the time, you would tell me, right? I could protect you, it would all be anonymous. You said yourself the cheer rules were," I pause, flipping through my notes on Savannah's conversations with me to find the exact words, "misogynist and draconian."

"It's worth it," she tells me, then repeats it: "It's so worth it."

It sounds like she's trying to convince herself.

A sniffle crackles over the line and I hold myself still, worried about Savannah.

"Hey, you okay?"

"I'm fine." The words are soggy and she sniffles again. "It's just, you know, we work so hard. They pay us next to nothing, and they have the weirdest expectations. Be sexy. Be classy. Don't eat before weigh-ins. Do your hair just right. I love to dance, I love to perform, I love going out there in the uniform, but sometimes... I'm sorry. I'm just tired. It's an honor to dance with the Beaver cheer team." She sounds like she's smiling again, as if she can smile hard enough to erase the fact she's crying.

"Oh, Savannah." I sigh, wishing I knew the right thing to say. "It sounds like you're having a hard time."

"No, no, I'm fine. It's fine."

I raise my eyebrows because we both know that's a damn lie.

"I tell you what, Savannah, why don't we try to meet up for coffee next week, and we can talk more about it? It doesn't have to be on the record, not unless you want it to be."

"No, no, that's okay. Look, I gotta go, okay? But yes, you're right about the rules. If you want, I can send you the official handbook, okay? Just don't tell anyone you got it from me."

I do a fist pump, then take a deep breath, steadying myself.

"That would be great, thanks, Savannah. Take care of yourself, okay?"

"I will; you too."

With that, she hangs up, and I stare at the pictures of the cheerleaders from Vegas still emblazoned across my computer screen. In one, the women are all adorably dressed, pointing at a street sign that says Las Vegas Boulevard, blinking lights and tourists all around. I squint, leaning forward and zooming in on the photo.

Behind the pack of cheerleaders is a sign for a wedding chapel.

I stare at it, then at Savannah's bright smile in front of it. Her white-blonde hair is in a high, bouncy ponytail, and she looks like she doesn't have a care in the world.

"No fucking way," I say out loud. "No way."

I dismiss the wayward idea as completely out of hand. There are chapels all over Vegas. It doesn't mean anything.

Sure would be a twist to my piece, though.

I tap out a few notes, reply to a few emails, and start thinking about dinner. I'm smiling and humming to myself as I log out and shut everything down. My stomach explodes into happy butterflies.

I have a date with Daniel Harrison tonight.

# CHAPTER 26

## DANIEL

She opens the door on the first knock.

"Hi." Her hands run over the tight, creamy dress she showed me this morning, tugging it down.

"Kelsey Cole," I say, unable to look away from her.

"Do I look okay?"

Is she seriously asking me that?

I shake my head slowly, in disbelief. "Kelsey, you look amazing. You're stunning."

She is, too, her dark blonde hair falling in waves around her shoulders, her brown eyes sparkling, her lips painted a dark red that makes me think about how they'd look wrapped around my dick.

"I promised you I wouldn't have sex with you again until you begged me, and I meant it, but I didn't promise you I wouldn't be thinking about it," I say, my hands wrapping around her hips and pulling her close.

A laugh trickles out of her and I drink her in, her pretty, freckle-dusted nose, the quirk of her eyebrows as she stares up at me.

"Can I kiss you?" I ask.

She doesn't answer, simply pulls my face to hers, and just like that, the whole fucking day melts away. None of the shit with Rhett or the team matters. None of the crap my agent texted me today about retirement announcements matters.

Only this, right now, her mouth on mine, the delectable scent of her all around me.

"Hi," I finally say, breaking off the kiss. "You hungry?"

"Starving," she answers, her cheeks pinker than they were a moment ago.

I tuck her hand into mine and it feels better than any football ever has. It fits. She fits.

*She deserves someone younger. Someone less selfish, someone whose job won't leave her crying in a bar bathroom.*

My molars grind against each other and I push the thoughts aside. Fuck that. I want her, and I'll make Kelsey Cole mine.

"Did you have a bad day?" she asks, eyes narrowed, watching me.

I tuck her in close, and she lets out a tiny whuff of surprise.

"It's better now," I say. "With you."

"What happened?"

I sigh. I love how smart she is. I love how perceptive she is.

Fuck, I love that she cares enough to ask.

"You know how I got tackled last night? Illegally, I mean."

"Yeah," she lets out one of those small snorts I'm starting to get addicted to and then stops walking, staring up at me with those big brown eyes. "You're hurt. Oh god, how bad is it?"

"No, Kelsey," I say, and even though her worry shouldn't please me, I'm a selfish bastard because I love it. I fucking love that she's worried about me. "I'm not hurt. I'm fine. The guy who did it, Rhett Edwards? They traded him to our team."

"Oh no," she says, shaking her head. "Is he as big of a jerk as he seems?"

We walk down the stairs of her apartment, and I consider the question.

"Probably not," I say honestly. "I wasn't happy to see him, and for a second, I thought the Matthews brothers were going to kick his ass. He's part of the team now, though, and how well he fits in is up to him."

"That's mature of you," she says, elbowing me lightly in the hip.

"That's what happens when you date an old man."

Her smile turns into a scowl and I open the door to my truck, ushering her inside.

"You're not an old man."

"I'm fifteen years older than you, Kelsey," I say gently. "I *am* an old man compared to you. Too old for you."

As soon as I say it, I want to take it back. It might be true, but I don't want to fucking risk her thinking it.

"I'm pretty sure I get to decide if you're too old for me."

I pause, holding the door open as she buckles in, hanging on her every word, her every breath.

"I think you could be perfect for me," she says quietly.

My heart skips a beat at the words and I grin at her like a fool for a second.

She doesn't smile back, but watches me thoughtfully, her lips pursed. I'm okay with that. I'm okay with her hesitation.

Because I'm damn sure I can convince her I am perfect for her.

"You're going to give me an even bigger head if you keep up all this praise," I drawl, leaning against the truck, one arm overhead. "Won't be able to fit in the truck."

"Please." A smile turns the corners of her lips up, like the sun coming out from behind the clouds. "You already barely fit in my apartment."

I hold up an arm and kiss my bicep, flexing, and earn another snort from her.

"There's only one place I care about fitting," I say with a wicked grin, then do my best over-the-top wink.

Her laugh's the last thing I hear as I close her door and walk around to my side. When I open up my door, she's still laughing.

"You know, you are totally ridiculous."

"I think the word you wanted was charming," I tell her, unable to stop smiling. When I'm with Kelsey, smiling is about all I can do. Being with her is easy, and fun, and I haven't been this excited about the future in a long time.

"So charming," she says, stretching out the word. "Talking about fitting inside me."

The truck roars to life as I turn the engine over and I brace my hand on her seat as I check my blind spots and pull out of the lot.

"For someone who wants to take a step back from sex, you sure have a one-track mind," I say. "For the record, I was talking about the valet fitting my truck into the parking garages downtown."

"Oh, uh-huh, is that right?"

"Absolutely."

"Mmhmm."

"We already know I fit perfectly inside you." The words come out in a low growl, and the intensity of my need takes me aback.

She doesn't answer, and when I glance from the road to her face, she's blushing, her white teeth biting down on her lip.

"When you look at me like that, it makes it hard for me to think about anything but kissing you," I tell her.

"Kissing isn't off the table."

"It is while I'm driving, and if I pull the car over right now to kiss you, I'm going to have a hard time not pulling that dress up and tasting you all over again."

She sucks in a breath, the noise small and quiet against the sound of the road outside.

I'm going to lose my mind if I keep thinking about the sounds she makes.

I turn on the radio and music blares through the speakers. It's not a cold shower, but it's the closest thing I've got, and I'll be damned if I'm going to break my promise to have her begging me for sex.

It'll be so fucking worth it.

The music gets quieter, and when I look over, she's fiddling with the knob.

"I finally got a chance to look at the book. You know, the one you slipped in my bag? Your favorite?"

I make a turn, then promptly pump the brakes, running into good ole Philly traffic. "What did you think?"

"I was surprised, to be honest. I was expecting like… I don't know, Cormac McCarthy or something."

"Cormac McCarthy?" I huff a laugh. "Don't get me wrong, he's great, but not exactly a favorite of mine."

"Well, *A Wrinkle In Time* wasn't what I expected."

"I love that book," I say honestly. "I loved it as a kid, and it's one of the few that held up when I went back to read it a few years ago."

"I loved it too. I haven't thought about it in years, but now I want to reread it."

Warmth spreads through my chest, and the smile I give her now has nothing to do with how badly I want her and everything to do with the fact she wants to reread one of my favorite books… because it's my favorite.

"What's your favorite?"

"Oh, god. I can't pick a favorite book. That's like asking me to pick, I don't know, a favorite child."

"You never said you had kids. I had no idea."

Her musical laugh at my stupid joke is better than anything playing through my speakers.

"You know," I continue, "kids aren't a dealbreaker for me, but that is something that you should probably bring up before a fourth date." I can't seem to wipe the grin off my face. Can't seem to play it cool with her.

"Fourth date? This is our second date."

"Nah." I hold up four fingers. "The sandwich date." I tick one off. "The phone date." Another finger down. "And last, but not least, the sleepover date."

She's beaming up at me, and my chest is so full it feels like it could crack open.

"Four dates." Her eyebrows rise, and I make myself look back at the road. "That sounds pretty serious."

"Kelsey Cole, I wouldn't be taking you out tonight if I wasn't one hundred percent serious about you."

"Speaking of which, where are you taking me?"

I scrunch my nose as the stoplight turns red again. "I gotta come clean with you."

"Uh, that doesn't sound good."

"Trust me, I know you prefer me dirty, but…"

"Shut up," she says, laughing again. Her warm hand reaches for mine on the steering wheel and I grab it, pleased beyond reason that she wants to hold my hand.

"Fine, I guess I won't tell you."

She squeezes my hand.

"No need to beat it out of me, those are my moneymakers. Alright, so here's the deal: my agent set up this date. I needed some help planning, seeing as how I was out of town and pretty busy this weekend. You know, a work thing."

"Oh, a work thing, huh? I had no idea."

"Hard to believe, isn't it? The only good thing about working out of town is getting to have phone sex," I say, turning left. "Trust me when I say I'd prefer the real thing every. Time."

"Well, you'll have to wait another five months and twenty-nine days."

"If that's what it takes, that's what it takes. I'd wait five years for you, Kelsey Cole. But you gotta stop distracting me, or I'll never be able to tell you what my agent planned for us."

"Oh, it's my fault, huh?"

"Of course not. You can't help how sexy you are. He arranged something special for us, he said. It usually happens on the weekend, but he pulled some strings, and…" I pull the car to a stop outside the Masonic Temple. A guy in a valet uniform steps up to the curb and I flash a grin at Kelsey before putting the car in park.

Another valet jogs around the truck, opening Kelsey's door for her. I wait for her on the sidewalk, and she slips her slim hand in my elbow, staring up at the iconic Philly landmark in surprise.

"Are you inducting me into a secret society?"

"Yes," I tell her solemnly. "Before I can continue things with you, you must become a Mason."

She bursts out laughing, covering her mouth with a hand and leaning against me. Her shoulders shake as we walk up the stone steps.

"Honestly, if this is some kind of weird ceremony thing, I'm outta here."

"You don't want to be a Mason?" I tease. "Secret handshake, passwords, a cool hat."

"You wear a cool enough hat for both of us."

I tilt my head, guiding her to the front door, trying to figure out what she's talking about. "My helmet? You think my helmet is cool? Will wonders never cease?"

She squeezes my arm and grins up at me. Her eyes get wide as her gaze drifts beyond me to the impressive doorway of the Masonic Temple.

I've been by this place often enough, but up close, the stone arches are more extraordinary than they seem from the street.

"This is pretty incredible," she says. "You know I've lived in Philly for a few years, but I've never been inside this place? Maybe there is something to all this secret order stuff."

I laugh, pressing my hand over hers on my arm. "We're not here to join the Masons, I'm sorry."

"Cruel of you to get a girl's hopes up." She looses a dramatic sigh.

An usher opens the massive, ornate wooden doors, nearly three times as tall as I am, and we both fall silent, struck by the interior of the building. Her heels echo against the black and white floor inside.

"Wow," she says and we both stop, taking in the building. "They don't make them like this anymore."

"Hey, that's my line."

I savor the sound of her laughter bouncing off the marble entryway.

"Right this way, Mr. Harrison, Ms. Cole," the usher at the door says, and Kelsey startles at him, looking up at me with surprise in her eyes.

"You kinda came out of nowhere there, buddy," I tell him.

He doesn't smile. "I was standing behind you the whole time."

"Of course," I say.

Kelsey's cheeks suck in like she's trying not to laugh, and I twist my lips to the side, following the usher through the main hall and into one of the side rooms.

"Oh my gosh," Kelsey murmurs, standing stock still as she takes in the sight before us.

"My agent really outdid himself," I say, pleased as all hell.

Candles are everywhere, casting a soft, warm glow along the rows of white-clad chairs and on a raised dais underneath a stunning stained-glass window. A string quartet sits on stage, and a couple of them glance up at us as we enter, then return to tuning their instruments.

"The Masonic Temple has long been a fixture in the Philadelphia skyline," the usher says. "The Masons are an integral part of Philadelphia's history, and the city of brotherly love wouldn't be the same without them. Your... *agent* had nothing to do with this building, and it spits on the history of the very floor under your feet to make light of our contributions." With that, the usher turns abruptly, stalking out the door.

"Was that part of the initiation ceremony?" Kelsey asks drily. "Survive the angry usher?"

I laugh, then quickly close my mouth, the sound too loud in the hushed space. "Yes." I nod. "You are now a Freemason."

"Where's my hat?"

"I'll find you one."

We walk together, arm in arm, down the candlelit aisle to the front-row seats. The only seats, because my agent was able to swing this for the two of us.

"How did you do this?" Kelsey asks.

"I know some people. Or, you know, my agent knows people."

"How?"

"He got some kind of deal with the events company that throws these things."

Her eyebrows pinch together, her lips turning down in a frown. For the first time, I wonder if maybe getting my agent to organize these dates was a bad idea.

"It's beautiful," she says slowly, but whatever else she's about to add is cut off by a woman in black stepping onto the stage.

"Thank you so much for coming out tonight. We don't normally do Monday night concerts, but we couldn't say no to the opportunity to work with you, Mr. Harrison."

"Er," I say, my concern growing.

But the woman simply continues on, oblivious to my reaction. Or maybe she simply can't see it, considering how dim the candlelight is.

"We are so thrilled to have you both here for our concert tonight, featuring music from our most popular performance, a tribute to the Eagles."

Next to me, Kelsey goes still, too still, not just the patient kind of waiting-for-the-concert-to-start polite stillness.

"I didn't know you liked the Eagles," she says, her voice pitched low. "My dad loves the Eagles."

"Everyone likes the Eagles," the woman on stage says, glaring at Kelsey. "They're an American institution."

"Like the Masons," I whisper to Kelsey knowingly. She pinches my arm and I swallow a laugh.

The woman nods to the string quartet and points to someone in the back of the room. After a second, the cellist begins playing, and the three others join in for the strangest arrangement of "Hotel California" ever to make its way to my ears.

The woman jumps offstage, causing Kelsey to grab my arm in alarm.

"I thought she was going to fall into the candles," she murmurs.

"I think they're flameless," I tell her. "Is this… this is weird, right?"

"You and me, in the Masonic Temple, sitting in the dark except for hundreds of flameless candles, being played 'Hotel California' by a very enthusiastic string quartet?" She tilts her head, her lips quirking to the side. "Nah. This is a very normal date. Super normal. A nightly thing, really. Masonic Temple and chill."

I laugh, so loud that the cellist on stage misses a note.

The woman bustles over with a bottle of champagne and two glasses.

"If we could just get some footage of you two clinking glasses, it would be great. I know your agent sent the bottle over for you to do additional promo with."

"Footage?" I echo. Sure enough, another black-clad guy is creeping up behind Kelsey with a huge camera.

I sigh, pinching the bridge of my nose. I should have known.

"You're filming our date?" Kelsey's shoulders bow inward, her face pinching.

On stage, the quartet finishes up the song, and the lady grins down at us, pouring generous helpings of champagne in the empty glasses.

"That's so sweet," she tells Kelsey. "You think of these things as a date! Isn't she so cute?" she asks me.

Kelsey sucks in a breath.

The quartet starts playing a very sad, slow version of "Desperado," and the whole situation is so absurd that I can't help laughing again.

"Here, Kelsey, we'll cheers, drink the champagne, and then we've got to get to our dinner reservation in fifteen." I put my arm around her shoulders and draw her in tight, pressing a kiss against her temple.

The woman beams at me, and Kelsey and I take our champagne glasses like good little stooges. If these are the kinds of dates my agent set up for me this week, I'm better off taking my girl out for cheesesteak and beer on my own.

"Can you kiss her?" the guy with the camera says. "TikTok is thirsty, ya know, man?"

"I'm not going to kiss her for your footage," I tell him, sounding good-natured, but my annoyance is creeping up.

"Your agent said you would give us good footage to work with on soc med," the guy says.

"Soc med?" Kelsey repeats. She takes a small swig of the champagne. "Well, I'm starting to see why the Masons are into secrecy. This whole everyone knowing your business thing is a little much."

"I'm sorry," I tell her, putting my forehead against hers. "I should have known better than to let him plan anything."

"That's good," the woman crows, the cellist working hard through something onstage. "Keep looking at her like that, like you're in love with her. We really want to be Philly's premier romantic date night destination."

"Can we go?" Kelsey asks, and there's no humor in her voice, just exhaustion.

I feel like an asshole.

"Yeah, babe, of course."

She drains the rest of the champagne then stands, handing the glass back to the woman Brent must have arranged things with.

"But he promised we'd get enough footage—"

"Ma'am," I say carefully, my hand on Kelsey's lower back, "I didn't sign a contract with you. Whatever he agreed to I didn't know about. Use what you already have."

We walk out of the temple in silence, the beauty of the architecture dulled by the tired slump of her shoulders.

The valet does a double-take when he sees us and immediately takes off at a jog to go get my truck.

"You okay?" I place my hands on her shoulders, streetlights illuminating her beautiful face. She's more breathtaking than any building anyone could ever create, but there are dark circles under her eyes, and I realize how tired she must be.

"I shouldn't have brought you here tonight," I answer for her, tucking her into my body with a big hug. "I woke you up in the middle of the night after you were upset and worried, and then you worked all day too."

"Have you read any of the things they're writing about us?"

The question takes me by surprise. "Who's writing things about us?"

"Everyone. You heard what they said. Social media is shipping us."

"Shipping us?" I repeat, the words not computing.

The valet pulls up with my truck and I stare at her, totally confused.

"What does shipping us mean? Shipping something to us?"

A small laugh comes from her lips, and the look she gives me is incredulous.

I have no idea what she's talking about, and it's the first time I've felt older when I'm with her.

# CHAPTER 27

KELSEY

I climb into Daniel's huge truck while he holds the door open, a consummate gentleman. An out of touch gentleman, but a gentleman nonetheless.

When he gets in, his door closes softly and shuts out the noisy city.

Leaving me with the sound of his breathing and my thoughts.

"Shipping us is slang. It means people want us in a relationship. They ship us. They want us together."

"What's wrong with that?" he asks, that megawatt grin in full force. "I would like to be in a relationship with you, too. I ship you."

I bite back a laugh because damn it, he's cute, but this isn't funny. "No, like, do you not know what they've been saying about us? Some woman told me in a bar bathroom that I needed to keep giving you my magic beav."

His dark eyebrows rocket towards his hairline. "Your magic beav," he repeats. "And they want us to be together because—oh. I see it now. I get it."

"Yeah."

"They think you have a magical pussy." He nods, a serious expression on his face. "They're right."

Amusement wars with exasperation, and I give a reluctant laugh before settling against the leather seat and sighing.

"Listen, Kelsey," he says, his tone suddenly serious. "I know that this—that dating me—is a lot. I come with baggage. The Hot Dams…they can be a lot to deal with. I have an ex-wife, and a famous ex-girlfriend."

A nasty, thorny feeling unfurls inside me, bristling and tense. Jealousy. I blink, surprised at the force of it. I'm jealous of his exes? Since when?

"The thing is," he continues, watching me with his intelligent, lively blue eyes, "you're not in this alone. We're in this together. You don't have to navigate the pressure by yourself."

I nod, an unnamed and new emotion choking out the jealousy until the poison barbs recede completely, leaving me tired. I want to know where I stand with him. I want to know if he's as invested as I'm feeling, against all my best laid plans to never be with a football player, to never set myself up to get hurt again the way my dad's injuries hurt me.

"Kelsey," he says. His voice breaks, and my gaze darts from my hands wringing in my lap to his serious expression. "I want… I want you. I want to be with you. But I don't want to pressure you, I don't want you to feel like you don't have a choice. If it's too much, if all the bullshit that comes along with me is too much, just tell me and I'll drop you back at your apartment and let you go on with your life. But if there's a chance, a chance that you want me, too, that you want this… then I want to know that, too."

My jaw drops.

A soft smile plays across his lips and he brushes a lock of hair off my temple.

His touch feels so good. So right. So does every conversation I have with him, every silly little joke.

"Are you asking me to… be…" I trail off, not wanting to put

words in his mouth. I mean, I knew he was a pretty serious relationship guy, but this is fast. Fast fast.

"My girlfriend? Yeah, Kelsey Cole, I am. I guess I am." He seems somewhat surprised too, his thumb still stroking back and forth on my cheekbone.

"All or nothing, huh?" I say quietly, trying to sort out my feelings.

"I thought I would be okay with whatever crumbs you wanted to give me, but the more I spend time with you, the more I get to know you—I don't want scraps. I want it all. Maybe it's because I'm an old man compared to you, but you're funny, and smart, and beautiful and—"

I rise out of my seat and his expression heats as I halfway climb over the center console, smashing my lips against his.

He groans and I grip the collar of his button-down, pulling him closer to me, savoring the taste of champagne on his tongue, the delicious warmth of it in my mouth.

"Is that a yes?" His voice is gruff and he cups the back of my neck in his hand. "Will you be my girlfriend?"

"Yes," I tell him, and it feels like my heart's exploding with happiness. I kiss him again, peppering them all over his face. "Yes, yes, yes. I will be your girlfriend."

A cocky half-smile languidly grows on his face, and his attention slides from my mouth down to the cleavage now hanging in his face.

"You made the right choice," he growls.

Knuckles rap against the window.

I yelp in surprise, scrambling back into my seat.

Daniel chuckles, but the sound is dark, and I know he's as turned on as I am. He rolls down the window and the valet stands outside, a slightly sheepish look on his face.

"Hey man, would you mind signing this?" He holds up a Beavers cap, and Daniel takes it and the Sharpie he's holding, scrawling his initials across the bill.

"Also, you guys have to get moving. Sorry, Mr. Harrison. Sorry, miss," he says.

"No worries," Daniel says smoothly, handing him back the cap and pen. "We're on our way right now."

"Thanks, Mr. Harrison," the valet says enthusiastically. "You guys have a good night."

Daniel rolls up the window and I readjust my dress, clicking the seatbelt into place, trying to get my pounding heart under control.

"Do you think he saw us making out?"

"Nah, I have these windows tinted pretty good," Daniel says. "Why? Is my new girlfriend into that? A little exhibitionism?" He laughs at his questions, but I go silent, considering it.

Am I turned on by the idea of getting caught kissing Daniel?

"Holy shit," Daniel groans, turning on his blinker and merging into traffic, his eyes darkening as he glances between me and the road. "Fuck, Kelsey, you are, aren't you?"

"Erm." It's not an answer, and I'm not sure why, but I am. I *really* am.

"I am going to ask you something now, and then we're getting back to this. Do you want me to take you back to your apartment, or do you want me to cook dinner for you? No cameras, no fans, just us. You can spend the night, and I can drive you in to work tomorrow morning… or you can spend the day with me. We have Tuesdays off."

"You would cook me dinner?" It takes me by surprise. Star quarterback Daniel Harrison cooking me dinner, wanting to spend his day off with me?

"I would much rather eat you out for dinner, but yeah, I'd love to cook for you. I love to cook; it's why I like growing my own vegetables and gardening. Farm to table and all that."

"Yeah… yeah. I would love to have you cook for me. I'm starved… and a little buzzed after that glass of champagne, so I definitely need to eat." My cheeks are getting warmer by the second, and from the way Daniel keeps stealing looks at me, I'm convinced he knows that all I'm thinking about is him between my legs again.

"I want you to touch me," I tell him, suddenly desperate, suddenly wet.

"Fuck. Kelsey," he says. "Right now? You do like the idea of getting caught. Holy hell."

"You turned me on with what you said." I'm blushing furiously, heat rising all through my chest, but mostly rushing straight to my lower body.

"I told you I wouldn't touch you until you begged me for it," he says, and that husky growl is back in my face.

I shiver, and his eyes widen as he glances over at me.

"Kelsey, fuck."

"You're my boyfriend now," I say, feeling helpless and turned on and only thinking about wanting to get off immediately. "Isn't that point kind of moot?"

"Then beg me."

My fingernails dig into the seat and I squirm, desire racing through me. "I want you to touch me. Please."

"Hike up your dress," he orders, and there's no humor in his voice. He merges onto the highway, and my breath hitches as I lift my hips, pulling my sweater dress up, up, and up.

I'm wearing pink lacy underwear, and he swears softly as his eyes drift from the road to my bared lower half.

"Take your underwear off."

He doesn't watch, but I can't take my eyes from him. I ditch my heels first, then tug the underwear over one foot, then the other. The leather is cold against my bare ass, and it feels naughty.

I like it.

"Touch me, please, Daniel. Please."

"Like I'm going to say no to that. I've never been more grateful for long arms."

"Me too," I say, and I let out a small, self-conscious laugh. I'm really doing this. I'm really begging him to finger me while he drives us to his house. "Our bargain didn't last very long, did it?"

"And I, for one, am fucking glad." He watches the highway, not taking his eyes off it, his hand creeping over to my bare thigh. I suck in a breath, so keyed up and excited by the impropriety of him fingering me in the truck that my whole body clenches.

He groans and I watch him, his jaw tense, the muscles in his neck standing out as his fingers walk closer and closer to the short tuft of hair between my thighs.

"Kelsey," he murmurs. "Spread your legs like a good fucking girl."

A quiet whine leaves my lips and he grins. It's feral, and wild, and I want to come so bad I can't stand it.

I shift my body, suddenly not caring at all if someone sees me, not caring about anything but getting off as quickly as possible. Scooching as close to the center console and Daniel as I can, I prop my bare left foot up on the glove box, practically panting as his fingers trace over my pussy.

"You're the hottest thing I've ever touched, Kelsey. You're so fucking perfect." The words come out through gritted teeth and I moan, his fingers sliding through my wetness, dragging up and down my swollen clit. "You're close already, aren't you?"

"Yes," I admit, arching my back, trying to get more pressure.

"Fuck, yeah you are, baby. You're going to come all over my fingers, and then you're going to be nice and relaxed while I cook you dinner, aren't you? Then you're going to get nice and ready for me again, huh?"

"Yeah," I say, my head falling back, my legs opening wider as he makes quick, hard circles on my clit. "Keep talking," I urge him.

"You're so fucking close, aren't you, baby? Your legs are shaking. Fuck. I want to watch you, but I can't, so you need to tell me exactly how you're feeling. Can you do that, Kelsey?"

"Feels so good," I manage, my eyes squeezed shut. "I want you so badly. I wish you were inside me right now."

"I want to be in that tight little cunt, too. I want to fuck you until you're screaming my name." He changes his grip and a finger slides inside me. I buck my hips and a hoarse chuckle leaves his throat. "I fucking love how needy you are."

"I need you," I whisper, so damn close.

"Come for me, Kelsey. Let me feel this pretty little pussy come all over my hand."

His words send me over the edge, his fingers working me, thick and rough but just right against my wetness, and I climax, my entire body clenching as I shake, gasping.

In his truck.

On the highway.

"Mmm… did you like that, Kelsey?"

"Yeah," I say on an exhalation.

He removes his fingers from between my legs, and when he brings them to his mouth, licking them, my eyes get wide.

Devilish, he grins over at me, his eyes shining with lust and satisfaction all at once. "I'm really glad you said yes to being my girlfriend."

"Me too," I say, and his smile grows even bigger.

A few minutes tick by. I curl my legs up under me, tugging my dress down.

"Where are your underwear?" he asks. "Can I see them?"

I raise an eyebrow, but pick them up off the floorboards and hand them over.

He tucks them in his pocket carefully, one hand on the wheel. "Thanks," he says impishly, and I laugh in surprise.

"What are you going to do with those?"

"Keep them. They're mine now. My truck, my rules."

"Oh, is that right?"

"Yep. How does pasta sound for dinner? I make a mean fettuccine alfredo."

"Really good," I say, and my stomach growls in agreement.

"We should be there in about ten minutes," he says. "You know, making you come definitely made the trip seem shorter."

"It made me sleepy," I admit, and his smile turns sweet.

"Well, I have a huge, comfortable bed for you to curl up in. And I have this heater that works great in it, if you get chilly."

"Is that right?"

"Yep," he says, lifting the side of his shirt, exposing muscled abdomen. "See? Cuddling for warmth approved."

It should give me whiplash, how fast he goes from dirty-talking and fingering me in the front seat of his truck to being downright adorable, but it's so perfectly Daniel Harrison that I simply laugh.

It doesn't give me whiplash. It makes me feel like he's going to take care of me, no matter what it is I need.

And I could get very, very used to that.

# CHAPTER 28

KELSEY

By the time we make it to Daniel's house, it's pitch-black outside, stars obscured by thick bands of clouds that hang heavy in front of the nearly full moon. Bugs and nightbirds sing, and yet it's so quiet compared to the bustle of the city that I stand still in his driveway for a moment, breathing the crisp night air and reveling in the looseness of my body.

"Hungry?" Daniel asks, wrapping his arm around my waist and kissing my forehead.

"Starving," I say. "'Hotel California' did not serve the feast it promised."

A laugh booms out of him, and we make our way inside, through the front door this time.

"Your house is really nice," I say, and some of my awkward-ness comes back. It's more than nice, and it's a reminder of all the ways that we don't match well.

It's not a house. It's a mansion masquerading as a house, with expensive wood floors and plush carpets that probably cost more than my monthly rent.

"You're really nice," he says. "You make my house look good. Come on. You need food for what I have planned for you."

"Is that right?" I laugh, my momentary discomfort washed away by his easy-going nature.

"Yep. And I'm going to watch you carb-load to make sure you're ready."

"What do you have planned for me?" I follow him through the main foyer, past the library-slash-office he must have grabbed *A Wrinkle In Time* from.

"We're going to work out. Go over plays, discuss optimal positioning for our relationship."

I stare at him. "Huh?"

"I'm going to fuck you, Kelsey, and you're going to tell me exactly how and where you want it."

I squeak, then laugh, realizing what he meant. "I have to work tomorrow."

"We can just sleep, too, if you want. But I don't have work tomorrow…" He drifts off and his fingers find a light switch, illuminating a gorgeous navy blue and dark wood kitchen that somehow manages to be masculine and homey all at once. There's a huge copper farmhouse sink and an oversized fridge, like he's used to cooking for an army.

For all I know, he does.

As public as my new boyfriend's career is, I don't know nearly as much about him as I should.

"Sit," he says. "Water? Wine?"

"Water," I tell him.

"Sparkling or still?"

I tilt my head, unsure if the question is a joke. "Sparkling?"

"Good choice," he says and opens the fridge door to reveal rows of Topo Chico mineral water, protein shakes, and an assortment of fruits and vegetables. He pops the lid off one of the Topo Chicos and it fizzes as he hands it to me.

"Thanks," I say. "You know, I'm happy to help cook."

"Normally I would say yes," he says, unbuttoning and rolling up his sleeves, then leaning his muscled forearms against the counter, making unrelenting eye contact with me. "But right now, I want you to relax and I want to impress my girlfriend with my cooking skills."

"Is that right?" I can't help laughing a little, the bubbles from the water dancing along my tongue when I take a sip.

"I want to do everything I can to make being with me as easy as possible, Kelsey. Because it won't always be easy. But if making you dinner makes you smile, then I'll do it every night."

It's so sincere, the way he says it, his dazzling blue eyes full of heat and hope, that it takes me aback.

"I've never dated anyone like you," I finally say.

"Good. I'd be very jealous if you had." He bends down, pulling out a pot, and I settle back in the barstool, watching him work.

He floats around the kitchen with clear, efficient ease, obviously in his element and so competent that my eyebrows might be permanently lifted in surprise and awe. I'm not a great cook, but I can cook, and that's more than most guys I've dated. Then again, most guys aren't thirty-nine-year-old quarterbacks who like to garden because they like to cook, apparently.

I close my eyes and inhale, breathing in a delicious aroma of garlic and butter and onions. Water starts to boil in one of the pots, and Daniel's whisking together a cream sauce, pouring it into the butter mixture, alternating it with pinches of flour.

All while I bask in my post-orgasm glow and sip Topo Chico.

"You're spoiling me," I finally say.

"You deserve to be spoiled. That's what girlfriends are for."

I press the cool bottle against my cheek, practically glowing.

"If I haven't made this completely clear, Kelsey Cole, let me." He looks up at me from whisking the sauce, his blue eyes intense and focused. "When it comes to you, I'm in it to win it. I'll go as slow or fast as you want. You set the pace. You tell me what you want. But as for me? You don't have to worry."

I cough, choking on the fizzy water.

His expression turns to a grin, a rueful one. "Coming on too strong?"

"Maybe?" I say, but I'm not freaked out. I don't really know how to feel. I like it.

I like the attention. I like Daniel. I like the idea of him as my boyfriend.

"Let's just take it one day at a time."

"I can do that," he says, too quickly. Too easily. It's freaking adorable. "Like tomorrow? Can we take it tomorrow? One day spent apple-picking at a local farm, maybe spending the afternoon at a local winery down the road?"

I roll my eyes, my lips pursed to keep the idiotic grin off my face, and I tug my phone out of my purse. There are already thirty new emails in my inbox, but a quick perusal shows none of them are urgent. I stayed late today, anyway, and I don't have any meetings that can't be rescheduled.

Spending the day with Daniel sounds… unbelievably better than sitting in my tiny cube.

He's quiet, the only sound the gentle metallic noise of the whisk against the pan and the bubbling of the noodles in the pot next to it.

My fingers fly across the screen and I tap out an email in record time. *Taking a sick day. Be back later this week.*

I send it, and it kicks back an almost instant reply from my boss. *Feel better. Looking forward to hearing an update on the AFL cheer piece.*

My tongue swipes over my teeth and I try not to let that derail my excitement over taking tomorrow off and having fun.

"Is that a no?" Daniel finally asks, a note of disappointment in the question.

"I just called in." I hold up my phone, then squint at it. "Well, emailed, but either way, I'm off tomorrow now. We can hang out."

He beams at me, steam clouding the air between us. "That's great. I promise it will be a good time."

"I'm excited." I am. I feel alive, and awake. This is all so brand-new, this thing with Daniel, and even though his speech about being all in is… a lot, he's so easy to be with, so easy to like, that I can't help but feel excited, excited and so hopeful.

About him.

"Apples are great," he says solemnly. "They say one a day keeps the doctor away."

I laugh into the sparkling bottle of water, watching as he drains the noodles, then carefully spoons them into the cream sauce.

"Where did you learn to cook? Did your parents teach you? My mom was good in the kitchen, but with my dad and her job and me, I don't think she ever enjoyed it, you know? I picked up a little from her, but I'm not an expert. I wouldn't know how to do what you just did."

"Honestly?" he glances up at me from the pan full of noodles and aromatic white sauce and his eyes narrow, just slightly. "My college coach taught me one summer."

"What? Your football coach?" Confused, I lean across the island counter, my mouth pursed. "Is that normal?"

"No, definitely not," he says, laughing again. Graceful as a ballerina, he pivots to a cupboard behind him, which opens on silent hinges. Two large plates appear, clinking against the white marble counter as he piles noodles on each.

"Coach Morelle saw something in me I didn't know I had. Something I always wanted. My parents were… great, honestly, but they didn't understand why I wanted to play ball, why I had to. Coach did. Anyway, my parents wanted me to drop out and go into business with them, you know, take up the mantle of my dad's construction company. They were really old-fashioned, and my mom didn't teach me to cook because she always said that would be my wife's job."

He spears me with an apologetic glance and I dip my chin, signaling for him to go on.

"I didn't want a wife, not after the example she and my dad set. They must have loved each other once, but by the time I was old enough to remember, they'd settled into this toxic, bitter stale-mate." He blows out a breath, taking out silverware and carefully setting it all in front of me.

"I'm sorry," I say quietly. My childhood wasn't perfect, but there was never any doubt that my parents loved each other.

"Don't. Don't be. I went to therapy for years after my own divorce. It was always going to fail. I wasn't who I should have been for her. I was afraid to be what she deserved." He places his own plate next to mine, then turns to wash his hands.

I wait to dive into the delicious-looking fettuccine, the cream sauce clinging to the noodles like a lover.

"But back to cooking. My coach saw me starting to fall apart, the more pressure my parents put on me to come home. He took me out of the dorms, he moved me in with his family in this huge, fancy house, and he and his wife treated me like one of their own. Coach Morelle helped make me the quarterback I am and the cook I am, too." He grins over at me, and the look is warm and open, a man who knows who he is and is completely comfortable with himself.

I spear noodles on my fork, twisting them around it and taking a huge bite.

Daniel watches me, still smiling, and I put my hand over my mouth, trying to hide the fact that I shoved way too many noodles in at once.

"I like you with your mouth full," he says, waggling his eyebrows.

I slap his arm, trying to swallow and not choke while laughing.

"You like it?"

"Yeah, I like it. It's delicious." It comes out garbled, my mouth still too stuffed. Finally, I swallow, and he's snickering at me while chewing his own food. "Coach Morelle..." The name sounds familiar, and I can't quite think of why.

"The coach of the Wilmington Beavers," Daniel says, and it clicks in my mind.

"That's right. Oh, that's so cool that you play for him again," I say. "That must be really nice."

"It's like coming home," he says simply, and I smile at him.

He's just so warm and open and friendly. It's impossible not to get caught up in his good-natured enthusiasm.

And I am completely, definitely, absolutely caught up in it.

I'm caught up in Daniel Harrison, and I can't stop smiling at him.

# CHAPTER 29

DANIEL

I get to spend the day with her tomorrow. I get to spend *tonight* with her.

I don't know how I convinced her to be my girlfriend, but I'm damn happy I did. After her first adorably huge bite, she's now taking tiny bites, her satisfaction in my cooking evident in the look of pleasure on her face.

"Thanks for letting me talk about my parents," I tell her, slightly self-conscious at all the personal details I just shared. "That was off the record," I clarify.

She stops chewing, something like hurt passing through her warm brown eyes. "Of course, Daniel. I'm not just going to take your personal information and throw it out there for everyone. I'm not, I don't know, say, your agent."

I sigh. "Yeah, that was shitty of him to do that to us tonight. And I'm sorry. I shouldn't have said the off the record thing."

Some of the stiffness melts from her shoulders and she takes a sip of the bubbling water. "I wouldn't do that. I just need you to know that. Unless there is something you say to me that you want on the record, I'm not just going to turn around and use you.

Daniel," she pauses, shrugging her shoulders, "that's not who I am. I have morals."

I cringe inwardly. "Of course you do. I'm sorry."

"My last boyfriend worked for Frothwater Finance. You know, the group that went down for fraud a few years ago?"

Nodding, I take another bite. I don't remember, not really, but the name is familiar enough.

"He got paranoid, thought I was trying to catch him in a lie or going through his stuff." She slumps, then takes another bite, staring at the kitchen sink, chewing thoughtfully. "It got bad. I was so young, it was my first job out of college, and he wasn't much older than me. We both said stupid things to each other, but he accused me of selling him out for my job. I wasn't even working on finance stuff. Anyway... I guess I'm a little messed up from it still."

"Hey," I say softly. Wrapping an arm around her shoulder, I tuck her into me, unable to keep my hands from her. "I wouldn't do that. I'll prove it to you." I stop myself from telling her I'll kick the guy's ass if she wants me to, because I'm too old for that shit. Old enough to know it wouldn't solve anything.

Probably.

"What's his name and address? For research purposes."

"Shut up," she says, laughing and looking up at me with huge, reproachful eyes.

She's just so damn sweet.

"Okay," she says, then pushes her plate back, squirming out of my arms, taking her plate to the sink.

Quickly, I wolf the rest of mine down. She starts scrubbing at the plate, and I gently nudge her out of the way.

"You cooked," she says. "I can clean up."

"Nah, that's not how this is going to work tonight. I made you uncomfortable by taking you to that stupid concert, and now I'm going to clean up while you keep me company."

"Are you sure?" Her forehead furrows in confusion, like she can't quite believe I'm happy to do both.

"Babe, I want to take care of you. Do you want a glass of wine?"

She shakes her head, an incredulous look on her face as she tip-taps her way back to the barstool, her heels loud on the floor.

Fuck, her legs look sexy in those heels.

"I like to help," Kelsey says, and I glance at her over my shoulder.

Her gaze drifts up to mine and she scrunches up her nose, looking guilty.

"Were you checking out my ass?"

"I'm allowed to check out your ass."

"You are. What did you think of it?"

"I think you have a grade-A ass," she says.

"Not an A plus?"

"Mmm. I'll have to do some more investigating before I can bump your ass grade up."

"Ass grade," I say, then laugh, turning back to the dishes.

"Do you know Savannah?" she asks out of the blue.

"Who?"

"Oh, one of the cheerleaders. I had a weird call with her today, and I keep thinking about it."

"Honestly, I don't know any of their names," I say, scrubbing at a spot on one plate before sticking it in the washer. Cleaning up for two is easy, and it takes all of ten minutes to clean the kitchen and put the extra food away.

Kelsey's on her phone, the blue light illuminating her heart-shaped face, the swoop of her cupid's bow into her lips tantalizing.

I could stare at her all night.

She looks so fucking good in my house.

I like having her here. Fuck, I'm excited to spend the day with her tomorrow. I knew asking her to do girly shit like pick apples and drink wine would work. She'll get to do something she wants, and I'll get to do her.

Win-win.

"I have to say," I drawl, drying my hands on the kitchen towel, "I'm fucking glad you decided to beg me for sex already."

Her eyes go round and the blue light dies, her phone sliding against the counter as she puts it down.

"Is that right?"

I stalk towards her, Kelsey the only thing on my mind. Not football, not cooking, nothing but Kelsey.

"Kelsey, I would have waited as long as you wanted. But am I fucking glad I get to touch you? To taste you? Hell yeah."

Her hair falls over her face as she slides off the barstool, and I catch her up in my arms as she closes the distance between us.

"Kelsey," I say, running my hands up and down her back. The soft fabric of her dress catches on my callouses, and I remember with a start that I have her underwear in my pocket. A groan tears out of me. This whole time, I've been walking around with her fucking panties in my pocket, and she's been sitting there in that dress without underwear on.

"I want you," she says, and I kiss her ferociously, no gentleness left in me. Just raw fucking need.

"Good," I say. "I want you."

I kiss her again, her tongue sliding against my lips, and I nip at it, catching her hair up in one hand. It's dominant and possessive, and I fucking love how she melts against me when I take control like this.

"I want to take you right here," I tell her, my cock hard and straining against my pants. She moans, her fingers pulling at my shirt.

I can't get it off fast enough. When I do, her hands run down my chest, her gaze admiring and hot against my skin.

Carefully, I tug at the hem of her dress and she puts her arms up, letting me pull it all the way over her head. When I'm done, she stands there in my kitchen, nothing on but her high heels, and I'm struck all over again by how beautiful she is.

Pretty little breasts, full hips and a thick ass just begging for my hands on it.

I lift her up, putting her on the kitchen counter. She squeals, clutching at my bare shoulders, and I laugh at the sound.

"I've got you," I tell her. "Open your legs."

She does, and her head falls back as I put my mouth between them, savoring each taste I take of her.

Her fingers dance along my scalp, her breath turning ragged.

"Fucking love the way you taste," I tell her, sucking at her clit. She's soaking wet again, and I'm not sure I can wait until she comes again. "I need you," I say, nearly panting.

I'm addicted to this woman, and I'm totally fine with that.

"Then take me," she says, her voice husky.

It's the only urging I need. Stroking her wet cunt with one hand, I use the other to take my pants off.

She scoots down, licking her lips, and I pump my hand down my cock, wanting to be inside her so badly it hurts.

"I want you," she says, her voice desperate, and precum beads at the tip of my cock.

"Kelsey." My voice is ragged. I grab her hips, hoisting her up. "Wrap your legs around me."

She groans and does as I ask, her warm wetness rocking against me.

"Fuck," I grit out, holding her up with one arm and lining my cock up to her entrance with the other. She sinks onto my length and I close my eyes, trying not to come right away.

"Daniel," she moans, and I swear my name has never sounded as good as it does in this moment.

I can't move, I'm afraid I'll come too quickly, so I stand there and pant, getting used to the hot slick of her.

Until she squirms against me and I lose all semblance of control.

I take a few steps, pinning her back against the kitchen wall, bracing myself against it before driving into her, hard.

"Daniel." Her voice is strained, and for a second, I think I've gone too far, that I've been too rough with her. "Harder," she says.

And I fucking lose my mind.

# CHAPTER 30

## KELSEY

This is amaziiiiing!

My entire body's completely keyed up, some primitive cavewoman part of my brain delighting in the fact that Daniel's strong enough to hold me up and fuck me against the wall. It feels like heaven, the angle he's pumping into me hitting everything just right, and it's all I can do to hold on as he slams against me.

"Feels so good," he says, his voice rough.

My legs are shaking again and my head tips back. His hand catches it, cradling it, as his hips continue to drive into me, filling me.

"So good," I echo.

His hand moves from the back of my head, circling around my throat, and my eyes go wide.

"Too much?" he whispers.

I kiss him hard, biting his lower lip, and he groans into my mouth.

"I like it," I tell him, and I do. My orgasm is right within reach, and I don't want him to stop.

He doesn't, a primitive sound tearing out of him as he speeds up, our bodies making slick noises as he slides in and out of me, my butt slamming against the wall.

I come with a sharp cry and fling my arms around his neck, and a second later, I feel him come too, his movements turning jerky as he thrusts in and out.

He holds me like that for a few minutes as we both catch our breath.

I'm surprised by the force of it—my need for him. My desire. I've never disliked sex or anything, but this is… this is like the sex Olympics. It's like a drug.

I want more.

I pull back slightly, my body sticking against his.

"Fuck, Kelsey," he says, then kisses me hard again, claiming my mouth. He finally softens, peppering my mouth with kisses. "You're fucking perfect."

"Do you think we'll ever get tired of that?" I say, and my voice sounds dazed.

I feel dazed.

"Hell no," he says and then beams at me, his smile so huge that it makes my heart hurt. "Come on, babe, let's get cleaned up. I knew there was a reason I got a huge bathtub. I just didn't know it was you."

With ridiculous, athletic ease, he lifts me up and then bridal carries me out of the kitchen and back into the master bedroom I remember from only a few days ago.

I smother a laugh as I remember my thoughts from that night. A one-night stand. Ha.

So much for a one-night stand, because Daniel?

I could fall hard for Daniel Harrison.

I already am.

# CHAPTER 31

## DANIEL

I wake up to Kelsey Cole snoring quietly next to me. Light brown hair sticks to her lower lip, moving as she breathes in and out.

It's the best fucking thing I've ever seen.

We fell asleep fast after a long, hot bubble bath last night, and now I'm doubly glad the realtor talked me into this place. Fitting in a bathtub alone is usually impossible, forget with a woman.

But Kelsey and I fit in the oversized tub I'd never used before just perfectly.

I trace circles on her stomach, not wanting to wake her but unable to keep from touching her. The sun filters through the curtains, the warm light a caress on her skin.

She looks impossible, so perfect she shouldn't exist, much less be snoring next to me in my bed.

Her eyes slowly open, and her lips curve up in a sleepy smile.

"Hi."

"Hi." She scooches closer, flinging one arm over my waist, her body warm and languid in my arms. she throws a leg over my waist, and then we both freeze as my hard cock rubs against her pussy.

"Sorry. Occupational hazard." It's the wrong word, and Kelsey's smile gets even sunnier, brighter than the light outside.

"I had no idea football players constantly had boners. Didn't know. No clue."

"I didn't mean it like that," I say, kissing the side of her neck, laughing while I savor every breath of hers that gusts against my chest.

"Mmhmm, sure. Now I know. Football players have stiffies all the time. Occupational hazard."

"Stiffies?" I choke out, my chest shaking with laughter. "Who calls it that?"

"I just did." She smirks up at me.

"It's a good day to go apple picking," I say, still running my hand up and down the curve of her side. "It's a good day to hang out with you."

"Mmm." She presses even closer to me, and when her hand wraps around my dick, I jerk in surprise. "I'm more interested in this right now."

I groan, then nip at her shoulder. "You've turned me into a sex fiend."

"Occupational hazard," she says, and then snorts as I huff a laugh into her hair.

Our laughter dies, though, as she straddles me. I roll onto my back to accommodate her, and she slides the length of me into her.

"You're so beautiful. I'm so damn lucky."

I put an arm behind my head, more than happy to watch Kelsey ride the hell out of me.

I can't think of a better way to start the day.

Her hair is a tangled mess, wild and shining as the sun slanting through the curtain catches it, her eyes dark and lips full. I can't do more than stare at her.

And when she starts whipping her hips back and forth, I decide this is the only way I want to start the day ever again.

I think I'm a little bit in love with Kelsey Cole.

# CHAPTER 32

K elsey

It's literally the perfect start to the day. Daniel gives me an orgasm then coffee and eggs, and my cheeks hurt from smiling.

Being Daniel's girlfriend is good for my serotonin levels. Really good.

"You know, you still haven't given me my shirt back from last Friday," he says gravely, passing me some jam for the dry toast on my plate.

We're sitting at his kitchen table, my dress still in a heap on the floor next to his clothes from the night before. I'm naked under his fluffy, huge bathrobe, and I pull my shoulder out, just to tease him.

"It's mine now," I tell him, fluttering my eyelashes.

"Is that right?" his lips quirk to the side, like they do when he's trying not to laugh.

"Uh-huh. Possession is nine-tenths of the law. Kiss that shirt goodbye."

"Is that right? Then I'll have to steal it back or date you until you give it back."

"Oh, is that the game here? This is a long con to get my hard-earned shirt back?"

He breaks, laughing hard. "I would be the worst con artist ever. I'm too in love with you already."

The knife covered in raspberry jam clatters to my plate. My hand doesn't seem to want to hold it anymore.

I stare at him.

His throat bobs. He pushes his dark, silver-flecked hair from his forehead, his gaze darting back and forth between my eyes.

"Sorry," he says. "Forget I said anything."

"Daniel," I say his name slowly, trying to think past the pounding in my ears. "We just met, like a week ago. You can't be in love with me. That's not how that works."

"You're right. It was just a slip of the tongue. Don't worry about it. Pass me the jam? I'm still hungry."

Wordless, I do as he asks and we eat in silence.

Until I glance at my dress on the floor, then slap my hand against the kitchen tabletop.

"Shit."

"What?"

"I only have my dress to wear today to go apple picking. And heels." I scrunch my nose. "We'll have to run back to my apartment for jeans and boots." I give him a reproachful look. "And new underwear, since you've abducted mine."

"Yes. They were abducted."

"Stolen. Taken. Whatever." I laugh at him, rolling my eyes, and he grins right back.

It's just so easy with him. Everything is easy with him.

Because this is new. That's why. It's always easy at the start, before you know how to piss each other off and all the ways you can be hurt.

"I'll just take you into town and we can get you some new things on the way."

"Will I be wearing your bathrobe?"

"Good point." His eyes narrow, and he gives me a once-over. "What size are you?"

"Huh?"

"You go shower and I'll go get you a few things in your size. Then you can keep them here for when you stay over."

"Don't be silly. I have plenty of clothes at home—"

"And you have no clothes here, with me, at my home. And you're my girlfriend now, which means you are going to be staying here more, right?"

I don't know what to say to that. "I guess?"

"And I want to spoil you, so let this be one of the first times I spoil you. Text me your sizes, and I'll get you a couple things for today."

"What if I say no?"

"Then I'll look at the size tag in your dress and do it anyway."

His grin is infectious, and I have a feeling that despite the joking way he said it, he's not kidding around, not at all.

"Daniel... you know that's not why I said yes to being your girlfriend, right? I have a job. I have my own money."

"I know that. But I have a lot of money, and I want to do this for you. Unless you're actually saying no, in which case, I will respect that and we can go back into Philly and get your stuff."

I scrunch my face up, squeezing my eyes shut. Traffic into Philly right now is going to be the fucking pits on the bridge, and we both know it. I believe him, though, that he would drive me in if that's what I said I wanted.

I have a feeling he would give me whatever I wanted if he could.

If I just asked.

I have a feeling he meant it when he said he was in love with me.

I wish I knew how I felt about it all.

"Fine." I exhale, and it's long and loud.

He looks alarmed, his eyebrows raised. "You say that like getting some new clothes is a prison sentence."

I suck in another breath, holding it as I try to collect my scattered thoughts.

"I'm just... You have to understand, I'm not used to this. Not just having a boyfriend, but having a boyfriend who wants to, er, pamper me. It makes me nervous."

His eyes turn sad and he immediately walks over to me, pressing his hands against my cheeks. "You have no reason to be nervous, Kelsey. I'm not going anywhere. Well, other than to get you some appropriate apple-picking clothes. If you wear that fucking dress without panties, I'm going to get arrested for indecency."

I laugh, then nod. He catches my mouth in a hot, insistent kiss, and I groan before pushing him away.

"Fine then," I say, and this time it's with a smile. "Spoil me."

His gaze takes on a slightly wicked glint, and I hope I haven't just made a mistake.

———

By the time I get done in the shower, the entire bathroom's fogged up. Which, frankly, is incredible, considering the bathroom is humongous. Oops.

I didn't mean to take that long.

But my muscles were sore as hell from last night, and the hot water felt so freaking good. A little flutter of happiness works through me as I dry off with one of the oversized fluffy towels. It's as soft as a cloud, and like everything else about Daniel's house, it screams expensive.

A knock sounds at the door.

"Hey," Daniel calls. "I have a few things for you. The women at the store helped me. I'm going to hop in the shower while you get dressed and then we can go pick apples to our heart's delight."

I open it, and some of the steam drifts out the crack as he walks through it.

"Our heart's delight, huh?"

His gaze turns hot as he devours me, and I clutch the towel around me tighter.

"Well," he drags out the word. "Your heart's delight. Mine's right here, naked except for a towel."

I shake my head and roll my eyes, my stomach exploding into happy butterflies that seem to have taken up residence there. I should probably get that looked at.

"Go shower," I tell him. "You smell like sex."

"Don't threaten me with a good time," he says smoothly. "I'd kiss you but I'm afraid it will turn into me making you scream my name over and over again, and I know you're ready for apples."

I snort, then dance past his grabby hands.

He's laughing as the door closes behind him, and I hear the shower start up again not long after.

There are six huge paper bags on the floor.

"Daniel," I say, shaking my head. "What have you done?"

I dump one on the bed. Seven pairs of expensive designer jeans fall out, all in my size. My eyes grow wide. The next bag has several pairs of fleece-lined leggings, long socks, and cute cropped shirts and sweatshirts. The next is dresses, underwear, and some cute lacy bras. The fourth bag has two pairs of shoes. And the fifth contains two coats and cardigans.

There are enough clothes here that I could likely stay for a month and not wear the same outfit twice.

This isn't just a random outfit from Tractor Supply or Walmart, which is what I expected. No. He bought me an entire new wardrobe to keep at his house, and he must have gone to some nearby small-town boutique.

It's all really cute and good quality, and I can't help but be impressed.

I'm still goggling at it all when he reappears, towel drying his hair, another towel around his waist.

"You hate it," he says, catching sight of me.

"No… but it's too much," I say. "I can't accept this."

"You're my girlfriend."

"I can't take this, Daniel."

"You're not. It's staying at my house. For my girlfriend to wear. When she stays at my house." He draws each word out slowly, and it's so silly that by the time he's done talking I'm grinning again.

When he says it like that, it makes perfect sense. Of course he wants me to have clothes here. Of course he wants to buy me nice things.

Until I look away from his handsome face and back at the mountain of things on the bed.

"Are you sure?" I ask, biting my lip.

"Just pick something out for today, and if you don't want the rest, I'll take it back. I promise…. Unless… you know… you want to keep it here?" His fingers walk up my spine, between my shoulders, and I shiver at the touch.

"We'll see how I feel after our apple picking," I manage, trying to sound lofty and unaffected.

"Works for me." He grins, watching me carefully. "Do you like what they picked out? I told the shopgirls your size and they went a little crazy. I think they had fun."

"I'll say." I find a pair of fleece-lined leggings and pause before sliding them on. "Do you wear boxers or briefs?" I should know this. I should know what kind of underwear he wears, too.

"Briefs. Why?"

"Because I'm not wearing brand-new underwear without washing it. Can I wear your briefs?"

He grimaces, and it's not until he reaches between his legs that I realize I've gotten him hard again.

"Why is that sexy?" I can't help laughing.

"Because I'm obsessed with you, and the thought of you in my underwear is turning me on."

"Obsessed, huh?"

"Head over heels, you name it, Kelsey. Call it what you want. Yes," he croaks. "You can wear mine."

A second later, he returns from the closet in jeans, holding a pair of navy briefs out for me.

My mouth goes dry at the sight of him.

He's just so hot. He has the kind of muscle that guys my age usually don't, or if they do, it looks slightly unnatural. On Daniel? On Daniel it looks so good. He's cut, lean but thickly muscled, and his arms and shoulders scream power.

"You're hot," I say, unable to help myself.

His answering grin has me fanning myself. "You sure you want to go pick apples? I can think of something else we could do all day."

"You promised me a date!" I exclaim, wagging a finger at him. "You promised apples and wine and charcuterie." I reach for the underwear, but he holds it out of reach, an easy thing to do, considering his size compared to mine.

"I did not promise charcuterie," he says.

"I looked up the wine place. I'll buy the charcuterie," I tell him, doing a little jump for the underwear.

I grab the underwear. "Aha!" I yelp, throwing my hands in the air, victorious.

My towel falls down.

"Kelsey," Daniel says, and the next minute, he's kissing me. His hands wander all over my body and I groan as he pinches a nipple.

"Apples," I manage as he kisses his way down my neck, his mouth settling on one hard nipple, then the other.

"Fuck the apples," Daniel says.

We don't leave the house for another hour.

# CHAPTER 33

## KELSEY

I feel cute in my new clothes. Cute, and comfy. Or maybe it's the way Daniel keeps stealing glances at me, tickling me when I reach for an apple, making me sit on his lap, possessive, as the tractor pulls us back to the spot where we pay for loaded bags of them.

He helps me off and I jump down, glad the new boots are holding up and not wearing blisters. A hell of a lot better than heels, though. I can't imagine trying to do this in my outfit from last night.

"Thank you for the clothes," I tell him for the millionth time, and he silences me with a quick, stolen kiss.

"Gross!" a kid shouts and we pull apart.

"Hey, Harrison, man, good to see you," a voice booms out.

"Darius," Daniel turns to me, clearly pleased to see him. "Kelsey, this is one of my oldest friends, Darius. Kelsey, Darius. We are lucky enough to be playing together on the Beavers again."

I reach a hand out, but Darius shakes his head at me. "Nope. I was just wiping his nose," he points at a toddler on the ground, pulling up weeds. "Trust me, you do not want to do that. Hey, Shara, look who it is!"

The kid looks up at me, and sure enough, his little button nose is running.

"Don't worry, he just has allergies. Parenting, am I right? Did y'all already go picking? You could come with us, help us run zone defense."

Daniel laughs, and I grin in response. "We just got done. We're headed to the winery over on 322."

"Damn," Darius shakes his head.

"Daddy said a bad word," a second kid appears, as if summoned by it.

I bite my cheeks to keep from laughing.

"I'll put a quarter in the swear jar, honey."

"Hi, Daniel," Darius' wife makes her way to us, holding another baby on her hip, her fluffy black hair in cute pigtails. "And you must be Kelsey, right?"

"Hi," I say, holding out my hand again.

"No, trust me, you don't want to shake her hand either," Darius says. "She was just on diaper duty."

"Darius, please," Shara says, glaring at him and then rolling her eyes. "He might be right, though. This is Darius Jr." She jerks her head at the baby on her hip, who coos.

"I'm Layla," says the biggest kid, the one who called him out for swearing. "And that's little J. Short for Justice."

"Me!" The toddler on the ground throws a flower at me, and I grin at him.

"Are you guys ready to get some apples?" I ask them, charmed by the three of them and their happy parents.

"Yes," Layla tells me seriously, her dark eyes huge in her face. "We're going to make apple butter. It makes the whole house smell good, right, Mommy?"

"That's right, honey."

"That sounds really nice. You know the best trees with the most apples on them are all the way back there, right, Daniel?"

Daniel's staring at me, and his throat bobs before he answers. "That's true. The ones with the most apples left were definitely further back."

"Damn it," Darius says, then laughs.

"Daddy!" Layla scowls up at him.

"Another quarter."

"I'm keeping track."

Shara shakes her head, biting her lips as the baby tugs on one of her braids. "Hey, do you two want to come over for poker night on Friday? We've been talking about it for a while, but we keep forgetting to invite anyone."

I glance up at the white clouds dotting the sky, trying to remember my plans. Cameron and I have brunch Saturday, as usual, but as far as I can remember, I'm free.

"I'd love to," I tell her.

"You like poker?" Daniel asks.

"Texas hold 'em," I say, grinning at Darius, who's rubbing his hands together in excitement.

"You any good?" Darius asks, squinting at me. "We only play for jelly beans."

"Sour Patch Kids," Shara adds. "You know, the good stuff."

"I love that. I'll bring Reese's to bet with," I say.

"Reese's," Daniel echoes. "Those your favorite?"

"Who doesn't love peanut butter cups?" I ask, amused at his interest.

"Last call for apple picking!" the man on the tractor yells, and Layla scampers off, up into the trailer.

"We better go," Darius says. "Doing the farmer's job for them, if you ask me."

"Good thing no one asked you," Shara says, sighing.

Darius picks up little J from the ground, swinging him into his arms.

"It was nice meeting you, Kelsey. You better bring Junior Mints and Peppermint Patties. It's about to go down."

I snort. "You got it. It was nice to meet you both, too. I'll come hungry for Sour Patch Kids."

"Oh, is that right?" Darius calls out from the trailer. "Your new girl thinks she's going to come in and clean house, huh? Well, we will see about *that*, Kelsey."

The family of five take their seats as I laugh, excited about Friday.

"I haven't played poker in ages," I tell Daniel, hefting my bag of apples in my arms. He's staring down at me, silent, and I bite my cheeks.

"What happened? Did I say something wrong? You have a weird look."

"You like kids?" he asks slowly.

"Who doesn't like kids? Your friend and his wife seem awesome. It helps when the kids are cute, by the way, and that Layla, I loved her." I laugh. "I bet she gives them a run for their money."

"They all do."

We trudge through the soggy field towards the main farm, where we can pay for the apples, and the wind whips through the open space, sending my hair flying around me.

"This has been a great day," I tell him, my heart full. It really has. "It's been a perfect fall day."

"I agree," Daniel says, but his voice is quiet, different somehow.

When I glance up at him, though, his eyes are sparkling, his smile just as big as ever.

"Good thing it's not over. I'm ready for charcuterie."

"And wine?"

"And wine," I confirm.

"Good," Daniel says, then looks askance at me. "You sure you're feeling okay? I think maybe you're coming down with something."

"What?" I try to juggle the bag full of apples in my arms and he lifts it effortlessly from my embrace. I push my palm against my forehead, trying to figure out what he's talking about. "Do I look bad?"

"Really bad," he nods. "You probably should call in sick and spend the night again."

A laugh rips out of me and I roll my eyes. "You're ridiculous."

"Ridiculously into you," he says.

My cheeks hurt, and it's not just from the icy wind but from smiling.

Daniel Harrison makes me feel really good.

# CHAPTER 34

## DANIEL

I don't want to take her home. The day is done, the sun setting on the picturesque winery. A propane heater burns over our table, large outdoor lanterns lighting the path and hanging from the huge oak trees all over the winery. The charcuterie board is mostly empty now, I've devoured two of their flatbreads all on my own, and between the two of us, we've polished off a bottle of wine.

No more than that, though, seeing as how we both have to work tomorrow.

For the first time in my career, I'm not looking forward to it. There's an ache in my shoulder I don't like, but more than that, I want to spend more time with the woman sitting next to me with a glass of wine in her hand and stars in her eyes.

"I think I need to get home," she says softly, then covers her mouth as she yawns.

"I shouldn't have kept you out so late," I tell her. We've already paid, but neither one of us was ready to leave until now.

"You didn't." She shakes her head. "I wanted to hang out with you, just like you said."

She shifts, then flinches slightly.

"You okay?" I frown. It's easy to see when someone's in pain once you've been around pro athletes long enough, and Kelsey doesn't have a clue how to hide it.

Or a reason to.

"Just sore."

"Apple picking?"

"No," she says, a smirk on her face. "From last night. And this morning."

"Oh. *Oh.* I hurt you? Shit, Kelsey, why didn't you say something?" I grab her hand, kissing her knuckles and observing her face, looking for clues of what I've done wrong.

"It's a good sore, you goofball. You didn't do anything I didn't want you to do."

Possessive pride fills me at that, and I kiss her hand again, loving the way she looks at me when I do it.

This fucking woman. It's been all of a few days and I'm already in so deep that I'm not sure it's healthy.

When I saw her talking to Darius' kids, it was like a light bulb went off in my head. She was good with them. Natural.

She would be a good mother, if she wanted to be.

"Do you want kids?" I ask, the question blurting out of me. Damn wine. I wince.

"Kids?"

"Yeah, you know. Eventually." I tug at the collar of my shirt. I fucked that right up.

"I mean… maybe? I don't know. I like kids, but I'm only twenty-five. I want to do more things before I have a baby, you know?"

"Right," I say. "Absolutely. I respect that."

"You want kids." She says it slowly, with an air of disbelief that surprises me.

"Well, yeah. I love kids. I'd love to have my own. I love the idea of throwing the football around with them, coaching little league or soccer or whatever. Going to their dance recitals." My throat gets tight at the idea. A little version of Kelsey and me in a pale pink tutu, twirling around on stage while Kels sits next to me in a dark theater, holding my hand.

God, I want that.

The vision disappears and there's just Kelsey, blinking up at me, a curious expression on her face.

"In the future," I say, trying to backtrack.

"The future," she repeats. "Yeah. Kids. With the right person."

I want to be the right fucking person for her so bad that I can hardly stand it.

"Let's get you home." I force myself to say it.

"Yeah. Sleep sounds good. I'm so relaxed." She stretches her arms out, then yawns, and it's so fucking cute that my heart squeezes at the sight.

"Apples, wine, and multiple orgasms," I say, holding out a hand for her, helping her out of her chair. "The secret to a good night's sleep."

"Maybe I should do an investigative report on that," she says, and I laugh. "This just in: multiple orgasms and wine key to deep sleep. More at six o'clock."

"Is that your newscaster voice?"

"Oh yeah. It's good, right? Spent a semester refining it."

"Better than good. That's how I want you to dirty talk to me," I tell her.

"This just in: Daniel Harrison's dick." She's completely straight-faced and I burst out laughing. She squeals as I pull her closer for a tight hug.

"You better stop or I'll have to take you back to my house instead of your apartment."

She sighs, her body drooping as we make it to the parking lot. "Sadly, I have to go to work tomorrow. I'm going to have a ton to catch up on."

"Was it worth it?" I ask. The gravel crunches under our feet and I'm holding my breath, waiting for her answer.

"You're kidding, right? Today was… the perfect day. I'm not exaggerating. I had a great time… although—"

"Although?"

"I am sore from having the best sex ever and very, very tired."

I swing her around, picking her up, savoring the way she feels, the little sound of surprise she makes, the smile on her face.

"I'll just have to carry you then."

"Is that right?"

"That's right. Can't have you wearing yourself out. In fact, we'll have to work on your stamina."

"Oh?" She raises an eyebrow at me, smiling wide.

"Yep. Only way to get stronger and faster is practice, you know." I nod at my own advice, and her chest shakes with laughter. "We'll work on it."

"Hmmm, I think I can handle that." She stretches up towards me and I meet her halfway, kissing her deeply and unlocking my truck.

I don't want to take her to her apartment.

I want her to come home with me.

# CHAPTER 35

KELSEY

Despite the champagne bubble feeling in my chest, everything at work is normal as usual. My cube is still small and smells like the previous occupant ate too much tuna for lunch. My computer is still slow, my email inbox self-filling.

But I feel different.

None of those things bother me like they usually do.

I feel… really happy.

And I know it's because of Daniel.

I sigh dreamily, outlining a few ideas to pitch at the mid-week meeting in addition to an update for my boss on the AFL cheer-leader investigation piece that's been my focus for the past month.

No matter what, though, no matter how compelling the pitch idea… my thoughts keep wandering back to a certain salt-and-pepper-haired quarterback. My boyfriend.

Giddy.

That's the word for how I feel.

"Hey." Cameron's voice startles me out of my reverie, and I spin around in my chair.

"Good morning," I say, trying to sound normal. Trying not to sound like I'm about to burst with happiness.

"You skipped work to hang out with him yesterday, didn't you?" Cameron doesn't miss a beat.

"I took a sick day."

"Good for you. Fuck the man," Cameron hops up on my desk, crossing her legs and lacing her fingers over a knee. "How was it?"

My nose scrunches up and I bite my lower lip. "Really good."

"Yessssss," she says. "That's mah giiiiiirl."

"He asked me to be his girlfriend."

"Hell yeah, he did," Cameron says. "Of course he did. He's old. He's going to want to lock your ass on down. Put a ring on it. Wife you."

"Please don't use wife as a verb. Gross."

She shrugs a shoulder. "Whatever. It's true."

"He's so great," I gush. "I really like him. He's so funny, and handsome—"

"And good in bed," Cameron interrupts. "Right? That's a plus when you date an older guy. They know their way around your feminine bud of pleasure. Around the freshwater pearl."

"Oh my god." I stare at her. "Why are you calling it that? Please."

"I had to knock the watery grin off your face somehow. Get you back in game mode for our meeting."

"Please don't call it that again."

"Your aching bead. The center of your pleasure."

"Where is this coming from?"

"Listen, I'm happy for you. I'm glad someone's getting some." She sighs heavily. "Okay, so you're his girlfriend now. How's the whole I-despise-football-with-the-heat-of-a-thousand-suns thing working out for you?"

Oh.

My face falls, and my toes twitch inside my heels. "I don't

know yet," I admit. "I'm just kind of taking it one day at a time. It's easy to forget he plays football."

"That must be nice. The time I dated a football player, it was all he cared about."

I swing my gaze back up to her, but she has a faraway look in her eyes. "Is this the football player you're going to be avoiding at the Beaver Ball?"

"Maybe." She raises her eyebrows at me, and I know I'm right. "Are you going to tell me what went down between you two?"

"Nope," she says. A look of pure discomfort turns her lips down and she stands up abruptly, focused on something over my shoulder.

"Am I interrupting?" John, our boss, is standing behind me.

"No," Cameron says smoothly. "We were just discussing pitch ideas for the meeting."

"Good. Kelsey, I'd like to talk about your AFL piece. In my office."

"Right now?"

Cameron's gaze darts to me, then slides back to John. Clearing my throat, I lock my computer and gather up a legal pad and pen, just to have something to do with my hands.

"Yep. I want to discuss it with you before the meeting."

"Okay." Standing slowly, I follow him back to his corner office. I glance back at Cameron and she gives me a thumbs up, then pretends to slice her throat.

I have no idea what that's supposed to mean, but it makes me want to laugh.

The door closes slowly behind me, and I can't help but feel like I've been called into the principal's office.

I'm a grown woman, I'm secure in my career, but when the damn door closes in the boss's office I feel like I'm in trouble.

"Sit, sit," John says, motioning to a chair in front of his desk.

He doesn't close the blinds, which is a relief, at least. I do as he says, scooching around until I feel both comfortable and alert. I'm glad I didn't spend the night at Daniel's. I need to be alert, and I have a feeling we would have spent most of the night awake.

A blush starts to climb my throat and I clear it, trying to refocus.

"I wanted to see where you were on the cheerleader piece," John tells me, steepling his fingers and inspecting me from over the top of his glasses.

"I have a source sending me the Beavers' official rulebook, and I think there will be a lot of interesting ways to juxtapose it with the accusations from the cheerleaders. You know, the expectations of them versus the way the league uses them—"

"You have a new relationship with Daniel Harrison, right? Can you use him on the record to discuss AFL leadership's role in the exploitation of their cheerleading teams?"

I blink. I should have expected that. Still, it hits me like a blow to the gut, the memory of my ex's accusations ringing in my ears. I don't answer right away.

"Mr. Harrison has already given me a few on-the-record statements regarding the cheerleaders." The statement comes out slowly, woodenly.

"Is he willing to go on the record about the league's treatment of them?" John doesn't miss a beat and I have a sick feeling he's been waiting to pounce on me about this since Daniel and I started trending.

"I understand your reticence to discuss your love life with me, and frankly, I already know more than I'd like to." John leans back in his chair, crossing his arms and blowing out a breath. "But what you need to understand is that you have a unique opportunity at your disposal with your access to the quarterback of the Wilmington Beavers. I would be a shitty journalist and a shitty boss if I didn't push you to use it."

I clamp my lips shut, trying to keep the words in that will surely get me fired. My heart races and my stomach's in knots.

"Kelsey," John stretches out my name, taking off his glasses and cleaning them on his shirt before he perches them back on the bridge of his nose. "You have what it takes to make it in this business. You're a great writer, you have good instincts, and you're good at getting sources to trust you. Plus, you look great on camera. You test well with our audience. Don't let some whirlwind romance with a jock blind you to your career goals. Take it from me, these sorts of things… they don't last. He's older than you, and he's dated supermodels. Nah, I say get what you can from him, and do what you need to do to move up here."

I *cannot* believe what I'm hearing. At the same time, I totally can, because this is nothing if not on-brand for John. Cameron would probably have a snappy response, but my brain has slammed to a stop.

"Are you wanting to segue into sideline reporting? Sports beat? Is that what this is about? Because BeaverTok and the Hot Dams have made it clear they would like to see more of you." He scratches his chin and I try to formulate a response.

"I'm not sure I'm qualified to—"

"If you can do investigative reporting, you can be our sideline correspondent. You're a smart girl, you'll figure it out. You angling for that spot or not?" He narrows his eyes at me. "I bet we'd get great ratings if we had you at the post-game interviews with your boyfriend. Well, until he's had enough of you."

For fuck's sake.

"I'll give you an official update and draft of my AFL piece next week."

"Make sure you get a good sound bite from the quarterback, even if you have to lead him to it."

I stand up, unable to listen to any more of his nonsense, and plaster a smile on my face. "My piece has plenty of backbone without involving the thoughts of a quarterback who's not qualified to remark on the inner workings of the league's leadership. But thanks so much. I'll keep that in mind, John." I pivot, marching out of his office and back to my cube.

*These sorts of things don't last.*

*These sorts of things don't last.*

It plays on repeat in my ears, a high-pitched whine that has me sipping my water slowly, trying not to take it to heart. What the hell does John know, anyway?

I check my phone, half out of habit, half hoping that there'll be a text from Daniel.

But there's nothing but more work emails, and a text from Savannah. She wants to meet up.

It's not from Daniel, but it perks me up a little, anyway. Fuck John and his antiquated bullshit.

*These sorts of things don't last.*

# CHAPTER 36

## DANIEL

**M**y shoulder's fucked up again. That's the thing about ball and socket injuries. Once you've dislocated something once, you're way more likely to dislocate it again. Despite hearing the actual statistic more times than I can count, I can't remember the exact numbers. It doesn't matter, not really.

I've had my shoulder popped back into place at least a half dozen times now, and I'm not sure surgery did more than force me to rest and rehab twice as long as I would have liked to.

Days like today, when it aches and twitches, I know my time marking white dashes on a green field are numbered, same as the yard lines.

From the way the coaches are watching me in practice, they know it too.

Even Rhett, who's shaping up to be a great defensive lineman for us, eyes me with concern.

Different now that we're on the same team.

The whistle blows, signaling practice is finally fucking over.

I used to dread it, the moment the coaches decided we were

done for the day. Used to dread walking off the field, having to be someone besides the quarterback. On the turf, everything's easy. Easier than going home to a wife I could never figure out how to make happy. Easier than dealing with parents who didn't understand what I was doing with my life.

Now, I try not to count down minutes until they call it for the day. I'm tired. I'm not as fast as I used to be, and from the way my team's looking at me, I think they know it, too.

Plus, I want to see Kelsey. I want to go home and pull her into my lap, and talk about her day. Make her laugh.

Sweat soaks my lower back and I tug my helmet off.

"Harrison," the offensive coordinator, Dale Smith, yells. "With me."

With Dale, it's always with me, like we're fucking walking into war together. Usually, it makes me laugh.

Today, I just want to get in the shower and head the fuck home, call Kelsey, and ice my aching shoulder.

I jog over to the sidelines where he stands, though, like a good little soldier, and he claps a hand on my bad shoulder.

I hide my wince.

"Coach Morelle wants to talk to you."

My stomach sinks.

"Yes, sir," I tell him. Can't say no to the coach. I cast a longing gaze at all the other guys, who are chatting and walking off the field, headed for the locker room. Instead of joining them, I walk side by side with Dale, who likes to try and edge in front of me. It's some weird power move, but I never quite let him push past me.

Finally, we're in front of Coach's heavy wooden door, a brass plaque engraved with his name shining in the fluorescent hall lights. It smells like cleaner and cigar smoke, the latter a scent that will always remind me of the summer I lived with the Morelles in college.

I knock on the door, and Dale nods at me once when Coach yells out, "Come in," in his gruff smoker's voice.

"Daniel, Dale, take a seat, gentlemen."

We do as he says, because that's what you fucking do when Coach Morelle tells you to do something. He's in his late sixties now, a giant string bean of a man, all lean muscle and sharp green eyes that we used to joke could see everything like a hawk. He doesn't look old, though, just tougher. Meaner, even, like time's tried chewing on him and just spit him back out.

"How are you, Coach?" I say, settling back in my chair.

"I'm fine, son, just fine. Daniel, do you know why I called you in here today?"

"Can't say that I do," I reply. It's a little dance we've done since I was nineteen and greener than the turf that stained our pants and skin. He asks if I know why I'm in trouble, I feign innocence.

"Neither of us are as young as we used to be," Coach Morelle says, pushing back in his chair, relaxing his hands on the arms.

"That's true enough," I say, and Dale laughs.

*Fuck you, Dale,* I think at him. His job isn't any more secure than mine, but age isn't going to be what gets him cut.

"You looked good on Sunday, son. I'm real proud of what you did out there. That was the champion Harrison."

I grit my teeth, steeling myself for what I'm pretty sure is coming. "Thank you, Coach," I say blandly.

"You got hit hard by Rhett Edwards." He shuffles some papers on his desk, his gaze dropping to them.

I follow the direction of his eyes.

It's my fucking medical records.

I swallow. I might be half ready to retire, I might have one foot out of the league already, and deep down, I know my heart hasn't been in it the same this season, but I want to retire on my own fucking terms. I don't want to be forced out like this.

Not like this.

"I'm going to be real with you, Daniel, because we have a history, and that's what you deserve."

He's about to put me down like a fucking prize stallion. I can just fucking feel it.

"Doc says you aren't progressing like you should in rehab. Doc says your shoulder isn't looking good, that you need some time off."

He pauses, waiting for a response. I just stare at him. I'm not going to say shit. I'm not some fucking rookie looking to impress him or mouth off.

I wait.

He sighs, glancing at Dale.

If Dale delivers the news, I'm going to have to try not to sucker punch the fucker.

"Do you think it's time to bring in Gustafson?"

I blink. He's asking me if I want to step down and let the second-string quarterback take over?

"I believe in you," he continues, and I'm too taken aback to do more than watch him. "I believe that you can lead this team to victory, like you did at State, like you did with the Mustangs. Do we have a shot at the playoffs? Maybe. Either way, I want you to tell me if you're too hurt to keep grinding out there. I trust you. I think you're the quarterback and team captain we need."

Warmth and relief war in my chest. He's not cutting me.

"My shoulder's fine, Coach," I lie. "Never been better."

He puts an elbow on the desk, then points at me. "You won't let me down, Daniel. That's why I brought you on. You and me? We're practically family. I know I can count on you to do the right thing."

It feels good. I might be pushing forty, but Coach has always been more like a father to me than anything else.

It feels good to hear him say it, and fuck, maybe I needed to hear it.

Because now? Now I want to get back on that field and prove him right about me.

"You got it, Coach. I won't let you down."

"That's all then, Daniel. See you tomorrow."

I nod, ignoring the way it pulls the muscle, pain slamming down my arm.

"Tomorrow," I echo, and with that, I've been dismissed.

I don't want to let Coach down.

I want to win.

I want to go out on top.

# CHAPTER 37

KELSEY

By the time Friday rolls around, I've never been more ready for the weekend. Daniel and I have both been busy, and though we've texted, we haven't seen each other since Tuesday night.

I miss him more than I thought I would.

A bag sits at my front door, full of weekend stay-over stuff. A slumber party bag. My skin care products packed away neatly. Pajamas. Underwear so I don't have to wear his again. I've packed *A Wrinkle In Time*, too, which I reread this week, smiling at the dogeared pages and underlined passages.

I love that he loves that book. It was better than I remembered, too, and the thought of him reading it again as an adult makes me like him even more.

His texts have been so cute this week, too. Flirty and sweet, the perfect mix of sexy and kind.

I'm grinning when he knocks on the door, and I fling it open, jumping onto him.

"Oof," he says. I slide off him, worry lancing through me.

"Are you okay? What's wrong? Did I hurt you?"

"No, not at all, Kelsey." He grins down at me, but his eyes are tight, strained. His strong jaw is tight, and a muscle tics in his forehead.

I frown at him, but then he circles his arms around my waist, his lips meeting mine, and my concerns melt away. My fingers dig into his leather jacket, pulling him closer.

"You look gorgeous," he tells me, finally pulling back. "I have two bags of Reese's in the car for you."

It takes me a minute to catch my breath. He's just that damn good of a kisser. John can say what he will about Daniel being older, but knowing his way around the bedroom?

It's a definite fucking bonus.

Literally.

"You look gorgeous," I echo, and his smile gets even bigger. "I bought candy too." I pat my purse, where the candy's just waiting to be eaten. "You remembered I like Reese's?"

"Yep. One bag to buy-in with, and another bag to bribe you for kisses with."

"You don't need to bribe me." I kiss him again, and again, until he groans.

"We're going to be late if you keep doing that."

"Have I told you that you have the best smile I've ever seen?" I ask.

"Have I told you that you're the best thing I've ever seen?" he replies, and we grin at each other like a pair of fools. "Is this your bag?"

"Yeah, I hope that's okay."

"Babe, it's more than okay. You don't even know how okay it is."

"I don't even know," I repeat jokingly, doing a bad impression of him.

"Is that what I sound like?"

"No," I admit. "You sound way sexier." I drop my voice an octave. "You don't even know," I growl.

He barks out a laugh, then stoops to pick up my overnight

bag. Something flashes across his face and he switches arms, putting the bag over his other shoulder.

"You ready to play poker?"

"Daniel… are you sure you're okay? You look like something's hurt."

"If anything's hurting," he drawls out, his gaze heating as he looks me up and down, "it's my balls, because my dick's been hard all week without you around."

"You're ridiculous," I say.

"It's a good thing you're not wearing a dress," he says with an arch look.

"Is that right?"

"Oh yeah. If you were in a dress? I'd already have taken you in three different positions on your couch."

"I'll have to remember that for next time," I say, trying my best to give him a saucy wink.

He grimaces. "Do you have something in your eye?"

"No, I was trying to wink."

"Oh, is that right? Is that code for 'take my pants off and make sweet love to me'?"

"No, you have to win that tonight." I start to wink again, but then think better of it.

"Was that another wink? It was just a slow blink." He chuckles, and I can't help laughing alongside him.

"Oh, I meant to ask you—should we stop and get flowers for Darius and his wife? Or wine? I don't want to show up emptyhanded."

"I'm way ahead of you, Kelsey. I've got a bottle of wine and flowers in the car. And some chips, too, along with the candy."

"Oooh, what kind of chips? Jalapeño are my favorite."

"Well, maybe you better stay here. I don't know if I can date a jalapeño chip lover."

"What? What's wrong with jalapeño?"

"I don't want it jalapeño business."

"Oh my god," I suck in a breath, biting my cheeks. "That's the worst dad joke." I finally laugh, turning the lock as we head for his truck, my bag over his shoulder.

"What can I say? I'm in training."

"Huh? In training?"

He glances down at me, an amused look on his face.

It dawns on me what he means then, my brain putting it together with what he said on the last night I spent with him. He wants to be a dad. Like… he really wants to be a dad.

"You know I'm on birth control, right? I might want kids someday, but I'm not ready for them right now." I bite my lip, turning over the words after they come out of my mouth. "I might not ever want them."

"Hey, no, Kelsey, I'm sorry." Frowning, he tosses my bag in the back seat of the truck, then opens the door for me.

I wring my hands together, trying to make sense of my racing emotions.

"I wasn't trying to pressure you. It was a joke. No, Kels," he pauses, cupping my face, running his thumbs over my cheekbones. "When it comes to you, I want it all. I hope you know that. But I would never pressure you into anything like that. Hell, I'm willing to wait for you as long as it takes. Just means I get more time with you, just the two of us." He kisses me, big body pressing against mine, and I sigh happily when he pulls away. "I have to say, I'm pretty greedy for you. I'm not sure if that will ever change." He purses his lips. "You sure you want to go to Darius' house tonight? It's not too late to skip out, go back to my house and have fun, just the two of us." He waggles his eyebrows and I roll my eyes.

"I want to hang out with your friends. Are you afraid I'm going to beat you? Is that what this is about?"

"Oooh, fighting words from the tiny Texan."

"That's right, don't you forget it. A Texan raised on poker." I poke him in the chest. "And I'm not that tiny. You're just a giant."

"You're just right," he says, then easily lifts me up, like I weigh nothing, and buckles me into the seat.

"Hey," I object.

"Just helping my pocket-sized girlfriend into my oversized truck."

"Oh yeah? I've got a pocket for you," I grump, then twist my lips to the side. "Wait—"

"Oh, you have a pocket for me, do you?" He's laughing, his shoulders shaking with it, leaning over me and planting another kiss on my forehead.

I scowl at him, or try to, but it's impossible to even pretend to be mad.

"I would love to help you out with your pocket later, baby," he says, so ridiculously handsome that I give up.

"Fine! Help me with my pocket! I'd like that, too."

It just makes him laugh harder, and he closes the door.

———

Darius and Shara's house rests against a sea of yellow and orange-leafed trees, the picturesque home illuminated by bright lights that show off the gorgeous exterior.

"Wow." It's about all I can say as Daniel pulls the car up the circle drive, parking next to a top-of-the-line SUV. The drive's crowded with cars and I tug at the hem of my blouse, feeling self-conscious.

Shara and Darius and their kids were so adorable and welcoming I forgot that tonight would be full of other AFL players and their dates.

"Do I look okay?"

"You are the most stunning woman I've ever seen," Daniel says easily. He glances over at me, then does a double-take. "Are you nervous?"

"A little," I admit. "What if they don't like me?"

"That's not even possible. You're smart, you're kind, and you're funny. Will they be intimidated by your beauty? Probably.

But they're used to it, because they're around me all day." His eyebrows move up and down, his wide grin contagious.

My lips twist to the side and I let out a laugh before studying his face. "You're good at that, you know?"

"At being really, really ridiculously good-looking?" He squints, sucking in his cheeks and making a kissing face.

"Huh?" I wrinkle my nose. "I meant at making me feel better. At putting people at ease."

"So I'm not really, really, ridiculously good-looking?"

"What are you talking about?" I ask, because it's clear he's trying to make me laugh, but I don't get it at all.

"You haven't seen *Zoolander*?" He lets the weird expression go, surprise taking its place.

"No. Is it on Netflix?"

"I think I have it on DVD," he says ruefully, yanking the shifter into park. "Don't worry, we'll correct your education this weekend."

"Is it good?"

"No, it's horrible. You'll love it."

I huff out a laugh. "If you say so."

A moment later, our arms are full of candy (for betting) and flowers (for Shara) and wine (for everyone), and Daniel strides into their house like he's been here a million times.

"How well do you know them?" I manage, trying not to stare as he bypasses knocking and simply opens the door.

"Darius and I played on the Mustangs together in Colorado," he tells me. "It's rare for players to manage to play on more than one team together. Usually, we get friendly with each other only to move away with three hours' notice. You get used to saying goodbye. Having Darius here was like…" He pauses and I tear my gaze away from the lavish but tasteful surroundings to glance up at him. "It was like a sign. That this is where I'm supposed to be." He squeezes my hand and loud laughter spills out of a doorway. A little kid—the middle one, I think—appears, pushing the pocket doors wide open before launching full speed toward Daniel.

"Hey little man," Daniel says, ruffling his hair.

"Daniel. Daniel! DANIEL'S HERE!" the kid screams, and I try not to wince, slightly shocked by the amount of volume coming from such a small body.

Shara beams at us as she follows her son through the doors.

"Hey there, you two. Kelsey, it's good to see you again. Please tell me these flowers aren't for me."

"They're for you," Daniel says. "We brought enough candy to buy in a few times and enough wine to have a rough morning."

"Daniel's here," her son announces, pulling him towards the doorway, the light spilling into the darker, more formal living room.

"The flowers are gorgeous."

"Thanks for inviting me," I say, feeling really awkward and out of place. Daniel clearly knows them really well, and I don't. At all. "Your house is beautiful."

"Thank you. Daniel, I like her," Shara tells him, giving me a huge smile. "You better not mess things up with this one. And if he does, Kelsey, you come over here and we'll set him straight."

"Who am I setting straight?" Darius booms from the other room.

"Daniel, if he screws up with his cute new girlfriend."

"Don't worry," Daniel yells back, letting himself be pulled into the gleaming kitchen, Shara and I following in their wake. "I'm not planning on messing anything up. Just the opposite, actually."

A warm glow settles through me, and I'm smiling to myself as I make my way into Darius and Shara's stunning, immaculate kitchen. It's like something out of a movie, pristine white and massive, with the largest range I've ever seen in my life.

But as I take in all the people standing around the kitchen, laughing and talking with drinks and plates heaped full of food, I understand why.

If the cheerleaders made me think twice about my makeup

routine when I interviewed them, these guys make me think twice about my protein intake. They're huge. I feel completely out of place. Daniel's tall and muscled, yeah, but some of these guys look like they could eat Daniel for breakfast.

"Kelsey," Darius yells, a huge grin on his face. "Welcome to our home! There's a ton of food on the island," he jerks his head, and indeed, there's an entire meal laid out. A smoked brisket, barbecue ribs, potato salad, fruit salad, regular salad. A cheese plate. More fruit. A huge glass container of water with lemon slices and flowers floating in it. "There's beer in the cooler, and wine in the butler's pantry. Or, I can make you a famous Darius cocktail."

He tilts his head and raises his eyebrow, giving me a sneaky smile.

"What's a Darius—"

"DARIUS COCKTAIL!" half the room shouts.

"I guess that settles it," I laugh, the knot of tension and worry easing inside me. It's hard to be nervous when everyone is having a good time. No one is looking at me like I don't belong, and Darius nods at me, approval in his eyes.

"One Darius drink coming up."

"Be careful with those," Daniel leans over, whispering in my ear. "I trust your judgment, but they'll sneak up on you, and I have big plans for us tomorrow."

"Oh, do you now?" I ask, poking him in the ribs.

Laughing, he squirms away.

"One of these days, you're going to have to fill me in on all these big plans you have. Including the ones about me."

His gaze heats, blue eyes twinkling, as he cups my cheek, his breath gusting across my lips. What a tease.

"Kelsey, I've been pretty up front about my plans with you."

"Oh?" My heart thumps wildly against my chest. "Have you?"

"Mmhmm," he says, a cocky half-smile on his face. "I'm going to make you watch *Zoolander* with me, on this nearly obsolete form of technology called a DVD, and then you're spending the rest of the weekend with me."

He kisses me, swallowing the laughter bubbling out of my mouth, and a raucous cheer goes up all around.

I break off the kiss, tucking a piece of hair behind my ear, slightly embarrassed.

"Oh, young love, young love," Shara says, putting the flowers in a vase.

"Here you go," Darius says. "Drink up!" He hands me a cocktail glass and I eye it speculatively.

Without further ado, I take a deep swig, and Darius thumps my back when I cough.

"It's good," I rasp, the alcohol burning all the way down.

"Of course it's good, I made it."

"I'm ready for poker!" one of the huge men says, dressed in jeans and a Hot Dam t-shirt.

"That's Tyler, Ty, one of the Matthews brothers," Daniel tells me. "He's young, but he's a good one. He'll go places if he can get traded—" He clamps his mouth shut, then shoots me an apologetic look.

I squeeze his hand because I know he wants to tell me all about his friends, and I also know he doesn't want to hurt any of their feelings or talk shit about their team.

"Is your girl ready to get her ass handed to her at the poker table?" Ty says, a mischievous glint in his eyes.

"Oh," I say, making my own eyes as round as possible. "I'm terrible at poker." I bat my eyelashes, suppressing an evil grin. "I always forget which is better, the one with all the same colors or the one with the same numbers."

Ty laughs, and he sizes me up. I try to make myself look more innocent.

I'm going to win all the fucking candy tonight.

"Be careful with her," Daniel says to Ty. "She plays dirty."

"No," I say, swatting at his elbow. "I promise I won't get the cards sticky from the candy. Sheesh!"

Daniel snickers, then leans down and whispers. "Nice act. I'll be watching you, Cole."

"Well," Darius says, "if everyone's eaten enough, we can head to the poker tables. Let the games begin!"

The men and their dates, except Ty and a guy on crutches—the other Matthews brother, I remember—who seem to be alone, make their way out of the crowded kitchen. The next room is a two-story great room where a few tables have been set up, each with a couple decks of brand-new cards on them and a set of poker chips.

Well. Looks like they take their poker pretty seriously.

I have to say I approve. A pang goes through me, a bout of homesickness that takes me by surprise.

"What's wrong?" Daniel asks, and I realize I've stopped as everyone takes a seat, frowning at nothing.

"My dad would love this," I finally say. "It just... it made me miss him. It's been too long since I've been home to see him and my mom."

"Then go make him proud. You can send him a picture of all your ill-gotten candy gains at the end of the night."

That makes me laugh, taking the edge off some of the residual guilt that slides through me whenever homesickness hits for moving so far away from them. Not that they've ever made me feel like they're anything but immensely proud of my career and accomplishments, and me as a daughter... but sometimes I wish West Texas wasn't so far away.

A kids' movie plays on the TV, the sound turned down but the colors and cartoons still garish, and it's such a funny mix of things, all the candy being used to buy chips, the huge football players sitting on small folding chairs, the groups of players' kids running around happily between the tables, that I can't help feeling... good. Like I could belong here, too.

It's not fussy or fancy or any of the things I worried it would be.

It's still a hell of a lot nicer than any poker game I've ever been to, but they're all just people, all just families trying to have a good time together.

It's really nice.

"Kelsey, come play at our table," Ty Matthews calls out, a shark's grin on his face as he pats a chair next to him.

"I'm going to play at Darius' table," Daniel tells me. "You can sit with me, or you can go show the Matthews brothers what a pair of rookie idiots they are."

I rub my hands together as I square off with Daniel. "There's nothing I love more than when someone underestimates me."

"I fucking love that about you, baby." He kisses my forehead and I pivot, ready to take the Matthews brothers for all the sugar in the world. I yelp in surprise as he smacks my butt. "Go get 'em, tiger."

Shara catches my eye, laughing and shaking her head, and I grin at her before resuming my look of gullible innocence and taking my place between the massive Matthews brothers.

"Is this the one where I ask you what you have?" I say, sitting down carefully so as not to jostle the older brother's wrapped up ankle.

The one with the lighter hair laughs, giving me an incredulous look. "Go Fish? No. This isn't Go Fish."

"I know, I know, I was just kidding. I know this is poker. I'm not good at it, but…" I drift off, the handful of times I did nearly this exact same bit in college racing through my memories. "I'm Kelsey, by the way."

"Jacob Matthews," the lighter haired, injured one says, offering a hand the size of a freaking dinner plate to shake. "And that idiot's my little brother, Tyler. We all call him Ty, though."

"You're a reporter, right?" Ty interjects, shuffling the cards with ease.

He's good at it, the cards making the familiar snick against each other as they bridge between his hands. Could be Ty's sand-bagging too. I watch him, curious.

"Yeah, I am," I finally answer.

Another player sits down, twice as wide as me, the chair groaning.

"Rhett," Jacob says. "Didn't think you were coming tonight."

"Here I am," the guy says gruffly. There's no way he's not a linebacker. He's huge. Surly.

"You trying to play nice after what you did to Daniel last week?" Ty asks him, shuffling again.

He pushes the deck out to me and I nearly cut it out of habit, but remember I'm trying to win and stare up at him in confusion instead.

"Cut the deck," he says.

"Hmm?" I ask.

"Cut the deck?" He grins at me, and despite the fact he's objectively handsome, he doesn't hold a candle to my Daniel. "Show her, Jacob."

Jacob sighs, then cuts the deck, an exasperated expression on his face. Even so, when he leans back against his chair, he gives me an appraising stare, like he suspects me already. Whatever. It'll make it more fun.

"Does she know how to play?" Rhett grumbles, glaring at me. "I thought this was going to be fun, not beginner hour."

"Oh, gosh, I'm sorry. If y'all don't want me to play, I'll go sit with Daniel." I pout. "I'll pick it up fast. I promise."

"No, no, no," Ty says. "This'll be fun. You'll get it."

Rhett grunts.

Obviously, playing nice with a poker novice isn't his idea of fun.

"It's just for candy," I say, but these guys don't play games for fun. Not the same way regular people do. They're out to win, same as me. They're just telling me a whole lot more about themselves than they realize right now. "Right?"

"Like from a baby," Ty says, laughing. "Okay, sweetheart—"

"My name is Kelsey," I tell him, dropping some of the act. "Not sweetheart."

His eyebrows rise and his grin deepens.

"Don't be an ass, Ty," his brother tells him.

Rhett sighs.

"Before you play, you put in the ante. That means you pay to get dealt in. We each get three cards to start. We do a round of bets based on our cards. The dealer, that's me, flips the first three off the top of the deck. That's called the flop. After the flop, we'll take turns betting again, based on both our hands and what we think other players might have in their hands."

"Do I have to bet?" I interrupt, blinking rapidly.

"No, you can fold," Jacob says slowly, and I glance at him. He's really staring at me now. Maybe I'm laying it on too thick.

"Once that round of betting is done, one more card goes out, and then we bet again, or you can fold. Whoever has the better hand after that last round wins whatever's been bet."

I fish a box of Junior Mints out of my purse and a bag of Reese's Peanut Butter Cups. I'll save the peppermint patties in case I need another buy-in later.

"Sounds fun." I shrug.

Ty whistles. "Reese's? Harrison, your girlfriend's packing some serious heat."

Daniel catches my eye then winks at me. I toss my hair over my shoulder as Ty continues to explain the winning hands. I let him go on as Jacob puts a stack of chips in front of me.

Besides, maybe Rhett needs the refresher.

He definitely needs an attitude change.

"Ready?" Ty finally asks, laughing as it becomes clear I'm not listening to a word he's saying.

"Sure," I say, scooting forward to sit on the very edge of the chair.

"Ante up," Ty announces and I follow their lead, putting one of the chips in the center.

Ty deals us all three cards and I make a big show of picking them up off the table, holding them right in front of my eyes even as the guys all barely touch theirs, staring at me incredulously.

"Were we supposed to leave them on the table?" I set them back down reluctantly.

Rhett groans.

"Does he talk?" I ask Jacob. "Do you talk?" I direct the question at Rhett.

He glares at me.

"Riiiight," I sigh.

"Bets?" Ty asks, all business.

Oh, this is going to be too much fun. I make my face as sunny as possible, then glance at my cards again, the same way the men did, peeking at the corners.

"Check," Rhett says.

"Check," Ty says.

"How many is this?" I ask, throwing in a couple chips off my stack.

"If it was money, that would be about a hundred bucks."

"Cool," I say.

"You want to bet?" Ty's laughing. "All right."

"All right," I repeat.

"Call," Jacob says.

"Call," Rhett pushes his chips in.

"Call," Ty agrees, and we're all in it now.

I look at my cards again, biting my cheeks.

Ty turns the card, and this time, Rhett bets. Ty calls. I push in a few more chips.

"You want to raise?" Ty says. "You sure?"

"Oh yeah. I like these cards. Girl power," I say stupidly.

Jacob snorts, gives me one look, and folds. He's onto me. Whatever. It's still fun.

Rhett calls, Ty calls.

Last card.

Ty and Rhett bet. I glance at my cards.

"Bet?" I ask, then push a stack of chips into the center.

"That's a raise, Kelsey," Ty says slowly.

"Oh. Okay. Raise."

Jacob's smirking at me, and I know for sure now he knows I'm messing with them. He nods at me as if to say, go on then, and I wink at him before turning back to the other two. It would be a better play to lose the first hand, make them think the worst about my skills, but winning outright is fun too.

Besides, I don't want to make them hate me. Just keep them on their toes.

"I feel good about this." I grin.

Rhett sighs, then calls, and Ty narrows his eyes at me, then calls too, pushing his chips into the middle.

"What have you got?" Ty asks, and he has a pretty good hand, two pair, tens and jacks. Rhett's got jack shit, a pair of queens, a lucky one on the river. Hm.

"Oh, you had queens too?" I make myself ask. "Girl power."

I flip my cards over. Pair of queens, and a jack.

On the table, a jack, a queen and a couple of lower number cards.

Rhett curses. Ty laughs, his eyebrows high on his forehead.

"Did I win?" I sip my Darius cocktail, only wincing slightly as it burns down my throat. Probably a bad sign that I'm no longer choking on the alcohol content.

"Full house," Jacob says.

I set my drink down and pull the chips in towards me, then stack them neatly.

"Well, sweetheart," I say to Ty. "That was like taking candy from a baby."

He laughs, shaking his head. "You could have just told us you knew how to play."

"Nah, this was way more fun, wasn't it, Rhett?"

Rhett's glaring at me from over his beer and I wink at him, which simply intensifies the glower.

"I had a feeling you were sandbagging," Jacob says. "That was pretty fun to watch, though."

"What gave it away?" I ask, putting in the ante as Ty shuffles up for the next round.

"Go Fish," he says, laughing. "No way would Daniel date a girl who confused Go Fish and poker."

"That's fair," I say, laughing.

"You could've told your own brother," Ty grumps at him, dealing us in for the next hand.

Rhett grunts again.

"Dude, use your words," Ty tells him, clearly annoyed. "If you're going to be part of the team then don't act like we all forced you to come out here."

"Did you just get traded?" I ask him, and when he narrows his eyes at me, jerking his head in what I assume to be a yes, it clicks. "Oh, you're the asshole that hurt my boyfriend? The Miami Reef Shark?"

"Kelsey," Jacob says quietly.

"Sorry," I say, gritting my teeth, white-knuckling my cup. "Sorry. That was rude of me. We're going to have *fun*!" It comes out manic, though, and Rhett's eyes go wide.

When he barks out a laugh, it catches the three of us by surprise.

"He does know how to laugh," I make myself say, and just like that, a lot of the tension dissipates, Rhett even giving me a ghost of a smile. "Well, you're a Beaver now."

He just shakes his head silently, checking his cards again.

It's fun. We play hand after hand until it's down to Ty and me, Jacob and Rhett watching, along with a crowd of players knocked out from their respective tables.

Someone refills my cocktail and I sip it as I bet, Ty's stack of chips dwindling until he finally goes all in and I put him out of his misery.

Applause breaks out.

"Winner, winner!" Darius shouts. "And look who she'll be going up against."

The mountain of football players parts and Daniel walks through the crowd, so fucking handsome I can't help but sigh.

"Wait," I say. "You won too?"

"Yup. You and me, Shara and Jimmy L. We're the winners. You ready?"

I nod, grinding my molars, and sip the lemony cocktail again.

"I'm ready."

An hour and a half later, there's a kid dozing in Daniel's lap, face slack and heavy with sleep. Daniel holds him with one arm, playing with his free hand, completely unbothered by him.

Part of me wonders if he's doing it on purpose, holding the kid, because it's distracting as hell. The kid stirs in his sleep as Shara flops the cards, and my ovaries explode a little as Daniel pats his little back until he quiets again.

Daniel and I are the last two playing, and most of the team's already headed back to their houses with their families, save the Matthews brothers, who are in deep and enthusiastic conversation with Darius while we play.

"Bets?" Shara asks.

"Check," I say.

"Bet," Daniel announces. "I'm all in."

My eyebrows rise, then my eyes narrow. His pretty blue eyes are clear, and while his expression's serious, it's good-natured and soft. I don't think he's bluffing, and I could fold and let him take the pot, or… or I could play my okay hand through, and we could get back to his house.

Either way, I'm winning tonight.

"Call," I say, pushing my chips into the center.

"Ooooh," Shara says, laughing. "Now things are getting interesting." Her child makes a small noise and she finally stands, taking the sleeping toddler.

"Darius or Ty, you take over while I get this guy to bed," she says softly. She rocks while she walks him upstairs, and the Matthews brothers and Darius fill in at the table.

"You going to take the old man out, Kels?" Ty asks.

Darius flips the turn and I settle back in my seat, ignoring Ty, surprised at my good luck. Darius starts to flip the river, and Daniel clears his throat.

"Not so fast," he says. "Raise."

"You're outta chips, Harrison," Ty tells him.

"If I win, I get to take you to the Beaver Ball. I'm giving a speech, and I want you there with me," Daniel announces, ignoring Ty, focusing all that intensity on me. I go hot beneath his scrutiny.

"I'm already going with Cameron," I say.

"Cameron," Jacob blurts, sitting up straight. "Cameron Brooks?"

"Yeah?" I momentarily forget the game as I focus on Jacob. His cheeks are flushed, his pupils dilated. "She's my best friend."

"Cameron Brooks is your best friend," he repeats, his tone disbelieving.

"Do you know her?" I say rhetorically, because there's no way he doesn't, not with the hungry way he's looking at me. "How do you know her?"

"She broke his heart," Ty chimes in.

"Shut the fuck up, Ty. You don't want me to start talking about your *girlfriend*, do you?"

"She's not my girlfriend," Ty mutters, looking for all the world like a little whipped puppy.

"Are you… did you do something to her? To Cameron?" I half-stand, maybe a little more buzzed than I meant to be. Damn Darius cocktails. "She told me I had to be the anti-wingwoman between her and a football player there. Is it you?"

He hangs his head, his dark eyes sad, and I almost feel sorry for him.

"Cameron is brilliant, and so pretty, and she's my friend," I whisper shout, at least not drunk enough to forget the fact there are little kids trying to sleep in this huge house. "What did you do to her?"

"I fell in love with her," he says quietly. "That's what I did. I fell in love with Cameron Brooks, and she didn't want to love me back."

Darius clears his throat. "As enlightening and depressing as this is, folks, I am old and I want to get to bed soon. My kids wake up like clockwork at six AM, and if I don't get sleep, tomorrow morning will be a bloodbath. With my blood. Let's finish this up so I don't have to kick you out." He slaps a hand on the table and the alcohol in my glass sloshes with the impact. "The gentleman quarterback has raised your bet. Do you have an answering bet, Kelsey?"

The first idea that pops in my head has me covering my hand to smother wild laughter, and Daniel shoots me a semi-concerned look as I giggle.

"Well?" Darius prompts.

"I call. If I win…" I trail off, taking a deep breath, making sure this is really the bet I want to make. "I get to write your speech for the Beaver Ball." I dissolve into fresh laughter because the speech already writing itself in my mind is completely absurd, as absurd as the fact they have a formal fundraiser for wildlife they call the Beaver Ball.

Did absolutely NO ONE think that through?

"Deal," Daniel says, and extends a hand.

I stand up, reaching across the table to shake it, and Darius flips the river.

It's an ace of spades.

I double over with laughter, tears starting to stream from my face. Ty reaches over for my cards, but I slap his hand away and do it myself.

"Royal flush, ace high," I announce. It's an impossible hand, the odds so ridiculous for me to get the ace of spades on the last fucking card that I'm choking on laughter. It's the best hand, and the fact that I was betting on an okay hand only to end up winning is… hilarious.

"I am not gonna lie, man, I'd be pretty worried about what-ever she has planned for your speech." Ty scratches his beard, amusement clear in the crinkle of his eyes. "Kelsey, it was nice to meet you. I've heard nothing but good things from my… about you. From Daniel."

"A royal flush?" Daniel's still staring at the cards, and when he flips his, he has a good hand too, a straight, not surprising, considering what's on the table, but my hand's unbeatable. "Damn baby, I'm so proud of you."

"And that's what we call sportsmanship. Kelsey, you get all the candy."

"Keep it," I say as Daniel sprints around the table to wrap me in a huge hug. "I still have a bag of peppermint patties in my purse."

"Yeah, and she's already sweet enough," Daniel says. I groan.

"Shara and I will be making a donation to the Beaver Ball in your name."

"That's amazing. Thank you... But seriously, does no one think the name Beaver Ball is hilarious?" I ask, my voice muffled in Daniel's still enthusiastic hug.

"I think it's pretty funny," Ty says.

"Are you going to tell Cameron you saw me?" Jacob asks, and I peek out from Daniel's arm at him.

"You better believe I'm going to interrogate her about you. And if I find out you did something fucked up..." I manage to pull a hand out from Daniel, shaking it at him. "I'm going to find out where you live."

"I already know where they live," Daniel says. "We can egg their house."

"Eggs are too expensive to waste," I say. They all look at me like I've grown a second head. Right. That's not a problem they have.

I detach myself from Daniel.

"Can I help you clean up?" I ask, then feel doubly stupid when I see that a crew of people have been cleaning up the party already. "Oh. Thank you for inviting me. I had a great time."

"We're good, Kelsey, but that's really sweet of you. You got a good one, Daniel," Darius says. "And you do too," he directs at me. "No QB in the league is a better man than the one staring at you like he's a fool in love."

I put my purse over my shoulder, unsure how to answer that.

Daniel's smile gets even wider. "Then let this fool in love take you home."

"Okay—aghh!"

He picks me up, chucking me over his shoulder like a fireman.

"Shit, Harrison, your shoulder," Ty says, and from my perch on his back, which seems really, really high, Ty looks worried.

But Daniel spanks my butt and before I can think too hard about what Ty said, Daniel's running out of the house with me. My purse flops against his hip as he sprints, and he practically throws me in the truck.

He races around the car, diving into the driver's seat.

"Are you drunk?" I ask him, blowing my hair out of my eyes. Or trying to. It just settles back on my lips. "I'm a little drunk."

His smile fades, replaced by a concerned scrunch of his forehead.

"You're really handsome," I tell him, stretching out over the console to smooth the wrinkles above his brow. "I think you're just really handsome."

"I'm not drunk, but I can definitely tell you've had a few too many Darius cocktails."

He leans over me. "Oooh," I breathe. "Are we going to get frisky in the car again?"

He pushes the seat heater button. "Nope. Just trying to make you comfortable."

"Why not?"

"Because you just said you're drunk. I'm going to make sure you hydrate, and then we're going to cuddle until you pass out, which... based on the way one of your eyes is slightly more closed than the other, won't take long at all." He opens up the center console and my eyes widen as cold air spills out of it.

I peek inside and it's full of sports drinks and water bottles. "You have a fridge in your truck?"

"I know." He sighs. "It's over the top. But... why not, you know? Gatorade or water?"

"Do you have blue Gatorade? That's my favorite."

"You got it."

"How come I didn't know this was here?"

"You never asked." He pulls out a blue bottle, twisting the top off before he hands it to me. "Be a good girl and drink up, Kels. You're not going to want a hangover for what we're doing tomorrow."

I drink as much as I can, living for the approving look in his eye. He screws the top back on.

"See? I can be good," I purr, running my fingers up and down his bicep as he finally puts the truck in gear and pulls out of the driveway. "I won."

"That you did. I still can't believe you managed a royal flush."

"You and me both. I mean, I had a king high flush already, but when I got the ace on the river? Whew!" I clap my hands. "My dad's going to be so proud. I can't wait to tell him."

"You said he taught you to play?"

"Oh yeah. He would stack the deck for me at first, and it wasn't until I was older that I realized it. Apparently straight flushes weren't as common as I thought." I'm grinning at the memory, but the bubble of happiness fades all too quickly. "I worry about him, Daniel."

"I know," he says, and his tone is sympathetic. "I know you do."

*I worry about you,* I want to tell him.

I don't want to worry about either of them.

I want them both to be okay, and for us to all be healthy, and if it weren't for fucking football, I might actually get that wish.

But that's not reality.

I lean back against my seat, and at some point, I must fall asleep, because when I wake up again, I'm wearing only my underwear and a t-shirt, snuggled up to Daniel in his bed.

I get up to pee, then stare at myself in the mirror for a long time after I wash my hands.

Daniel's breathing is deep and even in the next room, and my heart aches with feeling for him.

I really care about him. More than I would think possible after such a short amount of time. But he's funny, and real, and kind, and so quick and handsome that the thought of him getting hurt makes feel physically sick.

I wish he didn't play football.

By the time I finally get back in bed, my feet are cold as ice.

# CHAPTER 38

DANIEL

"Wake up, sleepy head," I whisper. There's a latte in one hand, one from the local coffee house down the road, and a breakfast sandwich in the other. I wasn't sure which kind she liked, so I bought three and a cruller. They're in the kitchen if sausage, egg and cheese isn't her jam.

Her brown eyes open slowly. I thrust the paper cup at her.

"Drink it. Then more water."

"Huh?" she smacks her lips, stretching long in my bed.

God, she looks so fucking good in my bed. I never want her out of it. It's too soon, too fast for me to feel so strongly about her.

But I know a good thing when I see it, and Kelsey is like all the good things wrapped up in a perfect package.

I kneel next to her, brushing my forefinger over the tip of her cute nose. "It's a latte. I remember you saying you liked hazelnut lattes the other day. Extra hot." I hold up the bag. "Breakfast, and then you gotta get dressed so we're not late. I have your outfit all ready for you."

"Huh?" she repeats, then takes a long swig of the coffee. "Mmm."

My dick gets hard at the little sound. I ignore it, loving how she looks right now, disheveled, undone, gorgeous.

She drinks a bit more, then glances over at me. "Thank you."

"I would do it every morning if you let me," I tell her honestly. She throws the sheets off, pointing her feet as she stretches some more, so fucking cute that it takes nearly all my willpower not to try and tackle her back to the bed right now.

We don't have time for that.

Kelsey takes the bag, opening it carefully. "A sausage, egg and cheese?" she asks, and her voice is delighted and slightly more awake.

"Did I do okay?"

"Heck yeah. This is the perfect breakfast after too many Darius cocktails."

"Are you hungover?"

She shrugs. "Not really. A little, maybe. I only had three or four."

"Ah, to have the liver of a twenty-five-year-old," I say dramatically.

"With great power comes great responsibility," she says knowingly.

We grin at each other like idiots for a moment.

"Well," I say, getting up and slapping my hands together briskly. "We gotta get going."

"What time is it?"

"Seven AM."

She blinks at me, her eyebrows rising. Fuck, she's so cute.

"Where are we going at seven AM on a Saturday?"

I point to a pile of clothes on the chair in the corner. "You'll see."

Kelsey gets out of bed gracefully, sipping her latte and then taking a bite of the sandwich. I can't stop watching her. I keep waiting for the bloom of my fascination with her to wear off, keep thinking that it's some kind of infatuation, but the more I get to know her, the more obsessed with her I feel.

Today's going to be so fucking fun. I love bye weeks.

She bends over and the t-shirt I put her in to sleep last night rides up, showing off the thick curve of her ass.

"What's this?" Her voice is still fuzzy with sleep, but slightly more alert now that she's out of bed.

"Your uniform," I tell her gleefully.

"My what?" she glances at me over her shoulder, and there's slight shock in her expression. Ha. I love surprising her.

"Your uniform," I repeat.

She chugs the latte, and I don't hold back my laugh as she sets the cup down, then holds up the royal blue shirt. "Assistant Coach Kelsey?" she reads off the back.

Her eyes are narrowed.

"You're going to be helping me coach youth football this morning."

Her expression darkens slightly, and I hold up a hand.

"Don't worry, it's no-contact, and it's hilarious. The kids are like little feral animals. They're going to love you. We play games with them, it's a lot of fun. I promise you'll have a good time. Do you trust me?"

Her lips twist to the side and she eyes the empty coffee cup where she set it on the floor. "I'm going to need more coffee." She puts the whistle on over her shirt, though, tugging her hair through it.

"More coffee. You got it, Coach."

She rolls her eyes, but grins in spite of herself. "This is not what I was expecting to do today."

"You mad?" I ask, my heart sinking. Maybe this was a terrible idea.

"No, not at all." She tilts her head, her expression thoughtful as she watches me stand next to the bed she was just asleep in. "You just continue to surprise me."

"What, you still think I'm a meathead jock?"

"I never thought that."

I give her a look.

"Okay, maybe I did for like five minutes after you tackled me. But I haven't since then." She opens her mouth again, like she's going to say something else.

I stare at her, tension building between us, waiting. Not wanting to interrupt. Ever since last weekend when I told her I loved her, when it slipped out way too early and impulsive, the words hanging between us. I haven't mentioned it since, but it hasn't changed how I feel.

"It sounds fun," she finally says. "I haven't volunteered with kids since college."

"Then you better suit up, Coach. We've got to be there by eight."

"Sir, yessir." She snaps off a passable salute, then returns to chomping on her sandwich, staring down at the shirt on the chair.

The strangest thought goes through my mind, and it's that I wish her shirt didn't say Coach Kelsey.

I wish it said Coach Harrison.

# CHAPTER 39

## KELSEY

I t's chaos. Utter chaos.

Kids spill out every which way, all in a multicolored rainbow of shirts matching their coaches. Daniel and I have the royal blue team, who are currently pretending to be lions in a drill on the Wilmington Beavers football field.

They are too fucking cute, and watching Daniel hold a little boy's hand as he finally works up the courage to participate is absolutely sending me head over heels.

He's too good to be true, and it's fucking scary.

Darius and Shara are here, too, coaching a group of yellow-clad kids, and the Matthews brothers are too, coaching a group of pink-shirted kids. Their groups are older—Daniel and I appear to have lucked out with the five and six-year-old group.

They're a mess, and it's taking all my strength not to simply laugh at their antics. Three or four of them don't want to partici-pate at all and are rolling around on the turf like wriggling snakes instead. Another kid's doing forward rolls instead of acting like a lion, and I giggle as she throws her arms in the air like an Olympic gymnast with every new roll.

"Coach Kelsey. I need water!" A red-faced girl with drooping pigtails pulls at my shirt. I tear my attention off the group of lions as Daniel leads them across the field.

The girl looks like she's been to war. She looks like she's seen things no child should see. "I need water!" she screams.

"Okay," I tell her, then blow the whistle.

"Water time!" I yell, making the time-out sign.

"Water!" the kids yell, and it's a lion and snake stampede.

Daniel also looks to either be holding back a laugh or tears, and the look he gives me sends me over the edge. I clap a hand over my mouth, turning away from the kids as they flop onto the grass next to their brand-new Wilmington Beaver water bottles.

I'm staring up at the ceiling of the Wilmington stadium, trying not to absolutely lose it laughing. I don't know if it's the hangover or the kids, but I can't seem to be anything but silly today.

"Having fun?" Daniel asks, gripping me around the waist and kissing the back of my neck.

"The time of my life," I say honestly, turning to kiss him.

"DISGUSTING!" one of the kids yells at us.

"MY MOMMY SAID THAT'S HOW YOU GET BABIES!" another joins in.

"COACH KELSEY IS HAVING A BABY!" a third screams.

I moan and bury my face in my hands.

"Coach Kelsey is not pregnant, oh ye agents of chaos," Daniel tells them. "And that's not how we talk to our coaches, right, kids?"

"You shouldn't kiss your assistant coach," one of the cherub-faced devils says.

I bite my cheeks, but a snort comes out anyway.

"Don't encourage them, Kels," Daniel tells me out of the side of his mouth.

I turn back around and stare at the ceiling some more, trying my hardest not to lose it completely and laugh.

A little hand tugs on my shirt, and I look down to see the pigtailed girl again.

"Coach Kelsey," she says, her eyes huge in her face. "Can I have a hug?"

"Sure," I say, and she holds her arms up. I bend down to pat her shoulders, and she launches at me like a spider monkey.

"Unf," I say, stepping backwards in surprise as she clambers up, gluing herself to my hip, her hands, inexplicably sticky, gluing themselves around my neck.

"I love hugs," she yells, and I wince.

"Okay," I say, supporting her weight with one arm. "I think you should go get some more water."

"No," she says. "I don't want to. I want a hug." She draws the word out like a threat.

Daniel's staring at me, that massive grin on his face, like he's never seen anything better.

It makes my heart flutter.

"How about we play a game of defense-defense-offense?"

"Yeah!" the kids chorus.

I have no idea what that is, but if it keeps the kids happy, I'm game.

"Who here has played duck-duck-goose?" he asks, and ten of our twenty kids launch into the air, their little bodies unable to contain their excitement. "Right," he continues, cutting me another amused look. "Let's get in a circle."

He pats the ground, and to my surprise, the kids listen to him, falling over themselves in their hurry to sit next to him.

"No, a circle, guys, you know what a circle is..." He pauses and they scooch out from the clump they've made around him. "Good job. A good athlete always listens to their coach. Now make room for Coach Kelsey."

A little boy holds up his hand. "Can you sit next to me, Coach Kelsey?"

"Sure," I manage, suddenly overcome with unexpected emotion. I must be PMSing because my hormones are raging. Despite all the chaos of this morning—and there was a lot of chaos—Daniel is... so good with these kids, so warm and sweet and patient, that I swear, it's making me think twice about all the times he's mentioned wanting them.

He would be an amazing father.

He would be an amazing husband.

He's an amazing guy.

A lump forms in my throat and I sit down quickly, the little girl shuffling so that she's in my lap instead of glued to my hip.

Daniel's staring at me and I grin at him, swallowing down the tight knot.

"Are you married?" the little boy on my left asks, a serious expression on his sweet face.

"Not yet," Daniel tells him, then winks at me. "Alright," he continues before I have a chance to respond. "Here's how this is going to go."

The whole time he's explaining defense-defense-offense to the group, I'm barely listening.

Not yet.

*Not yet.*

# CHAPTER 40

## DANIEL

The next few weeks slide by in a blur of pain and texts to Kelsey. I don't get nearly as much time to see her as I would like, between her work schedule and practice and away games.

Every day, practice feels harder. My motivation is slipping, the pain in my shoulder worse. Every day, Dale looks at me like a fucking vulture ready to pick the meat from my bones.

Every day, I pop the ibuprofen they give me and strap an icepack to my back as soon as I'm home. Game day, they'll shoot me up full of pain killers and I'll be okay.

I'll make it work. Coach is counting on me.

My phone vibrates against the locker and I pull it out to see a message from Kelsey that takes the bite off the pain.

I miss you

> Miss you more. Sorry we haven't been able to meet up this week

Me too

> It's not your fault, either. My schedule is awful right now too

> How's the piece coming

> Good. Really good. I think it's going to piss your bosses off

> That's great

I roll my shoulder, pain radiating all the way down my back, down to my fucking hip. You'd think I'd be used to it now, the relentless aches. I don't think the human body ever gets used to the kind of beating we take, day after day, month after month, year after year.

> How's your dad?

Kelsey's dad's been on my mind a lot lately. I looked him up after she told me who he was, and the whole story is sickening.

And as much as I loved working with the kids on the field two weekends ago, I hate that injury and pain might be in their future, too.

> He's okay. Why do you ask?

> Just been thinking about him. About you, too

> You ready for the Beaver Ball

> You ready to read my speech at the Beaver Ball?

> Absolutely fucking not

> But I'm a man of my word

> I know. That's one of the things I love about you

My heart feels like it fucking grows in my chest, inflating with hope and that gold shimmer of love I've felt for Kelsey since my first date with her. The woman has me wrapped around her little finger, and I've never wanted to get wrapped tighter.

I tap out three words, three words I've been scared to say to her again. I delete them. I don't want to fucking say it again over text. That's not the right way.

The Beaver Ball is this weekend. Sure, she's going with her friend, Cameron, but she'll be there, it will be romantic, and I can tell her then. At the right time.

God, I can't wait to see her all dressed up.

She's perfect in nothing but my ratty old t-shirt, but she's going to shine this Friday. I'm proud to be her boyfriend.

> I can't wait to see you Friday

Big same

> What are you wearing

I'm at work

> I meant to the ball

Oh lol I rented a dress from this designer rental place online

I'm a little nervous because it gets here on Friday afternoon

Don't worry though, I won't look embarrassing

> You could wear a paper bag and I would still be proud to call you mine

I wince. I keep telling myself I'm not going to scare her off, and then I send her over-the-top shit like that.

"Harrison," a voice calls, and I put the phone back in my locker. "Time to rehab that shoulder."

I curse under my breath, steeling myself for more pain.

Pain's the name of the game lately.

# CHAPTER 41

**F**uck. Fuck.

The package from the runway rental place sits on my bed and I jump around like an idiot, trying to wriggle my ass into it.

Cameron's on the phone and the more I cuss, the more she panics.

"You are not abandoning me tonight, I swear to god, Kelsey, pull the fucking dress over your hot ass! Make it FIT!"

I give up, collapsing on the floor, sweaty and disheveled.

It's four thirty. I left the office early to pick the package up from my front desk, excited to get ready for the stupid Beaver Ball. The Beaver Ball, which I need to be at in an hour and a half.

And I can't even get the damn dress on.

"It doesn't fit," I moan. "There's no way. I don't understand, this is my normal size."

"It's not you, it's the stupid dress. You're gorgeous. Fuck that dress!" Cameron rages. "Okay. Look in your closet. What can you wear? Do you have a formal gown?"

"Why in the world would I have a formal gown? I have suit

dresses. A sun dress." I wriggle over to my closet, my movements hampered by the dress stuck at mid-thigh. "This is a nightmare."

"Do you have a tux?" Cameron screeches, completely losing her mind. "YOU ARE NOT ABANDONING ME TONIGHT!"

I glare at the phone. "Why would I have tux, Cameron?"

"I don't know! I don't know what you and that stupid quarterback are into!"

"He's not stupid," I grit out, then shake my head in confusion. "What the hell happened between you and Jacob, anyway?"

The line goes silent.

"I never told you his name."

"I'm an investigative reporter, Cameron."

"You need to focus," she snaps. "You need a dress, or I'm picking your naked ass up and we can tell everyone nudity is the new black."

"I honestly don't know what to say to that."

"I'm calling your boyfriend."

"What?"

The line beeps and I stare at my phone in shock. "Cameron? How did you get his number?"

"He gave it to me a couple weeks ago when he was trying to take you out the first time. He was calling the office, got me instead. He told me to give it to you."

"You never told me that," I say, stiff with surprise. Then I melt. It's so cute. I had no idea.

"Yeah, well, I thought we were both on team no-dating-football-players."

"Hello?" Daniel's voice comes through the speaker, and I sigh happily.

"Daniel, it's Cameron. Kelsey's friend."

"Where is Kelsey? Is she okay? What hospital—"

"Calm the fuck down, cowboy. Kelsey's fine. Tell him, Kelsey. Proof of life," Cameron barks.

"Hey, Daniel. I'm fine. Cameron is being dramatic."

"Kelsey is going to show up nude unless you can find her a

new dress in less than an hour. Kels, do you have your makeup and hair done yet?"

"Nope," I say, popping the p. "I'm screwed."

"I'm on it," Daniel says smoothly.

"Good," Cameron starts, then pauses midsentence. "Did he hang up?"

I fold back to the floor, fighting to get the dress off. Panting, I lie back, my strapless bra digging into my shoulders, and wriggle my toes.

"He hung up. Good man. He's going to take care of you."

"He's amazing." I shimmy my butt, trying to ease the death trap of a dress down.

"You seem really happy."

I pull at the fabric, and it finally gives. "I love him."

I sit up, forgetting the dress cutting off my circulation for a minute. "I love him?"

Cameron squeals. "KELSEY COLE!"

"I love him," I say again, and break into a smile. "Wow."

"Are you going to tell him?"

"You think I should?"

"Yes, you little Beaver lover, you should tell him."

"Tonight?"

"Tonight. But you're going to have to do it with me as your third wheel, because you're not fucking leaving me alone with Jacob Matthews for one FUCKING second."

"You sound really unhinged."

"You're the one falling in love after a month."

"That's why we're besties," I say. "Fuck, the dress finally came off. I'm sweating."

"Gross. Clean yourself up and get ready." She sounds for all the world like a drill sergeant.

The line goes dead, and I make it to where my phone lies as the nice robot lady asks me if I'd like to make a call.

I kick the dress on the floor, then think better of my desire to rip it into shreds with my bare hands and instead hang it back up in the bag with extreme prejudice.

My hair's damp from the shower, and I head to the bathroom to finish blow-drying it. Maybe I'll put the beaver in Beaver Ball, but at least my hair will be dry.

When I'm done, it looks like I stuck my hand in an electrical socket, and I plug my straightener in, careful to unplug the damn dryer first so I don't throw the breaker. Again.

A knock comes at the door, and it startles me so much that I scream.

"Kelsey Cole? Mr. Harrison sent us. Are you decent?"

I throw a robe on, a threadbare one I've had since high school, and pad to the door of my apartment and look out the peephole.

"Oh my goodness," I say on an exhale.

There are four people standing outside my door. One has a rolling suitcase. One has a silver rolling rack of dresses, and the other two are chatting excitedly and scrolling through their phones.

I open the door a crack. "I'm Kelsey?" It comes out like a question, and the lean guy closest to the door grins at me.

"Hi, sweetie, I'm Charles, from the Neiman Marcus Salon. This is Christophe, he runs the women's formalwear department, and Suze and Megan are makeup artists that I work with. Mr. Harrison called us and told us we needed to meet you here to get you glammed up for a ball." His eye turns professional, and he gives me a once-over. "This is going to be fun."

"Can we come in?" the guy with the rolling rack says. "We don't have a lot of time."

"I can't... I can't afford whatever this is going to cost."

"Of course you can't. Mr. Harrison already paid us. You just need to sit back and let us take care of this." He motions to my robe, and I pull it tighter around me, hoping he doesn't notice the fact that the seam is totally split at the armpit.

"I'm thinking the mauve Marchesa," the guy named Cristophe says, squinting at me.

"Oh, that will be gorgeous with her coloring," one of the women says.

"Did you just dry your hair? It's such a great color."

I'm staring at them, and I finally open the door wide and gesture for them to come inside. They're all chatting happily with each other like they do this kind of thing all the time, and I'm totally thrown.

One of the women pulls a dining chair from my kitchen table and sets it in the middle of my small living room.

"Do you like lavender, hon?" the dress guy easily pulls the rack of clothes more expensive than my entire apartment through the door. "We could do lavender."

"I couldn't get my butt in my rental gown," I blurt out, and they all smile at me, exchanging knowing glances. I scrunch my nose, so self-conscious I want to melt away.

"Don't worry, sweetie, we brought a couple sizes. Every designer runs different. It's the dress, not you. You're going to be even more gorgeous when we get through with you."

"Okay."

"Okay!" Charles claps his hands. "Sit, sit."

So I sit, and they make easy conversation with me and each other, dolling me up like a Barbie. The suitcase contains an entire Sephora's worth of cosmetics, and the two women wield the makeup sponges and false eyelashes like warriors as Charles works a curling iron through my hair.

It makes me feel like a princess, and I'm wide-eyed when they finally show me my reflection.

The look is surprisingly natural, but super glamorous. My eyes are dark, more cat-eyed than normal, but not too over the top. My lips are a shade pinker than normal, and one of the makeup artists presses the lipstick into a clutch, along with a few other items.

"For touch-ups," she says.

"This look will go with any of the dresses," the other says. "And don't worry about getting makeup on them, we'll help you in."

Charles just keeps messing with my hair, and the feel of the comb and his fingers has put me in a total trance.

"I think the Marchesa is too frilly. I don't want to overwhelm you," Christophe says, holding up the dress in question.

"It's gorgeous."

"How tall are you?"

"Five-seven."

"I just think it's too much dress. No, you're so pretty, let's get you in something slightly simpler. Your face will be the star."

"Heck yeah, it will." The makeup artists high-five.

"I think the champagne, don't you, Charles?"

"Yes."

Christophe pulls a garment bag off the rack, unzipping it.

My breath catches as he pulls it out. It's stunning—strapless with little draped sleeves that hang off the shoulders.

"She likes it," Christophe says, delighted by my response.

"She does," I agree, and he laughs.

"Put it on," Christophe says. Charles' hands leave my head and I stand up.

"Don't worry, it's nothing we haven't seen before," Charles says and I laugh, ducking behind the clothing rack for a semblance of privacy all the same.

I hold my breath as I step into the silk, pulling it up over my hips and putting my arms into the little draped sleeves.

"It fits," I announce, relieved as hell. "I need help with the zipper." Half my hair is up in curlers, and they press uncomfortably into my scalp as I emerge from behind the rack.

"Oh my GOD."

"Stunning."

I turn, and two pairs of hands help zip the dress up, which fits... like a fucking glove. A silk, golden glove.

"Show, show, show us!"

I tug the boned bodice up a little, and everyone does a little sigh at the same time when I finally turn.

"Is it good?"

"Good? This is a knockout. Touchdown. Homerun. Whatever the football one is," Christophe says. "You look amazing. You're going to be the belle of the Beaver Ball."

"I truly don't know how anyone says that with a straight face," I mutter. My eyes widen as I notice the slit that goes well past mid-thigh. "Holy leg."

"Yes, mama, work that skirt," Charles says. "Now get over here and let me get those curlers out."

A pair of gold heels emerges from a black duffel hanging on the rack, and Christophe straps me into them as Charles uses his fingers to comb out my new curls.

"Goddess," he finally says, and when they give me the mirror this time, I do a double-take.

"Knock 'em dead," Charles says cheerfully, packing up his stuff.

And within ten minutes, with lots of hugs and thank yous, the glam squad departs, leaving me alone in my apartment to grapple with my makeover and the amount of money Daniel must have dropped to make it happen for me.

I love him.

I can't wait to tell him tonight.

# CHAPTER 42

## DANIEL

The tux feels like a foreign object around my body. Despite the best tailoring possible, I'll never be comfortable in shit like this. The Matthews brothers seem similarly uncomfortable, and Jacob in particular looks especially out of his element.

"Where are your dates?" I ask them, and they both glower at me. "I see the resemblance."

Jacob walks off, his ankle much better thanks to ice, rehab, and likely a shit ton of injections.

I roll my shoulder. I know how that goes all too well.

"I didn't mean to be rude," I tell Ty.

"He's sensitive tonight. He knows he's going to see his ex."

"Cameron. Kelsey's best friend." God, I can't wait to see Kelsey. It's been a little over a week since we both were able to carve time out for each other, and I'm half-feral with need for my girlfriend.

"Yeah. They dated in college, he wanted to propose, she didn't want to get married. He never got over her."

"What about you? Why didn't you bring someone?"

Ty's face crumples, and then he pinches the bridge of his nose. "Things are, uh, complicated with my… my girlfriend. Too complicated."

"It shouldn't be hard," I say, thinking back to my ex-wife, then my famous ex-girlfriend. "If it's hard, it's not right."

"She's not the problem… it's uh, it's her job."

"Oh. She's busy."

"Something like that." Ty squirms, and I narrow my eyes at him.

"What does she do?"

"All kinds of things," he says vaguely. "Hey, holy shit, there's Kelsey."

I look away from the receiver towards the entrance.

"Wow, man, you did good. She's beautiful."

"She's mine," I tell him through gritted teeth, a possessive part of me roaring to life, a part of me I didn't know existed.

She is beautiful, though, it's a fucking fact.

I am awestruck by her. Gold fabric hugs her waist, flaring around her hips, a muscled leg flashing through a high slit in her dress as she walks.

She hasn't seen me yet, but makes easy conversation with the dark-haired woman with her. Cameron, I realize. I notice her peacock-blue dress, but hardly register her before my gaze goes back to Kelsey.

Fuck.

I want to eat her up. I want to take her home right now and get that dress off her, or better yet, hike it up.

I want to hold her.

"You really love her, huh?" Ty says, and when I look back over at him, he's staring at me with a strange, wistful expression I haven't seen him wear before.

"Why do you say that?" I say, taking a drink of my sparkling water.

"You have a look." He jerks his head at where Jacob watches the two women too, though his eyes are only on Cameron. "He used to get that look. Like the whole world stopped. Good for you, man. I'll look forward to a wedding invite."

He laughs like it's a joke, but I don't. It's not funny to me.

Nothing I feel about Kelsey Cole is a joke.

I move towards her like I'm in slow motion, like the whole world's tilted and time's slowed. There's nothing here but her, nothing that matters.

Her eyes light up when she sees me and I walk faster, people parting before me like water before a ship.

When my hands close on her hips, her lips on mine, it feels like home.

"Hi," Kelsey says, and I press my forehead to hers, so fucking glad to see her I can't even talk.

It's only been a week since I saw her last.

The force of my feelings surprises even me.

"You two are so cute it nearly makes me sick," Cameron says. "Seriously. People are staring."

"Let them," I say, and Kelsey squeaks as I dip her over one arm, then press another kiss on her perfect fucking mouth.

A few people standing nearby laugh and applaud as I pull her back up. Her cheeks are flushed, her eyes bright and beautiful.

"Hi," I tell her casually, pretending like this is all completely normal.

"She's my date tonight," Cameron tells me. Kelsey takes my elbow and I walk her over to the bar, Cameron trailing behind us. "I knew I was going to be a third wheel but this is a bit much."

"Cameron."

Kelsey stops, her eyes wide.

"Jacob," Cameron says tartly.

"Can I talk to you?" he asks.

Fuck. I do not want to deal with drama tonight. I want to dance with my gorgeous girlfriend, and give a speech, and go home and make love to my gorgeous girlfriend. Drama is not on the agenda.

"I don't have a lot to say to you, Jacob." Cameron crosses her arms over her chest. Jacob's gaze is pinned to her face.

"Five minutes," he says, and his voice breaks.

Her expression softens, the tightness in her mouth turning into sadness. "Fine."

"You sure?" Kelsey asks, putting her hand on Cameron's arm.

"Yeah. He won't leave me alone until I do." She looses an exasperated sigh, then nods to Jacob like she's expecting the worst.

We both watch them walk off in silence to a corner of the huge room, opposite where we stand.

"Do you want a drink?" I ask Kelsey.

"What are you having?"

"Sparkling water." I hold up the glass.

"I'll have that, then," she says. "You sure you don't want something stiffer for your speech?"

I cock an eyebrow at her. "I'm pretty damn nervous about this speech."

A devilish grin lights up her face. "You should be."

I signal to the bartender for two more waters, and she opens her tiny sparkly purse with a laugh, pulling out a folded-up square of paper.

"Don't worry, I'm texting it to you, too. You'll have no excuses not to be able to give this beautiful little speech."

"Am I allowed to read it before I have to say it in front of the whole room?"

She narrows her perfect brown eyes at me, then her features soften into a smile. "You don't really have to read it, Daniel. As *the* speech, I mean. It's ridiculous."

I give her a speculative look, unfolding the paper and smoothing it out along the bar top. The bartender sets two glasses of sparkling water in front of us.

"Thank you," Kelsey tells him, tugging hers close to her and leaning against the marble counter.

"It is an honor to be asked to speak tonight on behalf of Beavers everywhere. I always have a ball around beavers, so being fingered to give a speech about the importance of preserving the untamed wilds is a true pleasure," I read.

I look up, and Kelsey's shoulders are shaking with laughter, one hand over her mouth.

"Is this whole speech a long beaver pun?"

"Keep reading," she instructs.

Shaking my head, I do as she commands.

"The Beaver Ball has a long history, but it's nothing to be blue about—" I pause. "Is that a blue balls joke? You can do better."

A laugh tears out of her, and she does that adorable snort that means she's really amused.

I rub my jaw, freshly shaved, and take a swig of the water.

"I am always hard... pressed to find a bad thing to say about the nature of the beaver. The soft pelt, the way it loves wood and water. The beaver is truly a noble animal, and being able to care for these creatures and their homes is something everyone should get off on."

I level a look at her. "Get off on?" I repeat.

"It's one long vulva joke," she finally says, then takes the paper from me, folding it back into a square and sticking it in her tiny purse. "I'm sorry. I'm not going to make you read it. I just don't understand how no one else finds the name of the team and the mascot ridiculous."

"The Beavers are a time-honored institution," I tell her seriously. "To mock the beaver is to mock Wilmington, no, the world itself."

"Did you like the speech?" she asks. Kelsey's still biting her lip and holding back laughter, and it's so fucking cute that I pull her close to me.

"It was low-hanging fruit, but you grabbed it and squeezed." I nod sincerely, and she erupts into more laughter. "Truly admirable, your commitment to the bit."

"I'm glad you liked it," she says. "But seriously, you don't have to read it."

"You think I'm a chicken?" I brush the tip of my nose against hers, then stand back up, knowing if I don't put some space between us, I'm liable to throw her over my shoulder and into my truck.

"Of course not," she scoffs. Her gaze skates over my body and my hand flexes on the glass of water. "I love a good cock, but you're definitely no chicken."

I tip my head back and laugh. "Are you done yet?"

"Nah. I'll let you know when I am, though." She glances around and presses closer to me as the crowd at the bar grows. "There are more people here than I expected."

"You nervous?" I ask her, surprised. She's always so self-possessed, so poised, and I wonder how much of the filthy humor is her way of coping.

"A little," she admits, and I reach for her, unable to stop myself. My palm skates over the silky material of her dress, her hip warm beneath it.

"You are the most beautiful woman in the room. In the whole damned state. You are brilliant, and clever, and funny."

She tilts her chin up, staring at me with round eyes.

I press a soft kiss to her lips, brief and gentle.

"I love you, Daniel Harrison."

The sound of chatter and the low undertone of jazz music die. My heart pounds in my ears, and my fingers squeeze her hip.

I blink, completely taken off guard.

I've spent my entire fucking life with armor around my body, getting slammed to the ground by guys twice my weight.

And all it takes to completely blindside me is a small woman in a dress the color of morning sunlight telling me she loves me.

"I love you," she repeats, her gaze flicking back and forth between my eyes.

Turning away, she grabs her glass of sparkling water, her shimmering purse dangling from her other hand, and takes a long sip.

"Kelsey," I finally manage, my heart so full it might burst. I lean down, her waving hair tickling my nose as I press my lips against her ear. "Kelsey Cole, I love you too."

She laughs, and the sound is pure magic. Pure joy.

"Do we have to stay?" I ask her. "I have some ideas about how to show you I love you."

"Yes, you have to stay," she says, lacing her fingers into mine. "You are giving a speech. Not the speech I wrote, for the record, but a speech nonetheless."

"No one really cares about what I have to say." It's true. None of these people care about anything other than a tax write-off and the fleeting sense they've done something good. They care more about getting dressed up and showing off.

"I care," she says. "I want to see you shine. You're great at this." She gestures broadly, and I wonder what she means.

I must look like it too, because she puts her small hand on my cheek. "You're good with people. You're good at making people feel good, at leading them. You look like you belong here."

"I belong with you, Kelsey," I say. "Wherever you go, I want to be with you."

She beams up at me, so goddamned pretty it makes my heart hurt.

"Then we'll make it happen."

It's all I need to hear.

It's all I ever want to hear again.

# CHAPTER 43

## KELSEY

Cameron won't tell me what happened between her and Jacob.

She doesn't seem thrilled by it, but she's not crying or ranting, so I'm going to count it as a win. We sit at one of the tables in the back, separated from the actual donors who purchased tables at the benefit and the football players... most of them, at least.

Rhett's at our table, and from the sloppy way he's eating, and chugging a beer, he's drunk.

And he's not any more pleasant for it, either.

The music and conversation slowly dies off, and Daniel walks onto the dais at the front of the room.

"He's your boyfriend?" Rhett asks, a disgusted look on his face. Or maybe that's just his normal expression.

"You're unpleasant," Cameron tells him.

Rhett grunts unpleasantly.

I sigh. It's just the three of us at this table. Whoever else was supposed to sit here didn't show up. I don't blame them. I feel gorgeous, and Cameron is usually great company, but overall?

This is not exactly my scene.

Rhett puts a fist over his mouth and Cameron grimaces, skewering him with a look.

"You have the table manners of a rabid dog," she tells him.

He glares at her. "Your friend is mean," he tells me.

"Shush," I say. "Daniel's going to give a speech."

"No one gives a fuck," Rhett says, taking a long draw from his bottle of beer.

"I give a fuck."

"That's because you're fucking him." Rhett gives me a meaningful look, and a smile breaks across his face.

I blink. It's the first time I've seen him smile. Ever. Not even during the poker night did he grin. There were a few times I thought he might, but nope.

It would transform his face from brutal into handsome, were it not for the glimmer of cruelty in his dark eyes.

"You know, princess, if you wanted to take a real footballer for a ride, I wouldn't mind helping you out."

"The fuck?" Cameron scoots further away from him. "Shut up."

My jaw flexes as I pointedly ignore him, trying to listen to Daniel. The stage is too far away, though, and I all manage to catch are snatches of words. Based on the reaction of the audience, though, he's killing it. They laugh, make murmurs of approval or sympathy.

"I mean it, Kelsey Cole," Rhett says, leaning over the table. "I may not be the pretty quarterback, but I could show you a good time."

"Not interested." I stand up, annoyed that I can't hear my boyfriend and grossed out by Rhett's drunken perving. "Cameron, come on, let's go to the bathroom."

Applause breaks out, and I make a beeline for the ballroom door, which, thankfully, isn't far away. Cameron's on my heels, or at least I think it's Cameron.

Until Rhett's hand grips my shoulder, spinning me around.

"What is it, Kelsey? Am I not good enough for you?"

I stare at him, caught between real fear of him and disbelief that he won't leave me alone. "It has nothing to do with you, Rhett. I love Daniel."

"You could love me," he challenges, and real pain flashes through his eyes, making him look worse than tipsy.

It makes my throat tighten in dread, especially as his fingers tighten on my bare skin.

"Take your fucking hands off her," a low voice booms out in the quiet of the hallway.

Daniel. He's racing towards us and Rhett backs off, laughing, his hands in the air.

I take a breath, going limp with relief. Daniel's here.

"I didn't mean any harm, Harrison. Just curious what princess here sees in your old ass."

"Touch her again, and I will make sure you never see a minute of game time, mother fucker," Daniel growls. My eyes go wide. I've never heard him like this. He's usually so easy-going, laid-back and fun.

This Daniel sounds like he's ready to kill Rhett. For touching me.

"Daniel, stop." My heels click along the slick floor as I close the distance between us. He catches me with one arm, then pulls me behind him, putting his body between Rhett and me. "Please don't fight him."

"He's not going to fight me, princess," Rhett drawls, advancing towards us. "He's too cowardly to try to take me—"

Crack.

Daniel's fist makes contact with Rhett's jaw. He staggers back a couple steps, then swings his gaze back to us.

"Fuck, good hit," Rhett finally says.

I'm clinging to Daniel's jacket like it's a lifeline.

"Go home, Rhett. Don't let me see you near her again," Daniel's voice is low and dangerous, and I shiver. "Don't even fucking think about her."

Rhett gives us one last look, then pulls the doors of the ballroom back open, disappearing inside.

"Fuck, babe, are you okay?" Daniel wheels around, inspecting my shoulder, my face, like he's expecting to find evidence of Rhett's hands on my skin.

"I'm okay." He's shaking his hand and I grab it, looking for damage. "Are you okay?"

"We're leaving," he says. "Text Cameron when we get in the car. We're going home."

I nod, because I sure as hell don't want to spend another second around Rhett.

"I can't leave Cameron alone with him," I say, but Daniel's already pulled out his phone.

"Jacob, hey, listen, it's Daniel. Rhett's drunk and he just tried to fuck with Kelsey. Get to Cameron and make sure he leaves her alone. Get her home, and get Ty to take care of Rhett. Got it?"

He's steering me down the hall while he talks, and I'm grateful for his hand on my back because I'm shaking like a leaf.

He hangs up and I stop, my teeth chattering. Daniel pulls me into him, and I breathe deeply, trying to calm down, his sandalwood scent surrounding me.

"It's the adrenaline," he murmurs on the top of my head. "The chattering. It's the adrenaline leaving your body. I'm so fucking sorry, Kelsey, if I knew he was capable of that kind of shit I would have made sure he was nowhere near you."

"It's not your fault," I force out between my clacking teeth. "You can't blame yourself for someone else's actions."

"But I can blame myself for not protecting you."

"You did, though," I say, finally relaxing enough that my teeth stop. "You did protect me. You shouldn't have hit him, Daniel."

"Fuck that, Kels," he says, staring down at me with those intense, piercing blue eyes. "He's lucky I didn't fuck him all the way up. You're *mine*."

At those two words, all the feminism leaves my body.

"Take me home," I demand. "Take me home right now."

# CHAPTER 44

## DANIEL

I can't even talk the whole way home. Kelsey's quiet too, and I'm thankful the stupid fucking ball wasn't more than thirty minutes from my house.

I keep glancing over at her, making sure she's okay. Making sure that fucking dick didn't do more than scare her. What a fucking asshole.

I wanted to hurt him. I wanted to make him regret even thinking about her.

Mine.

Kelsey Cole is mine. She said she loves me.

I'm going to marry her, and the idea of anyone else fucking touching her is making me insane.

Finally, I pull into the driveway and the truck jerks as I throw it into park.

"Daniel," she says softly, her eyes wide with concern.

"I'm going to carry you inside."

"I can walk. I don't need help—"

"I need to carry you inside. I need to make sure you're okay." I have to hold her. I have to touch her. I don't know how I can fucking look at that bastard Rhett again. The whole way here, I just got angrier and angrier.

I throw the passenger door open, and Kelsey's bare thigh is the first thing I see.

I want her so bad I can hardly fucking stand it.

"Need you," I grit out. I put my hand under her thighs and lift her from the truck, barely registering the strain on my bad shoulder.

Barely registering anything beyond her. Her arms go to my neck, wrapping around it, and I'm glad to see she's at least stopped shaking.

"I need you too," she says on an exhale, and I jog to the front door, sliding the key in and unlocking it in record time.

"You're all wrapped up like a fucking present," I tell her. "I can't wait to take this dress off and see what's underneath."

"I forgot my coat at the ball," she says.

"You're not going to need it tonight."

The door slams shut behind me, and my fingers fumble on the lock before I charge into my bedroom.

Kelsey's breathing hard, her breasts straining at the top of the gold-colored gown. Groaning, I set her down on the bed and she bounces slightly, staring up at me with desire in her eyes, everything I want.

"I love you," she murmurs, so soft it's barely audible.

The words reverberate through me, though, and I hike her skirt up, tugging at the delicate fabric.

She lets out a little laugh, her hands skimming over my shirt, untucking it from the waist of my pants. Her hands are cold on my skin and I shiver as she runs them up my torso.

"I love you, Kelsey Cole," I tell her, and then my fingers find the delicate hidden zipper at her back, and I slowly pull it down, reveling in the bare flesh it reveals.

A low sigh tears from her lips and I groan as the dress falls away from her.

She's nude underneath.

"Fuck."

Kelsey kicks out a leg and the dress pools on the floor. I trace my fingers over her bare leg, kissing then biting her inner thigh, her calf, until I get to her shoes and take those off too.

"You're still wearing clothes. I want to touch you," she says, and her voice is sexy and hoarse and drives me crazy.

I take my jacket off, unbuttoning my shirt slowly, unable to look away from her.

"Touch yourself," I tell her. "Show me that pretty pussy."

She groans and I push her legs apart. Biting her lip, her fingers fall between her legs, and I suck in a breath as she slides them through her already slick flesh.

"So fucking perfect," I say, unbuckling my belt and getting undressed in record time. "I want to taste you."

I start to dive between her legs, but she puts a hand on my chest, stopping me.

"What's wrong?" I ask, confused but not willing to push her further than she wants to go. Ever. Never that.

"It's my turn. I want you in my mouth."

"Kelsey," I say, and it's a growl. "Such a good fucking girl."

Kelsey moves to the edge of the bed, then sinks back onto her heels, fisting her hand over my rock-hard cock. A feral noise rips from me and she looks up at me with a sexy, amused grin on her face.

"I can't believe I haven't done this yet," she says. "It's a little intimidating. I want it to be good for you."

"Anything you do is going to feel good." I rock forward as she rubs her hand up and down. When her mouth closes around the tip, licking the bead of precum at my slit, I groan.

"Look at you, taking me so good, you gorgeous girl," I say, and she moans.

I love that she likes it when I talk dirty to her. I love that I know she's getting wetter every time I call her my good girl. I love the way her mouth feels around my dick.

My hand curls around her hair and she makes another noise

that vibrates along my cock, making me clench my butt as tension builds through my body.

She works me with her mouth and I resist the urge to hold her still and fuck it. I don't want to come in her mouth.

I have other plans for tonight.

"Enough." It comes out a rasp.

A pop sounds as she back off, wiping the back of her hand over her mouth. Her lips are red and swollen, and the image of her looking up at me sears itself into my memory.

I pull her up to me, leaning down and kissing her fiercely until her fingernails bite into my skin.

"Remember how you used a vibrator on the phone with me?" I murmur.

She nods, and I grin at her.

"Well, I liked that. I liked that a lot. I bought some toys this week, to keep at my house."

Her eyes go wide and I kiss her again, tasting the champagne they gave out at the ball and the strawberry flavor of her lipstick.

"Do you want me to show you?" I'll let her decide. I want to use them, fuck, I want to drive her out of her mind with lust, I want to make her feel so good she doesn't have any room for anything else, but she has to decide.

"Show me," she says.

I retrieve the box from my bedside table, and her eyes go wide as I open the lid and pull out a bright pink silicone plug.

"Is that what I think it is?"

"It's going to feel so good," I tell her. "I want to fuck you while you have this inside."

"What if it doesn't?"

"Then we stop," I say, enunciating carefully. "You are in charge. I want to make you feel good." I kiss her shoulder, wanting to bite her. Wanting her so bad that my cock aches with it.

"I trust you," she says, and her legs tremble slightly. I fucking love it. I love that she wants me so badly she shakes with her need.

Makes me feel like a goddamned champion.

"Get on your hands and knees," I manage. A bottle of lube's nestled in the box, and Kelsey does as I say, presenting her fuckable ass. "Tell me if it's too much. I'm going to go slow."

I'm so goddamned turned on by the sight of her, the tips of her breasts brushing over my bed as she arches into my hand. I rub the curve of her ass, loving the way it jiggles, then reach around, spreading her legs wider and massaging her soaked clit.

A wordless moan escapes her and I grit my teeth, making small, persistent circles that have her moving against my hand.

"Please," she says, and I suck in a breath at the word.

With one hand, I flick open the bottle of lube, making sure to coat everything. The last thing I want to do is hurt her.

"I want this to feel good," I remind her. "Tell me if it's too much."

I push the plug in gently.

She buries her head in the covers, her toes curling.

"You can take it," I growl. "Relax, Kelsey." I stroke her clit while I push it in, and when it's finally fully seated in her, she raises her head, panting.

"You good?" I ask, wanting to hear it.

"I'm so turned on," she says. "It's weird… but good." Kelsey wriggles her ass, and I squeeze it.

"That's my fucking good girl."

"I want you," she moans. "It feels good."

"I know you do," I say, and she rolls over, spreading her legs for me. "Fuck."

I throw myself on her, unable to resist any longer. I close my mouth around her nipple, my hand between her legs, wanting every bit of her, wanting to make her fucking scream my name.

"Daniel," she says, and she's holding on to me so tight, her teeth scraping against my chest as she grinds against my fingers. "Please."

I thrust into her and she goes still beneath me, her eyes wide, her breath coming in quick, hot pants.

"You okay?" I say, kissing the side of her mouth, her forehead. Sweat beads on my temple and I watch her carefully.

"It's so much."

I pull out slowly, and it's like a chain reaction goes off in her. Her hands grip at my shoulders, clawing into me, and she bucks against me.

"Oh fuck, Daniel, oh my god, yes."

Grinning, I wait for her to finish, her orgasm making her clench all around me, so fucking tight that I have to hold my breath to keep from coming too.

I want this to last.

"Was it good, Kels?"

Her lips are parted, a shocked, hazy expression on her face. "So good," she moans.

I thrust in her again, slowly, and it's my turn to moan. "So wet, you're so fucking wet for me. Look how good you're taking me. Like you were made for me. Fuck, Kelsey."

My control is razor thin, and she's holding tight to me, one leg looped around my waist as she meets every thrust with one of her own.

"I'm going to, oh—" She breaks off, sagging against me, her face flushed and eyes squeezed shut.

"Eyes on me," I command, and she does as I say.

"I love you," she cries out, and I fucking lose myself in her, pulling my body into hers until she's part of me and I'm part of her.

"I love you," I tell her. "I love you so much, Kelsey Cole."

I hold her for a long time after we come, for a long time after she's fallen asleep, overwhelmed by the depth of my feelings for her.

I only want Kelsey. Only Kelsey, and I don't want her to be Kelsey Cole.

I want her to be *mine*.

# CHAPTER 45

## BEAVERTOK

Video: cream vintage aesthetic overlay on photos of Daniel Harrison in uniform, throwing winning touchdown, Daniel Harrison and Kelsey Cole holding hands while eating ice cream, Kelsey Cole in his jersey at the Beaver Trap Bar and Grill cheering for him.

Caption: besties plz they shouldn't be so cute my heart can't take it

@hotdamyesmaam: I want what she has

@beav3rzf@n: I literally don't get it she looks like a busted door

@HoforHarrison: that man is so fine

@putmeincoach254: idgaf what she looks like, if he keeps playing like this then they need to get married

@hotdamyesmaam: holy sh1t did you guys see what she wrote about the cheerleaders and the AFL

@putmeincoach254: the fuk

@hotdam5ever: is she trying to ruin our team

@hotdam5ever: what a b1tch

@beav3rzf@n: I told you guys she was ugly. NEXT

# CHAPTER 46

DANIEL

E ver since the Beaver Ball, nothing seems to get under my skin. I've avoided Rhett, and he must be avoiding me too because I've barely seen the asshole.

Even the fact my shoulder's tighter than ever, the pain excruciating when I move just wrong, only mildly concerns me. Well, that's a little bit of an understatement, but when I think about my Kelsey, it puts me in a damn good mood.

My truck keys are in hand, my hair still damp from the shower, when my phone lights up right as I'm about to text her. Fucking Dale.

Coach Morelle wants to see you

Now.

Fuck. I don't even have to ask why.

I know why.

I told Coach my shoulder was fine, that the docs were just being cautious, and then I played like shit today. Kelsey even noticed it this morning, although all week she's been giving me concerned looks and asking if I'm alright.

I lie to her, too.

I tell her I'm fine, that it's an old ache.

The first part's a lie. It's not fine. It's an old injury, but this pain is fresh.

But I'm used to gritting my teeth and grinding through it. What's the worst that could happen? Pain is part of the package when it comes to pro football. We all know it. We're all lying about how we feel, except for maybe the greenest rookies.

I make my way to the coaching offices, soothing elevator music coming from the overhead speakers. It only makes me more on edge.

The door to Coach Morelle's office is wide open, and Dale's standing there, staring at me with a shit-eating grin on his face.

Fucking Dale.

"Did you see what your girlfriend wrote?" he asks. "Put a piece out about the league today. You're in it."

Surprise rocks me. "Is that what this is about?"

"No," Coach Morelle says, not bothering to look up from the shuffle of papers on his desk. "I don't give a shit about the cheerleaders. Dale, you can leave."

"But—"

"Get the fuck out, Dale."

I blink, then swallow. In all the years I've known Coach Morelle, I've only heard him use that word three other times. Once when he stepped in dogshit in the middle of the night and I was downstairs getting water. Second time was when a second-string kicker missed a field goal so completely that the word sprang out of him, surprising all of us. Third time was when he got too riled up in the locker room, then apologized for his vulgarity after the game.

Dale closes the door behind him, and if he shares my shock, he doesn't show it.

"I'm in trouble, son," Coach says, jerking his head towards the chair in front of his desk. I sit slowly, not wanting to further aggravate my shoulder. "We need a win. I need you to be on point for the game tomorrow."

"Yes, Coach."

"I need you here, leading the guys, like you have for me so many times before. I need you to give it your all. Am I clear?"

"Yes, sir."

His hawkish gaze drifts to my shoulder, my arm crossed over my chest to keep it from aching. "Shoulder okay?" Coach Morelle asks the question slowly, and I know he fucking knows.

I know the med team fills him in on our in-house rehab, and our health is discussed like cattle up for auction. I know Morelle knows I've signed waiver after waiver asking for the lowest levels of pain management, signing that I know the risks.

"It's good enough to win." The lie slips out easily, but I would fucking say it again for Coach Morelle. He stepped up for me when I had no one. If he needs me to give it my all at tomorrow's game, then I'm going to fucking give it my all.

"Good, son. Good. That's what I like to hear." He nods again and I stand, ready to leave.

"I'm proud of you, Daniel. You know that, right? You should be proud, too."

"Thank you, Coach."

My throat gets tight, and I walk out the door before I get any more sentimental.

I'll give the old man my best on the field tomorrow, that's for damn sure.

# CHAPTER 47

KELSEY

**E**very time a notification buzzes through on my phone, I'm torn between a serotonin boost and extreme anxiety.

The reaction to the cheerleader piece going live on USBC-Philly was immediate and explosive.

Half the Hot Dams are out for my blood. Literally, in some extremely disturbing cases. The other half of the Beavers fanbase is disgusted with the AFL's treatment of the cheerleaders. I scrolled the comments for half an hour this morning before Cameron finally told me she was going to take my phone away.

Now I'm sitting in the makeup chair usually reserved for the lead anchors, the weather dude, and the other normal correspondents, getting foundation caked on my face so that I'm "TV ready."

I'm scheduled to give a two-minute overview of the cheerleader piece, and my stomach's in knots.

My phone buzzes, and the makeup artist glances away from my cheek to my eyes.

"You gonna get that one?"

I choke on a laugh. "I think I'm going to be sick."

She takes a hasty step back, squinting at me. "I can get you some water. Trash can's over by the door. You're wearing water-proof mascara, so go for it."

She's so nonchalant about me puking before going live that I stare at her for a second in disbelief, the nausea replaced by surprise.

"Do the other correspondents barf a lot?"

"Cameron tends to puke every so often before she gets in front of the cameras. Gotta be prepared, you know?"

"Right." I frown, totally distracted from my own nerves as I wonder about Cameron. She never told me she was getting sick from nervousness. I had no idea.

I thought she loved being on camera. I thought she wanted to take over hosting the whole damn thing.

"You gonna puke?"

I shake my head and smile weakly at her. "I'm okay."

"You know, I read the article," the makeup artist says, resuming dabbing concealer under my eyes. I'm pretty sure she's using so much contour that I'm not going to recognize myself, but whatever. "I think what you're doing is great. I'm sick of assholes taking advantage of young women. Good on you for speaking up."

"Oh. Thank you," I say, surprised. A warm glow fills my chest, and I smile at her.

"Relax your face!" she barks, and I drop the smile.

"Yeah, I think it's brave of you," she continues once I've resumed my dead doll impression. "BeaverTok is already doing their absolute best to run your name through the mud and dig up anything nasty they can about you, and here you are, getting ready to go on camera and put your face out there even more."

My fingers clench the arms of the makeup chair.

I think I'm starting to understand why Cameron throws up before she goes live.

"That's not very helpful," I manage through clenched teeth.

"It's the reality of it." She swipes some heavily pigmented

blush over my cheeks, and I inhale sharply through my nose. "But you can rest easy knowing that you're doing the right thing, even if it means the Hot Dams find out where you live."

"Thanks-so-much-I-think-that's-enough-for-now!" I shout in one breath, pushing her away from me and running to the bathroom down the hall.

My phone vibrates against my suit jacket, and I brace my hands against the sink, my heart pounding.

Hands shaking, I retrieve my phone and dial the only person I want to talk to.

The phone rings, and rings, and goes to voicemail.

I hang up, knowing Daniel must be at practice still, and call my dad instead.

"Hey honey." His voice is a hot cup of cocoa, a warm blanket on a cold night, a fresh-baked cookie straight from the oven. A tear slides down my cheek, and I swipe it away before it leaves a canyon in the thick foundation.

"Hi Dad," I say, my voice wobbling.

"Honey, you okay?"

"Not really," I tell him. "I'm about to go on air and I'm freaking out."

"Well, make sure you take a parachute." He laughs at his own dad joke, and I hiccup a laugh, my heartrate slowing. "I read the article you put out this morning."

He pauses and I wait, unsure of how he's going to react.

"I know you have some really good reasons to hate football, but if the result is you speaking up for these women? I'm really proud of you, Kelsey. You know that, right? You're doing the right thing, even when it's hard, and your mother and I couldn't be happier that you're the woman we raised."

"Dad." My voice breaks on the single syllable and I sniffle, real tears threatening now.

"I mean it, Kelsey. You're doing good, important work, and no matter how it goes on TV, you should be proud of yourself too. I had no idea they were treating those women like that!"

"Thanks, Dad. That means… that means so much to me."

"Well, it's just the truth. And Kels?"

"Yeah?"

"I saw that doctor you told me about."

The line goes quiet and I breathe, too loud, the sound echoing around the hard surfaces of the bathroom.

"Your boyfriend called me too, said I should go see him."

I pinch the bridge of my nose, trying not to cry, trying not to ruin the last fifteen minutes I spent getting my face shellacked to withstand the washout of bright lights.

"Your Daniel… he's a good man. He told me it would mean a lot to you, so I went. They're going to put me in some rehabilitation programs, some new trials. I'm looking forward to meeting him one day. I'm so damn proud of you, Kelsey Cole."

"Thanks, Dad," I say.

"I love you. Your mom says hi. She might be crying a little right now. Happy tears, don't worry. She says she loves you, too."

"I love you both so much."

"Now you dry your eyes and get out there and kick some ass, okay, honey?"

I laugh through a sniffle, my mom's objection to my dad's language coming through loud and clear.

"Okay, Dad. Love you. Bye."

I end the call.

They believe in me. They are proud of me.

I take a deep breath and stare at my overly made-up face in the mirror.

I'm going to fucking do this thing.

# CHAPTER 48

## DANIEL

**M**y beautiful girlfriend's face fills the screen and I can't stop smiling.

What a fucking badass.

She's recounting the main points of her exposé on the AFL's treatment and mishandling of their cheer teams, and she's doing it like a fucking champion. It's the third time I've watched the recording from the six o'clock news, and I could watch it again.

I'm so proud of her.

I shift and pain slices through my left shoulder, radiating down to my fingers. Fuck.

The ice and the ibuprofen I took are only doing the bare minimum to numb it.

Kelsey's segment ends and I reach for the phone in my pocket, stiff, trying not to agitate the injury.

> You did so fucking good babe
>
> I'm so proud of you
>
> You're kicking ass

Thank you

I know you said you wanted to rest tonight before the game tomorrow, but what if I told you I just want to snuggle next to you

Also the makeup artist said the Hot Dams were trying to dox me and honestly I'm scared to go back to my apartment

Fuck. The idea of the stupid fans going after Kels for this makes me sick to my stomach. But I don't want her to see me like this.

She shouldn't be here tonight.

I close my eyes, the anchors on TV throwing the report to the sports guy, who's now outlining all the ways the game tomorrow could go fucking badly.

A few days ago, I called her dad. Told him she was worried about him, told him the new treatments for head injuries might help. Told him I had an idea I wanted to keep secret from her, an idea I needed his help with.

Kelsey's dad, Warner Cole, is a great guy, and it comes as no surprise, considering his daughter is incredible too.

But I do not want Kelsey in my house tonight.

If she sees how fucked up my arm is, how truly fucked up it is, she's going to freak out.

I know it.

I start to tap out a bullshit response about how tonight's not good, about how I need to focus on the game, then delete it.

She doesn't feel safe going home to her apartment. Fuck. If it's a choice between Kelsey being safe or Kelsey being upset at me, I'm going to pick her safety every fucking time.

Of course babe

Good, because I just pulled up

I laugh, and then grunt because fuck, even my ribs hurt. Carefully, I extricate myself from my mountain of icepacks and make for the front door just as a knock sounds.

Taking a deep breath, I try to relax my face, my posture, and pull the door open.

Kelsey's standing on the step, and my heart skips a beat.

"Hi, my love," I tell her, so fucking happy to see her that I almost forget about how much my shoulder's messed up.

"Hey." She smashes into me, hugging me tight, and I immediately tense up. "I hope it's okay that I just… you know, came here. The makeup artist, she freaked me out, said BeaverTok is out for blood. I knew I wasn't going to be able to sleep if I stayed at my place. I promise I won't bother you."

I bite my cheeks, because as much as I love the way she feels against me, as much as I love hearing that I make her feel safe… she's hurting me worse. Pain, electric and volatile, shakes me, and I stay silent, trying to master it the same way I have since the first time I took an unlucky hit and dislocated my left shoulder in training camp all those years ago.

"Daniel?" she says, and this time, her voice is full of concern. "What's wrong?"

"Nothing. Just took a hit. Sore. You know how it is." I don't even sound convincing to myself, and she immediately backs off, stepping back and scrutinizing me.

"Sore…" she echoes, and I notice for the first time that she has a to-go bag from a Vietnamese place down the road. "How sore? You look… you look like you're in pain."

"I am in pain," I say, letting some of the tough guy act drop. "What did you bring? It smells amazing."

"Stir fry, a couple banh mi, some vermicelli and pork." She's still staring at me, though, as if she can find the source of the pain by just looking.

"Come inside. Let's eat, and then we'll go to bed early, yeah?"

"Yeah," she echoes, and I take the bag from her with my good arm and lock the door behind her.

"You did so great, by the way. The AFL is going to have hell to pay with how they've used the cheer teams, and you did that. I'm so proud of you."

"Thanks," she says, but there's an undercurrent of tension in that one syllable that sets my teeth on edge. Well, even further on edge, considering every step brings a fresh bout of pain.

I've never looked forward to the pre-game pain killer injections more in my fucking life.

"You sure you're okay?" she says, and I realize I've stopped, closing my eyes.

"Stressed about the game. Normal things. That's why I don't like to do stuff the night before."

"Oh," she says, and hurt passes over her face. "I know. I know that. You know what? I can go to Cameron's if you really want to be alone. I don't want to mess with your routine."

"No," I bark out, the word coming out much sharper than I intended. "I want you here. I love being with you. I'm just sore and stressed. Not at my finest." I try to smile at her, hefting the bag of food. "Thank you for bringing this. I've been meaning to try this place."

"They have great reviews, and it smelled so good in there," she says, but her voice is strained and she's looking at me like she's seeing things she hasn't before. "Want to eat?"

"Yeah," I say. "Always."

"Let's eat then."

I set the food down and stare at the kitchen cabinet where all the plates are. Thank fuck it's my left shoulder and not my right. It's going to hurt like hell to throw the ball tomorrow.

But I owe it to Coach. I owe it to my teammates.

I'll get through it, just like I always do. I'll deal with rehab once the season's over. It'll be worth it.

I start to reach up for a plate, then stop midway, slowly letting my arm drop.

"I feel like you're mad," Kelsey says out of nowhere. "You're giving me a vibe."

"I'm not mad," I say, my tone more curt than I meant, the pain putting me on edge. "I'm just bad company tonight. I'm glad you're here."

When I turn around, I'm smiling, trying to fight past it. I want to be better for her. I don't want her to see how I'm feeling. I don't want her to worry. I know all too well how worried she is about her dad. She doesn't need me to worry about on top of that.

Kelsey's not smiling. She's frowning, her eyes narrowed, her focus on my shoulder.

"Tell me what happened," she says, and that's not Kelsey, my girlfriend, my lover, talking.

That's the voice of the bulldog reporter.

It makes me grin, and it's for real this time.

"You're a total badass, you know that?" I dodge her question. "Let's eat out of the containers tonight."

"Why?"

"Why what? Sometimes I feel like being uncivilized and eating straight from the takeout containers."

"No, not that. I don't care about the takeout containers." She pauses, and her stern persona slips.

There's fear underneath it. Real fear.

It makes me pause. Guilt ripples through me, viscous and sour.

"I care about you," she presses on. "I care about the way you're standing right now, like if you lift your arm and get out a dish, you might fall over."

I blink. I hadn't realized I was holding myself like that. I fill my lungs with air and try to relax, and her expression darkens further.

"You're hurt. You've been hurt for a few weeks, and every time I asked you said you were fine and I believed you. I *wanted* to believe you." She picks at the hem of her ratty sweatshirt, the one that says Midland Bulldogs in faded blacks and purples. "You haven't been telling me the truth."

"I am fine," I insist. "Do you want noodles, stir fry, or the banh mi?"

I grab a banh mi and put the rest on the kitchen table, gingerly pulling chopsticks out and setting them down for her.

"Your mouth is saying one thing and your face is saying something totally different." Kelsey doesn't budge from her spot in the kitchen.

"Am I in pain? Yes. Do I have an old injury that's irritated right now? Yes. Am I fine?" I pause because the answer to that, the real answer, is no.

"Yes." I push the syllable out.

"You're going to hurt yourself even worse," she says, her voice a whisper. "You're going to make it worse by playing tomorrow."

I sigh, unwrapping the foil from the crusty French bread, and a jalapeño falls out on the floor. "That's a risk I take every time I put my cleats on, Kelsey Cole."

Her foot stamps against the floor, and then she plops down in the chair opposite me.

Tears brim in her eyes, and real worry turns the corners of her mouth down. "Daniel, if you were really hurt, if you were really messed up, would you tell me?"

"Of course." I take a big bite of my sandwich. "This isn't serious. It's aches and pains. No big deal."

"Then answer me this: if you were really hurt, would you tell your coaches? Would you take care of yourself?"

I force myself to meet her pretty brown eyes, tears threatening, glassy and full against her eyelashes.

"No." I admit it on a whoosh of air, an exhalation so huge it takes me by surprise. "No, because that's the job. I'll play for Coach Morelle until I can't anymore. That's how it works, Kelsey." I jab a finger onto the surface of the table. "This is the dream, no matter how much it hurts. This has always been my dream. The pain is part of it."

A tear slips down her cheek. "And you wouldn't tell me, either. Not really."

That catches me off-guard. "I just told you I would, Kelsey."

She shakes her head and clutches a foil-wrapped banh mi to

her chest. "I don't think you would. I don't think you're telling me right now because you don't think it's a big deal. You really think this is normal." Another tear follows, and another, and she doesn't move to brush them away, just stares at me.

My chest hurts, and my shoulder hurts, and everything fucking hurts, and it makes me so *fucking* tired.

"This is what I signed up for, Kelsey. This is football." I'm not mad. I'm not anything but resigned. I understand how she feels. She's wrong, but I understand it.

"And what happens when you can't play anymore? What happens after football, Daniel?" Her voice is so soft I strain to catch the questions. The answers slip through my fingers, and I blink at her.

"What happens when the guy you're willing to ruin your body for decides you're done? What happens to you after that?"

"You happen after that," I say. The words bubble out of me, natural. True. "A family. A life. Whatever gig my agent has lined up for me. You're a part of all of it, all my plans."

"And what if you're hurt so bad that you can't enjoy any of it? What if *this* hurts me so bad I'm not with you anymore?"

"This is about your dad, Kelsey. This isn't about me and my fucked up shoulder. I'm not your dad, I don't have a head injury."

"Of *course* it's about my dad. Of *course* it is. But if you think what happened to him has nothing to do with you, with me, with *us*, then…" She shakes her head and a sob hiccups out of her.

I just stare, my heart ripping apart, the air suddenly hard to breathe.

"They will use you until they *break* you, Daniel. The AFL is a meat grinder, and they will take it all from you, and dispose of you once you're past your shelf life. They'll shoot you so full of meds on game day that you won't be able to feel the damage until it's too fucking late. You know this. All of you fucking know it."

She shakes her head, taking a shaky breath, using the palm of her hand to swipe at her wet cheeks.

"We do know it," I say. "And it's worth it. It's worth it. It's fleeting, and it's perfect, and it's what we've dreamed of our whole lives. We've spent long days and late nights and early mornings bleeding football because we love it. We *made* it. We're the lucky ones. Because when my feet hit the turf and the ball's in my hand, I feel alive. I feel in control. I feel like a god, and I fucking love it." The words are coming out harsh now, a staccato gunfire of emotions I didn't know I felt.

"It doesn't love you back," she says, shaking her head. "It doesn't love you back, and your fans have me scared to go home tonight."

She stands slowly and I grind my molars as she gives me a long, sad look.

"Don't play tomorrow, Daniel. Don't hurt yourself worse."

"I have to," I say, and my tone is firm. Resolute.

Inside, I'm anything but. I know she's right. I don't want to hear it.

"You don't." She shakes her head and one more tear falls, splashing against my kitchen floor. "You don't have to."

She turns on her heel and I blink. What the hell just happened?

"Are you breaking up with me?" I ask her and she half turns, glancing at me over her shoulder.

"No. I love you. I love you so much that I can't stand by you while you tear your body apart for a game. I love you so much that it makes me sick to think of you hurt. I'm going to Cameron's. Please, Daniel. Please take care of yourself. No one else can. No one will make you."

Just like that, she's gone.

The front door closes, and her headlights bounce down the driveway, leaving me with too much fucking food and even more regrets.

# CHAPTER 49

KELSEY

Cameron's singing off-key, coffee percolating in her ancient Mr. Coffee maker, and all I can do is stare at the ceiling.

"You okay, boo?" The pull-out couch squeaks as she sits next to me.

"No," I say, sitting up so I don't roll into her. "Thanks for letting me crash here, though."

"Literally anytime." She eyes me speculatively. "Actually, if you want, you could just move in here. Rent's going up in a few months, and I'm either going to have to move or get a roommate."

My mouth opens and I flop back onto the pillow. A mistake, because the bed is not comfortable and now my back's hurting again.

"Oh. *Oh*." Cameron's eyes are wide, surprise flickering across her face, chased by a worried frown. "You were going to move in with him?"

"He mentioned it once or twice." I roll over onto my stomach, but it makes it worse and I finally roll off the bed, standing instead. "I never really answered him. I was thinking about it, though, and now…"

"You said you didn't break up with him." Cameron stands, too, and I help her tug the sheets off the bed and we both grunt as we fold it back into a couch.

"I didn't. But it wasn't good. It's not good," I say, and my voice breaks on the last word. "I just can't sit back and watch him destroy his body. You know?"

"Then don't." She shrugs a shoulder. "I know we planned on going to the game today, and he was going to let us use his box, but what if we go get our nails done instead? Or we can drive to the shore, hang out on the beach. Fuck football!"

"I feel terrible," I tell her, cramming the heels of my hands into my eyes.

"You're going to give yourself wrinkles. I mean, we could go get Botox today, but that's not in my budget at the moment. But I can recommend ten med spas that will blow your mind!" she says, using her tried and true TV voice.

I give a wet laugh. "No, I feel like an asshole."

"For what?" Cameron tilts her head at me, then passes me a couch cushion. We put them in place, then plop down on it. "For telling him that you don't want him to get hurt? How does that make you an asshole?"

"Because he loves football. He's a grown man, I can't tell him how to live his life. Who am I to even try?" I take a deep breath. Everything feels empty inside, hollowed out and brittle.

"Who are you? Are you fucking kidding me with this shit, bitch?"

I raise my eyebrows.

"You're Kelsey fucking Cole, and he said he loves you and wants you to have his babies and move in. If you wanting him to take care of his body and not break in half like an ancient tree makes him pissy, then he's not worth two shits!" Cameron's shouting now, a red flush spreading across her nose.

One of her neighbors bangs on the wall, and she glares in the direction of the sound.

"You know, maybe moving out of this place won't be the worst thing ever. Okay, but back to you. No. You have a right to tell the man how you feel. He has the right to do what he will with this information. This is the thing, though, Kelsey. Relationships are a lot of fucking work. They're a lot of compromise. You have to decide what you're not going to give up, where your red lines are, and what you're willing to budge on. It sounds like him playing injured is a no go. And I don't blame you one bit."

"When did you become a relationship expert?"

She huffs, sending her dark brown bangs flying. "It's a lot easier to give it from the outside, Kels. I've fucked up enough good things to know that much, though. If you love Daniel, like really love him, then I think you two can work this out."

"Maybe," I say. I nudge a spot on her carpet with my toe.

"No, not maybe. If you both love each other, like you've been gushing at me about for the last few weeks, then you'll fucking figure it out. And if you can't, or won't, then it wasn't love in the first place. It was convenient and fun and there's nothing wrong with that. Maybe it was just a thing because you were both young and didn't know any better and none of it was real anyway."

I blink, my mouth twisting in confusion. "You lost me at that last part."

I get the feeling she's not talking about me and Daniel anymore.

"Right," she says, blinking rapidly and then grinning at me. "Your hot old manfriend is playing a game injured today. You want to not watch it. What do you want to do instead—"

My phone vibrates and I lunge for it, hoping it's Daniel. Hoping he's calling to say he's not going to play.

It's not Daniel.

"Why the fuck is our boss calling you on a Sunday morning?" Cameron scowls at the phone.

"I have no idea."

I accept the call and Cameron stands up, walking the few steps to her kitchen and pouring two steaming cups of coffee.

"Hello?" I ask, perplexed and tired. And sad. So sad.

"Kelsey, I need you to get ready and come to the station. Frank Devon has laryngitis. Can't fucking talk."

"Frank Devon?"

Cameron mouths the name at me too, a question in her eyes, as she hands me a cup of coffee.

I motion for her to be quiet with a finger against my lips and put the call on speaker.

"Yes, fucking Frank fucking Devon. He has laryngitis. He can't do the sideline report today for the Beavers game."

I press a hand against my forehead, a knot forming in my stomach.

"What about Tila? Doesn't she usually fill in for him?"

"Tila's on fucking maternity leave," John says, as though her baby is a personal attack on him.

"I'll do it," Cameron pipes up. "I can do it."

"Is that Cameron?"

"Yes," she says, and I stare at her, my thoughts racing a mile a minute.

"Cameron, I don't know why you're on this call, but absolutely not. I don't want you to do it, I want *Kelsey* to do it."

"The Hot Dams want to literally murder me over the cheerleader report," I tell him. "The last thing I want to do is serve myself up on a silver platter for them."

"I don't give a fuck what anyone wants. I only give a fuck about what the ratings want, and no one is going to flip to the other channel if you're the one out there on the sidelines. I don't care if they hate your guts, they'll watch you."

"I don't know enough about football—"

"That's total bullshit and we both know it. I know who your dad is. We all know who your boyfriend is. Fuck, Kelsey, you're from Texas, where they hold your eyelids open and make you watch *Friday Night Lights* until you've memorized it."

"That's so far from reality I'm not sure how to even respond to it." Well, it's not that far from reality, seeing as how schools in Texas are as big as they can make them just so they have a bigger pool of athletes, but the eyelid thing is a stretch.

"It was a fucking joke, Kelsey."

"You know, you could find a different adjective, John," Cameron says drily. "You're overusing that one."

"You try keeping everything running and then tell me about adjectives," he retorts. "Kelsey, you need to do this for me. I need you on the sidelines. You do a good job and I'll try to get you on air more. I promise not on the sports beat. Well, I mostly promise that. Maybe."

Cameron rolls her eyes at me.

"You do a good enough job on the sidelines and maybe the stupid Hot Dams won't be able to hate you so much. Flirt with the quarterback after the game, sex sells, blah blah blah."

"Gross," Cameron says. "Please never say that again."

"Seconded," I agree.

"Then we're agreed," he says airily, even though I've agreed to exactly nothing. "Be at the station in an hour and we'll take the van down to Wilmington."

He hangs up and I chuck my phone across the room, where it hits Cameron's favorite chair before clunking to the ground.

"Tell me how you really feel," Cameron says, then snorts.

"Fuck," I say, scrubbing a hand down my face. "I need to call my dad."

We both stare at the phone like it's going to walk back to me.

I take a long drink of my coffee.

"He's right, though, about a couple things."

"John?" I ask, incredulous.

She nods, sipping her coffee, too. "He's a total dick, but you do well on camera and the Hot Dams aren't going to want to click away from your reporting."

"I don't know enough about football."

"That's not true."

I take another long drink of coffee. "I would like to be on

camera more. But damn it, Cameron, I didn't want to even watch this game today, let alone be there in person."

"I know," she says quietly, tucking an errant strand of hair back into her bun. "Maybe it will end up being a good thing. You two didn't break up. Right? You just needed some space."

My chest straight up hurts from the force of my deep sigh, and I retrieve my phone, plunking into her uncomfortable chair. I take a long swig of my coffee and Cameron hops up, refilling both our cups as I stare at my reflection in the screen.

I tap my favorites, then my dad's number.

He picks up on the fourth ring, just as I'm starting to lose hope.

"Hey Kels, you're calling early today."

"Hey Dad, I need your help."

"All you gotta do is ask, honey. You know that."

I smile, and it feels good. It feels good to smile, and know that no matter what, my dad's ready to drop whatever he's doing this Sunday and help.

"I need to know everything you know about the Beavers game today."

"Well, that's the last thing I expected you to say, but I can't say it doesn't make an old man happy to hear it."

He laughs, and my grin stretches wider as he starts rattling off who's out with injuries, who's been playing well, which team has a better offense, how the coaches stack up against each other.

"You sound good, Dad," I say quietly, hope blossoming inside me, replacing the prickling anxiety.

"I'm feeling good. Feeling real good... Does this sudden curiosity mean I'm going to get to see you at the game today?"

"It should just be the local affiliates running it," I tell him, but I frown because I honestly don't know.

"I'll make sure to watch it through the app, then. Hey, Anna, our baby girl's going to be on TV at the game today!" my dad yells out to my mom, and I laugh, feeling lighter. Feeling better.

Maybe it will work out after all.

# CHAPTER 50

## DANIEL

I stand in line with the other players, all of us waiting to receive our daily allotment of Toradol, and in my case, a few other injections. The pregame atmosphere is tense, worse than usual, even though the line for shots never has quite the same vibe as the rest of the facility.

Something about the white walls and motivational posters and flimsy blue curtains and syringes laid out drives home the fact that there's a reality outside this stadium just waiting to catch up with us.

Finally, it's my turn, and I sit in the spot recently vacated by one of our offensive linemen, who stoically took a syringe to the knee like an old pro. Like this is fucking normal.

None of this is fucking normal.

Kelsey's words keep ringing in my ears, like they have since she left last night.

What's after football?

"Harrison?" the doc says, and it's clear he's been asking me something.

I grunt at him.

"I asked how your shoulder is today."

"I'll take whatever you can give me, doc. Stronger the better."

"You got it," he says, agreeable as ever.

That's the thing about the doctors here. They want to help, sure, but they know who pays the bills, and it's the franchises and the owners and the fans who want to see us fucking smash together like live crash test dummies.

I don't even flinch as the first shot goes in.

"Numbing agent," the doc tells me cheerfully. "Straight into the AC joint."

If I had a nickel for every time I heard that.

The next shot burns, familiar liquid heat spreading through my shoulder joint, a welcome sting that's gone nearly as fast as it starts. It reminds me all of this is fleeting. That I should be grateful to be able to do this job. That it can all be over in the blink of an eye.

"Toradol," the doctor's assistant says, handing him a third syringe. "NSAID relief."

He injects it perfunctorily, and I don't even bat an eye.

"Might take a few hours to kick in. Don't overdo it, sign here," he says, handing me an iPad with a release form.

Do I understand the potential side effects of these drugs?

Do I agree to not hold the AFL responsible if I'm further injured?

Am I signing this form of my own free will?

Do I agree that I am fit to play?

I initial each box, reading each question, actually reading them, for the first time since my first season with the AFL.

The average career of a pro football player is three and a half seasons.

I'm looking at seventeen. Seventeen seasons of this.

"All good?" asks the doc, and when I glance back at him, his eyes are narrowed, and I wonder how many of us he's seen fuck our bodies up beyond the limits of what we're supposed to endure. I wonder how many of us signed that we were fit to play before we did that.

"All good," I say, handing him back the iPad.

I'm one of the lucky ones.

I repeat it over and over, heading to my favorite trainer for tape. Inject it full of pain killers. Tape it up. Wrap it up.

Put on the fucking suit and give it your all.

I grit my teeth as the trainer stretches my bad arm out, the KT Tape irritating the already swollen joint as much as it is helping. When he's done, though, I stretch experimentally.

It feels somewhat better, the pregame injection cocktail and tape at least taking the worst of the edge off.

"How you feeling, Harrison?" Darius sits on the next table over, one of the trainers taping up his back. His hip's already taped up, and I make myself smile at him.

It doesn't reach my eyes.

"Same as always," I say, the words hollow. "Ready to go."

"I know that's right," he says, and he furrows his brow at me.

He looks tired. He looks how I feel.

"All done," the trainer tells me.

"Thanks," I say automatically.

"Go give 'em hell, today, Harrison."

"Always do," I tell him. "I always do."

I walk back into the locker room, ready to put the pads on. Ready to warm up. Ready to play another game, ready to try my hardest and leave it all on the field.

*What comes after football?*

# CHAPTER 51

## KELSEY

I managed to make myself a ream of flashcards with player stats and fun facts, Cameron providing the neon-colored cards while my dad ran through as much information as he could remember on each team playing today.

He loved doing it, and I loved the simple fact that he could.

I love that Daniel talked him into trying new treatments, something my mom and I haven't been able to do.

I love Daniel so much for taking the time to help my dad that it makes my heart hurt.

I'm shuffling through the notecards in the front seat of the van, murmuring each fact and player's stats under my breath as my assigned cameraman navigates the bumper-to-bumper traffic.

Finally, we make it into the stadium parking lot and I swipe my sweaty palms against the cream-colored pencil skirt I borrowed from Cameron along with a simple black silk t-shirt that will hopefully keep my nervous sweat from being too apparent.

Cameron helped me with my makeup too, and I flip the visor down, checking my lipstick in the mirror.

"You're going to be fine," the cameraman says.

"I hope so."

"You will be. Just remember, the fans care a whole lot less about what you say and a whole lot more about what the players say."

I study his grizzled profile and relax back into the seat. "You're right. You're right."

"Of course I'm right." He snorts and pulls the van into the one of the spaces reserved for media, alongside the larger networks' much newer, nicer vans. "Just smile and let the guys talk. You can do this."

"Thanks," I say, and strangely enough, I'm bolstered by his easy confidence.

I can do this.

I can ignore the weirdness between Daniel and me for the next few hours. I can ignore the ill will the Beavers fans feel towards me thanks to the reporting I've done on their cheer team. I can just be another reporter on the sidelines, interviewing football players.

I just need to let them talk and not say anything stupid.

I just need to let my feelings about Daniel and football go for a few hours. It's a job. It's just another job.

I can do this.

Probably.

# CHAPTER 52

## DANIEL

The pain is excruciating. The additional injections at half-time barely put a dent in it. I keep thinking I see Kelsey, too, which is more distracting than my fucking shoulder. If it's not her, it's a woman who could be her sister. But every time I try to look for her, for whoever it is, Dale seems to notice my lack of attention to the game.

A few minutes left in the fourth quarter, I sit on the bench, my helmet in one hand, my bad arm propped on top of it. I squirt sports drink into my mouth and my eyes drift over to where I keep thinking I see her.

She shouldn't be with the press today, though.

As far as I know, she's not even watching the game at home.

I swish the sports drink around, finally swallowing it.

The worst part, the part that's settled like a stone in my stomach since I pulled on my cleats and jogged across the field, is that she's right.

She may not understand everything this game's meant to me, everything my coaches and teams have meant to me, but she's right about one thing:

My body can't take much more of this.

I'm not sure I want it to, either.

Dale's shouting something at me and I make myself focus. A glance up at the huge scoreboard overhead shows we're in possession.

An interception.

I launch off the bench, heading to the huddle, knowing what they're going to decide, knowing what we need to do.

We're down by seven. A touchdown and a field goal would tie it up, or we could score a touchdown and risk a two-point conversion for the win.

I promised Coach Morelle I'd do my best this game. I promised him.

Dale's telling all of us what we already know, but we listen all the same, and I can feel the moment the mood shifts.

We could win this thing. We could *win*.

"This is what we've been training for," Dale is yelling, his face beet-red. "This is the moment you prove exactly what you're made of. Now get out there and do the damn thing!"

"Let's fucking go," I shout, adrenaline racing through me.

The next minutes somehow pass in slow motion and too fast all at once, the kind of passage of time that's impossible to explain to someone who hasn't felt the pressure of a stadium full of fans in face paint and jerseys with their name printed across the back.

The ball is part of me.

The game is in my blood.

*I'm one of the lucky ones.*

The seconds tick by on the scoreboard and I launch the ball, ignoring the fresh burst of pain that cracks across my shoulder, deep into my back.

Ty Matthews dodges one of the cornerbacks, fingers stretched out for the ball.

Touchdown.

The noise of the crowd comes back in a tsunami of sound.

We're one point down.

We know what to do.

In their favorite section, the Hot Dams are doing their normal chant, but this time, they've changed it. They're shouting my name.

*Harri-son! Harri-son! Hot Dam, he's the man, he's Harri-son!*

The offensive line pulls in for a quick huddle, and even though I know the coaches are warming up the kicker, he's not going in.

We're going to fucking go for the two points.

We're going for the fucking win.

"Ty. I want you wide open, you hear? Everyone else, get him open." I grab Jacob's shoulder. "We're doing the Matthews switcheroo."

It's a damned lottery. Trick plays can be a ticket to heaven or a ticket to hell, depending on the outcome.

Today, I want the miracle. I fucking need to be a believer again.

"Coach Dale doesn't want us to run that," one of the guys says. He's third-string. Too new to know that sometimes the fucking coaches, especially ones named Dale, don't know shit.

"Does Dale have the ball? Is he out here bleeding on the turf? We're running the play I called," I snarl.

The rookie backs off, his eyes wide with surprise.

The Matthews brothers are watching me with both respect and surprise.

"Jacob, is your foot good enough to do it? You still fast enough?"

"Yeah, I can do it," he says, and I believe him.

Maybe this is how Coach feels when I tell him I'm fine. He hears what he wants to hear.

"Don't fucking lie to me," I grit out. "If you're not fast enough, if your ankle is still fucked, we'll run it the other way. Ty can get the hand-off."

Dale's screaming something into my headset. I rip it off and throw it on the ground. The cameras all around must catch it, because the crowd goes insane.

"Time, *time*," the coaches on the sidelines yell. The clock's running down while we're in the huddle.

There's never enough time when what you love is on the line.

"I can do it," Jacob says, calm, steady.

I actually do believe him this time. I nod once.

"Break," I shout, and my team forms up, taking on the slightly different positioning to run the trick play.

Dale's screaming obscenities on the sideline, screaming the name of the play he wants us to run instead.

Fuck you, Dale.

I grin at the offensive coordinator as the center lines up to snap the ball, then return my focus to the game.

This is it. Now or never.

"Hike," I shout, putting my whole heart in the word, because this might be the last time I say it.

Ty runs straight to the end zone, and the ball meets my hands. The defense is scrambling to cover Ty and I jerk my arm up. The guys gunning for me mostly back off, switching gears and running for the receivers.

Jacob brushes past me and I pass him the ball I never threw.

He leaps over the pile of bodies on the ground, and the last thing I see before I get hit is him diving into the end zone.

We fucking won.

It's almost a good enough feeling to numb out the fresh hell of my shoulder.

I don't get up. I stay down. I stay down, and I taste blood on my tongue. I know that feeling, I know it better than anything. It wakes me up at night.

My shoulder's dislocated.

Again.

# CHAPTER 53

KELSEY

'm on autopilot, interviewing the players they'll allow me to talk to after the game. I ask them questions without listening to a word they're saying because I don't care.

I don't care.

I don't care if the Hot Dams eviscerate me online, I don't care if my boss never promotes me again. Right now, all I care about is going through the motions long enough to finish out this gig. I toss it back to the studio, and the recording light on the camera blinks off.

*I have to find Daniel.*

The cameraman's talking to me, the stadium slowly emptying of fans.

I don't hear anything besides the blood rushing in my ears.

I rip off the mic pack, tossing it to the cameraman. The mic follows, and I rush to where the stadium meets the field, to the door the players have disappeared through. The players and some of the press, the ones who routinely get locker room access.

My own press pass swings on a navy lanyard around my neck,

and my heels sink into the turf before clacking along the concrete ramp that leads to Daniel.

Daniel, who got hit, who got hit and didn't get up.

I don't want to cry. I don't want to cry, but I'm not sure I can hold back the tears.

A security guard yells something as I race by him, holding my press pass up and not breaking stride. Before long, I've found it: the locker room.

It's loud in there, the sound trickling out as another reporter heads in.

I follow before someone can stop me—but I'm not a pro athlete.

The security guard's hand wraps around my wrist and I yank it away, breathing hard.

"You can't go in there, miss," he says, sounding truly regretful.

"I have a pass." The words come out too loud, a near scream, and he blinks in surprise, then recognition.

"You're the girlfriend... Kelsey something, right? The reporter?"

"Yep, and I can be in there." I jab my finger at the door and he gives me a long, speculative look.

"Go on. Don't cause any trouble, though."

I could kiss him. But I don't, because the only person I ever want to kiss again is hurting, and I want to find him. I need to find him.

"I won't," I say, and I'm not sure it's the whole truth.

But he lets go of my arm and I push the door wide open.

The locker room is chaos. The players are half-dressed, some in towels, and the reporters seem to have pinned several down to talk to, including the Matthews brothers, who look tired but happy.

"Jacob," I yell, waving a hand.

"Kelsey," he says, whipping his head toward me, his eyes wide with surprise. "You came."

"Where is he?" I ask.

Darius makes his way to me, still in his grass-stained pants. "Come on, Kels, I'll take you to him."

He sounds serious, and despite his warm smile, my stomach churns.

"Is he okay?" I make myself ask, and the question comes out small. I wrap my arms around myself.

"He will be. He's tough."

I nod, and he gives me a long look. "Come on then," he says.

Darius leads me through the hallway into what seems to be a weight room, then into a smaller room where a guy with a stethoscope over his suit jacket's talking to Daniel.

He's naked from the waist up, his forearms bleeding in a couple places, and his arm's in a sling, icepacks all over his shoulder.

"Daniel," I say, and my voice breaks on his name.

"You came," he says simply.

The doctor smiles at me, and his eyes are tired. I brush past him, crawling up onto the exam table next to Daniel.

He hugs me close with one arm, and he smells like sweat and grass and hard work.

He smells like Daniel.

"Are you okay?" I ask, and a tear falls onto his bicep.

"Are we okay?" he says, and the door closes as the doctor leaves.

"I'm so sorry. I'm so sorry. I should have stayed last night. I wasn't being fair to you, or what you do, or to us. I was upset, and I shouldn't have left. I don't want to leave again."

"No," he says slowly, his good hand finding my chin and tilting it up so I have to look at him. "Kelsey, you were right. I wasn't ready to hear it. I might never have been ready to hear it, but I am now because of you. I'm sorry. I lied to you about my shoulder. I lied to you about being fine, and you were right to worry."

"I just didn't want you to get hurt."

"I know, babe. I know." He kisses one cheek, and then the other.

"I love you too much to let you go, Daniel," I force myself to say. "I love you too much to walk away from you, even if it means watching you get hurt. I love you, football or not."

"Kelsey," he whispers, "I love you." Then he kisses me, fervent and laced with the copper tang of blood. "We're okay. I'm going to be okay."

Daniel's lips meet mine once again, and I sigh into his mouth, so relieved and grateful.

He pulls away, and he regards me for a long time.

"I have to do the post-game presser," he says. "Are you going to be there?"

I nod, biting my lip as I eye his shoulder, so swollen under the icepacks.

"Do you want me there?"

"I want you by my side. Always."

"Then I'll be there."

# CHAPTER 54

## POST-GAME PRESS CONFERENCE WITH QB DANIEL HARRISON: BEAVERS V. SERPENTS

Daniel Harrison sits in front of a crowd of microphones, the Beavers navy and gold logo stretched behind him.

Interviewer 1: Daniel, congrats on a great game today—

Daniel Harrison: <holds up a hand> Ladies and gents, this press conference is going to go slightly differently than it has before.

Interviewer 2: Is this because of your injury? Do you have plans to retire?

Daniel: <raises eyebrow> Was there something about going differently that you didn't get, Steve?

<laughter>

Daniel: Today's game was unlike any other game I've played in my life. I'm proud of the men that I work with, proud of the choices we made out there today and the choices we've made all season long. Watching these guys come together and meld as a team is truly incredible, and something that even as I've gotten older still manages to inspire me every day.

Interviewer 2: Why was it unlike any other game?

Daniel: <deep sigh> Steve, would you let me talk?

Interviewer 2: Sorry.

Daniel: That's fine. I have been honored to wear the navy and gold this season, and to have the support of some of the most vocal fans in the AFL. But today's game was unlike the others I've played because it was my last.

<room erupts into questions>

Daniel Harrison: <holds up a hand> I have played for the AFL for nearly twenty seasons now. I have loved every second of it. It has been the time of my life. But it's time for me to step down and let another quarterback take the limelight. It's time for me to find out what happens after football. And it's about damn time for me to stop ripping my arm out of its socket.

<laughter>

Daniel Harrison: It's been an honor, and I'm grateful for all the coaches and team owners who've taken a chance on me throughout my career, but especially Coach Morelle, who's been like a father to me.

Interviewer 2: Does this have to do with the new woman in your life?

Daniel: <deep breath> It has to do with me. It has to do with the fact that I've spent so long loving this game that I forgot there are other things out there to love. It has to do with the fact that I made one of those things cry today, because she was so worried about how I might hurt myself worse. I've been in denial about how much fight I have left in me. I'm going to be forty in less than six months. It's been a good run, but I'm done now. It's time to let someone else throw the ball. You can go against the clock as long as you want, but the clock's going to win every time.

<phone vibrates across the table>

Daniel Harrison: <holds it up> My agent, folks. He's not going to be real thrilled with finding it out this way.

<laughter>

Daniel Harrison: That's all I'm prepared to say now, that and thank you to all of you, too. Have a good night.

Daniel Harrison stands up slowly, crossing to the end of the stage, before looking into the crowd. A small blonde woman pushes through the sea of reporters, and he tugs her to his body. The reporters cheer as he kisses her soundly on the lips.

# CHAPTER 55

KELSEY

Daniel's truck is easier to drive than I expected.

We're both quiet as I pull onto the Delaware bridge, the river dark and silent beneath us. Traffic's not nearly as bad as it was going to the game, and I ease my grip on the wheel.

"I love you," Daniel says suddenly, and I glance over at him.

He's taken whatever anti-inflammatories and pain meds the team doc gave him, and even though I know he's going to be okay, and with rehab his shoulder will heal, I can't quite dissolve the lump in my throat when I think about how hard he hit the turf this afternoon.

"I love you," I say. "You okay?"

"Yeah."

"Listen... Daniel. I know you said it was time to retire, but I... I feel guilty about it. I don't want to be the reason you gave up football."

I didn't mean to say it. I didn't mean to ever say it, but now it's out there, between us. I exhale into the heaviness of it, my gaze darting from the dashes on the road to his face.

"Kelsey, look at me."

I do, and his blue eyes are warm, a relaxed smile on his face. "Do I look upset?"

"No."

"If I look hurt, love, it's not because of that choice, which was fully my choice. My shoulder is in terrible shape. The rest of me is held together with K-tape and willpower, and I'm tired. I had a good run. I had an incredible run, and I'd rather retire on a win than retire when they have to cart me off the field on a stretcher."

I make a small noise of distress.

"It didn't happen, Kels. I'm in one piece, and even though I'm hurt, and have some long days of rehab and physical therapy ahead, I feel good. I feel better than I've felt in a long time. I did the hardest thing I've had to do in a long time, but when I looked at you in that crowd of reporters? When I saw you smile? You made it so easy."

"Daniel," I say on an exhale.

"I want to hold your hand so bad right now," he says, and a regret-filled chuckle leaves his mouth. The sling holding his left arm in place rustles as he readjusts himself on the seat. "You asked me: what happens after football? And I'm not going to lie, Kelsey, that question has scared the hell out of me for years now."

I tear my eyes from the road and look at him again, the lump in my throat slowly dissolving. "I'm sorry," I murmur.

"No. No, Kelsey, love, don't be sorry. Don't be sorry because you helped me find the answer. What comes after football?" He laughs, and it's deep, full of emotion. "The answer is you, Kelsey Cole. We do. I'll finally have time to do all the things I haven't had time for, or haven't had enough time to do well. You're the answer to a question I've been asking for years, so don't you dare apologize for that."

"Damn it, Daniel Harrison," I say, laughing as tears start to streak down my face. "I'm trying to drive over here."

"You're doing a great job," he says soothingly. "Don't forget it's the next exit."

I give him a rueful look. "I know."

"I had a feeling backseat driving would stop you from crying." He laughs again, the sound hitching as he sucks in a breath.

"Aren't you the master of reverse psychology?" I mutter, narrowing my eyes at him in concern.

I push the signal lever up, and the truck ticks as I merge into the exit, slowing it as we round the curve and make our way to the back road where Daniel lives.

"You know, I might need some help getting around the house with my arm so messed up."

"Oh gosh, I hadn't even thought of that," I say, worry for him spiking again.

"Yeah, you know, someone to help me pull the covers up in bed so I stay warm, or make sure I take my medicine at the right times... make sure I'm clean, give me a sponge bath."

I snort, and sure enough, he's laughing silently, his mouth twisted to the side as he tries to hold it in.

"Are you asking me to give you a sponge bath?"

"There is nothing I would like more than a sponge bath," he says. "Well, actually, I can think of a couple things I would like more."

"Oh yeah? I have no idea what those could be." I turn onto the long drive to Daniel's house, the spotlit trees glowing as we pass them.

"Well, the first on the list is you moving in with me," he says breezily.

The truck bounces roughly and I take my foot off the accelerator, trying to compute what he's saying.

"So you're asking me to move in and give you a sponge bath?"

"I was kidding about the sponge bath. Unless... you're into that."

"But the moving in part?" I ask, trying to wrap my head around it.

"Kelsey, I would marry you in a heartbeat if I thought you were ready. So yes, yes, I am asking you to move in with me because I don't want to wake up again without you by my side. I want to go to sleep with your body curled up next to me. I want to watch you wake up over coffee in the mornings, I want to make you laugh when you get home from work. I want you, here, with me for as long as you'll put up with me."

"Daniel…"

"You don't have to answer now," he says smoothly, misreading me entirely. "I know I'm moving fast. I know it's probably too fast. But I'm old enough to know what I want, and it's you, Kels. You."

"Yes," I say breathlessly. "Yes."

"Yes?"

"Yes."

He does a fist pump, then grunts. "Are sponge baths off the table? Because that might be more of a serious question than I thought."

I laugh. "I think I can probably give you a sponge bath or two."

He waggles his eyebrows at me. "I'll make it up to you."

The keys jangle as I remove them from the ignition, and I give him a long look, pursing my lips. "I think you need to concentrate on getting better first."

"There are plenty of things I can do that don't require my shoulder," he scoffs.

"Is that right?" I say, rolling my eyes.

"Yeah, and I can't wait to show you exactly what I mean."

"You need to rest," I say laughingly, but he's not laughing. His gaze is heated, his pupils dilated. When he licks his lips, a little shiver goes through me.

"What I need is you, Kelsey. You."

Before I can react, he's opening his door, still graceful despite his injury.

I follow his lead, jumping out of the truck, the distance to the ground much further for me.

"Hey." Daniel's leaning against the bed of the truck, a cocky half-smile on his face. "You ready for me to prove to you what I can do without the use of one arm?"

"Daniel," I huff, crossing my arms and slamming the truck door shut. "You really need to rest."

"I'm not resting until you've come at least once." He prowls towards me and I shake my head, unable to wipe the grin off my mouth.

"Seriously, you shouldn't."

"I might be retiring from football, but that doesn't mean I'm done wanting a challenge, Kels. You're going to give me what I want, and what I want right now is you naked on the edge of my bed with your legs spread wide." He's right in front of me now and heat rushes through me. Daniel puts a palm against the truck, caging me in with his big body.

"You can't tell me you don't want me to lick that perfect pussy until you come, can you?"

His voice is taunting and dangerous, and everything goes tight and loose inside me all at once.

He tilts my chin up with his good hand and I bite my lower lip.

A hoarse laugh comes out of him and he nudges my thighs apart with a knee. "Tell me you don't want to come on my tongue."

I swallow hard, then reach up and tug his head to mine, our noses touching. "I don't want to hurt you."

"You won't," he says confidently. "Just... maybe no knees on the shoulders this time."

I laugh, and he kisses me so fiercely that I'm melting with need.

"I love you so much," I tell him.

"Good." His grin takes on an edge and I suck in a breath because good grief, he's so sexy. "I want you to tell me that when you come in a minute."

How's a woman supposed to say no to that?

So I don't—I tell Daniel Harrison I love him over and over again instead.

And I can't say I don't love it when I make him say it back.

# EPILOGUE

## KELSEY

"You ready, honey?" My dad knocks on the door to Daniel's room —our room, now—and I grab my clutch, making a beeline for it. I don't care how old I am, I still don't want my parents seeing just how messy I make things when I get ready to go somewhere.

Dresses are strewn all over the bed and three different little purses are too, along with several pairs of shoes.

"I'm ready, Dad," I call out, opening the door and then slamming it shut behind me.

"You look beautiful, Kelsey girl," he says, beaming at me.

"You're not so bad yourself," I tell him, then wrap him in a hug. "You look great."

He's wearing a suit, his hair brushed neatly, mustache and beard trimmed up. His eyes have the sparkle I remember from when I was little, and he looks and seems younger these days. I hope it sticks, even though the doctors have warned us that he'll have bad days, too.

"I am so excited that you're being honored today, Dad. I'm so proud of you." I still don't quite understand what they've told me about the event tonight, and I've been too busy with work to do much research, but I'm happy to get dressed up and go into Philly for it with them tonight. I've been looking forward to it all month.

"You look stunning, Kelsey," my mom says, blotting her eyes with a tissue.

"Mom, don't cry," I tell her, then pull her into a hug too. "You look gorgeous. I love that color on you. I'm sorry Daniel can't make it tonight."

"Oh, I'm sure he's busy."

My nose wrinkles because my dad's right. Daniel's been very busy since retiring, busier than I expected. Between physical therapy and doctor appointments and whatever it is he's doing for his agent, we're lucky to see each other on the weekends and at night.

I'm so glad I decided to move in with him. I've loved every second of it, except for that one night I finally told him if he didn't start putting his socks in the dirty clothes hamper I would lose my mind. But even that wasn't a big deal, he just gave me a kiss and told me he'd do better.

And he did.

We load up into my car, my parents sitting in the back, making me feel a little bit like a chauffeur, but they're so cute, holding hands and chatting the whole ride, that I can't be mad.

"What's the address again?" I ask, and my dad rattles off a number on Broad Street. I throw it into my maps app at a red light, and confusion fizzles through me as I stare at it. "It's at the Masonic Temple?" I ask, biting back a laugh.

"Yeah," my dad gushes. "It's one of the most beautiful places in Philly, in my opinion. Your mom and I took an online tour before we decided on it."

"Before we came up, your dad means," my mom says softly.

My dad just laughs at his slip and I frown, trying to push down my concern.

"They have valet parking," my dad offers helpfully. "I'll pay for it."

"Oh, you don't have to do that, Dad. I can walk."

"You can, but I'm old. I don't want to walk, I want to valet," he insists. Stubborn as ever.

"Okay," I fold easily. Why not? Valet is nice. Plus, I know exactly where to expect this valet. "You know, Daniel took me here for a date once."

"Oh," my mom says, a wistful expression on her face in the rearview mirror. "Was it so romantic?"

"Well, it should have been." I laugh at the memory. "It was pretty weird. It will be nice to have a lowkey night here and enjoy the building with you guys," I tell them.

"Lowkey," my dad says, practically bubbling with excitement.

"Well, not for you," I manage, laughing as I turn onto Broad Street. "You're one of the guests of honor."

"That's right." My dad practically preens.

Finally, we're in front of the old stately building, along with a line of cars waiting to valet. To my surprise, there is also a news truck from my station.

"Is that Cameron?" I say, spying my dark-haired friend, mic in hand, looking glammed up and gorgeous.

"Pull up, honey, it's your turn," my dad says, too cheerfully.

I narrow my eyes at him in the rearview, suspicion rising. "What's going on?"

"You'll see," he crows.

"Mom?" I ask, but she just mimes zipping her lips.

I pull up to the valet stand, taking my keys from the ignition as a suited guy runs around the car and flings my door open.

"Our VIPs are here," he says. "We'll take good care of your car, now go have fun." He beams down at me and my suspicion grows.

My heels click on the pavement, and my mom and dad are arm in arm, waiting for me at the end of a red carpet. A red carpet?

Maybe that's normal.

But when Daniel emerges from a crowd of overgrown men, his

gorgeous, huge smile firmly in place, I know for sure I've been had.

I squint up at him, but it's impossible to not smile back at him when he looks like that.

"Hey, babe." His hands catch me around the waist.

"I thought you had a work thing…"

"Funny enough," he drawls, grin getting even bigger, "I do have a work thing."

He gestures to where my mom and dad are glancing back at us, grinning for the cameras lined up on the red carpet. "Welcome to the Inaugural Warner Cole Foundation Dinner."

I suck in a breath. "The Warner Cole Foundation?" My fingers flex on his suit sleeve and he presses a chaste kiss to my temple.

"That's right. Warner Cole, former pro footballer, father to the love of my life, and an all-around great guy, agreed to lend us his name, story, and undeniable star power in return for a spokesperson job and a fair sum of cash. Drives a hard bargain, your dad. And in return, my foundation for training athletes and coaches on safety and injury prevention has invited him to speak and be the face of it."

I'm speechless. Stunned. Flabbergasted.

My jaw opens, then closes because I can't think of anything to say.

"They're going to be taken care of, Kels," he whispers into my ear, hugging me tightly. "Your parents are going to be okay. And I'm getting to do something good for the sport and the next generations of footballers."

"I'm going to cry." I bury my face in his chest, and he pulls me closer.

"Don't cry, Kelsey, or I'll make you give me a sponge bath when we get home."

"You've been out of your sling for a month," I say, laughing through the tears that threaten. "Daniel, this is… I can't believe you kept it a secret from me!" I whack his hip with my purse and he laughs at me.

"It was worth it. I wanted to surprise you. I thought the… Masonic Temple would be the cherry on top."

I pull back from him, pursing my lips and biting back a laugh. "That depends on whether or not you've hired an Eagles tribute string quartet."

"Four words that will forever live in infamy," he says seriously. "Come on, Kels. Let's go inside. I can't wait to show you what our next chapter holds."

"What comes next?" I ask him, half-teasing.

"With you? Everything."

"I believe you," I whisper.

He laces his fingers through mine, and when our lips meet, my heart nearly bursts.

———

Thank you for reading AGAINST THE CLOCK! Be sure to follow me on social media or subscribe to my newsletter for the latest details on the Wilmington Football series.

# ACKNOWLEDGMENTS

Thank you to my biggest cheerleader, who reminds me to hydrate and eat (and that I always suffer at the 20,000 word mark) my husband- I love you. To my three boys- you're my whole world.

To the Clams: Stephanie Archer, Grace Reilly, and Bruce- you three are the BEST coworkers and support crew anyone could ask for, and I'm so glad I bullied you into being my friends. To Tiffany White and Ashley Reisinger- you are the sweetest, most thoughtful friends, and I will always be grateful Twitter brought us together.

To my readers, especially Caitlin Bailey-Garafola and Megan Alspaw, who tirelessly champion my work and are always there to help me dream up beaver backstory.

To my personal assistant Ally White, who keeps my head on straight, you're amazing. To my agent, Jessica Watterson, I am *so* lucky to have you in my corner.

scan to find me online

# ABOUT THE AUTHOR

Brittany writes spicy sports romance with an extra shot of humor.

When Brittany's not writing, she's usually taking her kids to sports practice, keeping them from jumping off things they have no business jumping off of, and daydreaming about going on a date with her husband.

For the latest updates, subscribe to her newsletter or follow her on Instagram and TikTok.

Head to www.brittanykelleywrites.com for more!